Shadows

SHADOWS

—Book I—

SCRUPLES ON THE LINE:
A Fictional Series Set During the American Civil War

Evie Yoder Miller

RESOURCE *Publications* · Eugene, Oregon

SHADOWS
Book I

Scruples on the Line: A Fictional Series Set During the American Civil War

Resource Publications
An Imprint of Wipf and Stock Publishers
199 W. 8th Ave., Suite 3
Eugene, OR 97401

www.wipfandstock.com

PAPERBACK ISBN: 978-1-5326-9901-6
HARDCOVER ISBN: 978-1-5326-9902-3
EBOOK ISBN: 978-1-5326-9903-0

Manufactured in the U.S.A.   FEBRUARY 26, 2020

Contents

LIST OF ILLUSTRATIONS

Maps

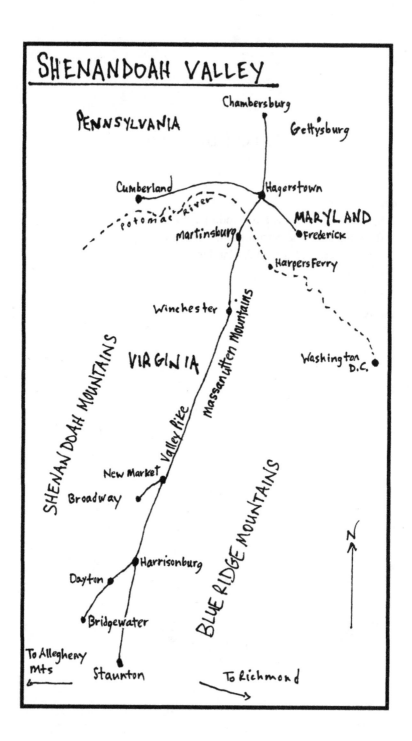

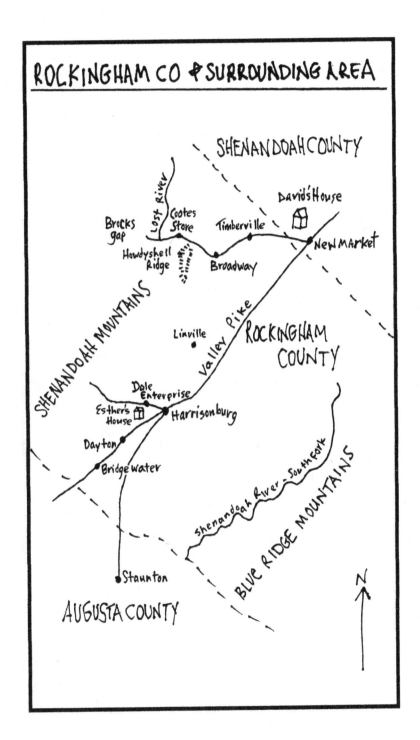

ROCKINGHAM CO & SURROUNDING AREA

SHENANDOAH COUNTY

Lost River

David's House

Brocks gap
Cootes Store
Timberville
New Market

Howdyshell Ridge
Broadway

SHENANDOAH MOUNTAINS

Linville

Valley Pike

ROCKINGHAM COUNTY

Dale Enterprise
Esther's House
Harrisonburg

Dayton

Bridgewater

Shenandoah River - South Fork

BLUE RIDGE MOUNTAINS

Staunton

AUGUSTA COUNTY

N

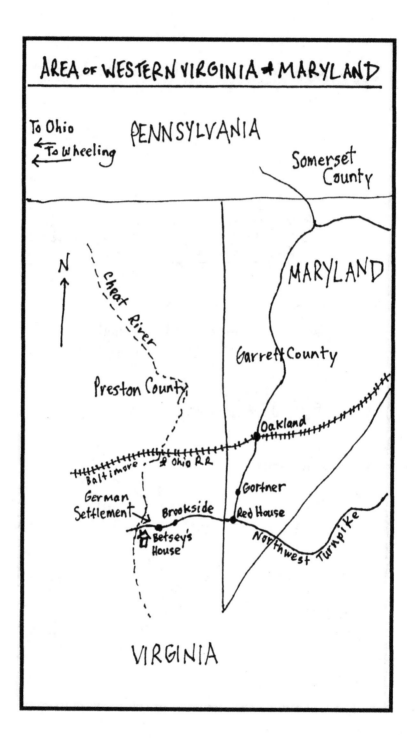

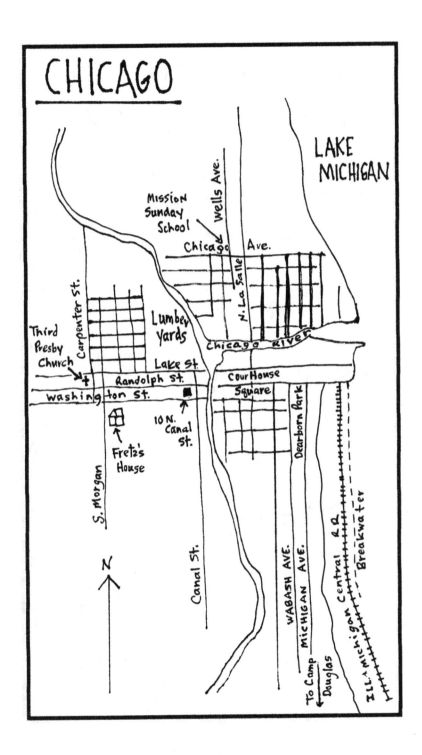

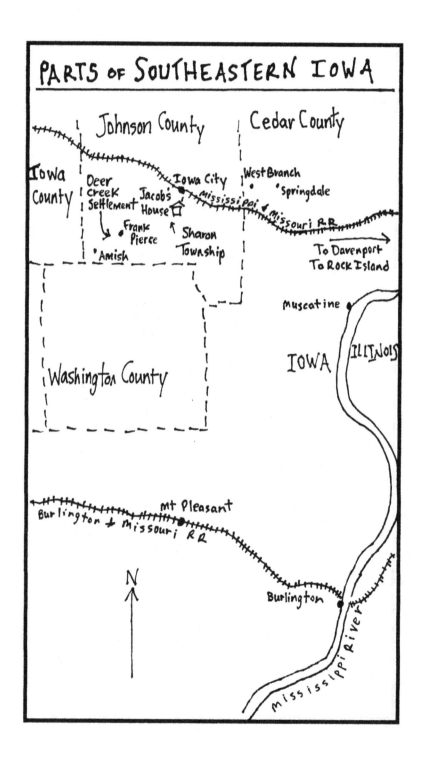

PARTS of SOUTHEASTERN IOWA

Johnson County   Cedar County

Iowa County

Deer Creek Settlement   Iowa City   West Branch   Springdale

Jacob's House   Mississippi & Missouri RR

Frank Pierce   Sharon Township

Amish

To Davenport
To Rock Island

Muscatine

IOWA   ILLINOIS

Washington County

Mt Pleasant

Burlington & Missouri RR

N

Burlington

Mississippi River

Jacob Schwartzendruber Family
(Select characters in novel)

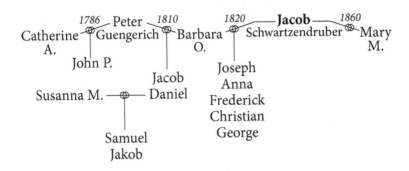

1786 — Peter — 1810   1820 — **Jacob** — 1860

Catherine ⊕ Guengerich ⊕ Barbara ⊕ Schwartzendruber ⊕ Mary
A.   O.   M.

John P.

Susanna M. — ⊕ — Jacob Daniel

     Joseph
     Anna
     Frederick
     Christian
     George

Samuel
Jakob

Fretz (John) Funk Family

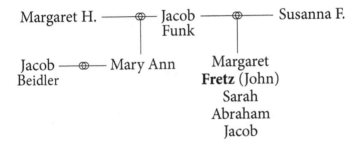

Margaret H. — ⊕ — Jacob — ⊕ — Susanna F.
                Funk

Jacob — ⊕ — Mary Ann
Beidler

Margaret
Fretz (John)
Sarah
Abraham
Jacob

Betsey Petersheim Family

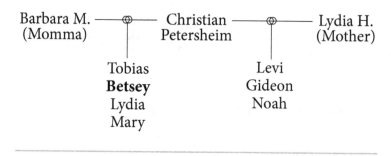

Barbara M. — Christian — Lydia H.
(Momma)   Petersheim   (Mother)

Tobias	Levi
Betsey	Gideon
Lydia	Noah
Mary	

David Bowman Family

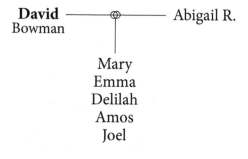

David — Abigail R.
Bowman

Mary
Emma
Delilah
Amos
Joel

Esther Shank Family

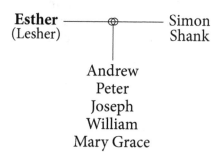

Esther — Simon
(Lesher)   Shank

Andrew
Peter
Joseph
William
Mary Grace

dedicated
to all who seek freedom for self and others,
refusing the power trappings
of weapons and words that kill,
of labels that divide and discriminate

dip your hair
in the rock of tears
and cry a song

—JEANIE TOMASKO

From "Sixteenth Day: Morning Prayer"
in *The Collect of the Day* by Jeanie Tomasko

Esther Shank — Shenandoah Valley, Virginia, October 1859

Mama used to speak of a bad death and a beautiful one. When I asked the difference, she only said, "Miles and miles."

Again, as an adult, I asked, but she shook her head. "You know when you see it."

I would not call hers beautiful, lingering till we thought to remove the pigeon feathers from her pillow. Papa had died with his shoes on, his head hitting a tree stump, his top splitting open. Mama never had to say what kind.

Yesterday a bird flew in our house, all silent. The boys had propped the door open for carrying in wood and stacking it under the window. One pile by the stove in the kitchen, another on the stone ledge by the fireplace. The bird was not to be had. Andrew said it had gone out when we turned our heads, but William spied droppings under a beam. The bird had found a crevice, its feet clinging. Peter brought a chair, thinking he could snatch the bird with his hands, but it took flight like a crazy one. I grabbed a broom and darted along.

By the time my man Simon came inside, the excitement had passed and only Mary Grace, my eight-year-old, set about to tell him the story. Her black eyes burned. He asked if it was a black crow, and she shook her head. "Only small and brown."

"But quick," I added.

"No more talk," he said. "A wren can bring good luck."

I live in our beautiful valley with Simon and our five youngsters. We've been able to keep disease at bay, unlike Mama and Papa, who lost my baby sister and brother to scarlet fever after they moved us from Pennsylvania to this wide valley. Mama complained about the work, a severe rockiness, but she never said aught against the surroundings. She would thrust out her arms, wider than her legs spread under muslin, her white clay pipe clenched tightly in her mouth. "Here we have room to spread out. Not bunched up."

We live near the settlement at Dale Enterprise with its huge thickets of mountain laurel. Our hills are tighter than out on the Valley Pike that goes north and south. Out there, strangers follow the wideness of our Shenandoah Valley. Yes, our mountains roll out like they see no hurry, Alleghenies to the West, the Blue Ridge to the East.

Simon says our valley is part of a larger one, going far to the north, even to where my brother Matthias moved with his family. There they call it the Cumberland Valley. Matthias lives near to Chambersburg in the state of Pennsylvania but to the west of where we came from. He sends a letter once a year. They have four Mennonite churches thereabouts. Here we go to church near to Harrisonburg, where Simon and the boys take grain and such to the market.

In his youth Simon saw the Potomac swell its wide banks far down north. I don't want to ever be near such rushing, but Simon has itchy feet. Once or twice a year we head to see his brother Gabriel near the trading post of Broadway. Simon wants our boys to know the river on the home place; he teaches them to fish and catch crawdads. Even Mary Grace had to learn the South Fork of the Shenandoah flows *down* the valley to the north.

"Southwest to northeast is how it runs," Simon said.

Simon's chin juts when a newcomer mistakes to say the upper Valley cannot be in the south.

Here at home, Simon takes pride in how he and our boys can do field work by themselves.

"Sufficient for our needs," he says.

Peter and Joseph, the middle boys, have the muscle, built big like my brothers. All my boys have fine brown hair like my family, but Mary Grace has coarse black hair like Simon. I wetten my comb with its missing teeth, but her braids stay bristly.

When the wheat was ready, Peter was strong at cutting with the grain cradle—as fast as Simon—and Andrew helped me bind and stack sheaves. Joseph and William kept up with the raking, unless William had to stop when he commenced sneezing. Then Mary Grace stepped in—long in her body already—and gave brief respite.

We teach our boys to be content as outsiders, not swept up by predictions of political disturbance, even war. Simon thinks I dwell too much on all that can go wrong. He doesn't want to hear about the Red Man being here first. He wants nothing of my fear, I may have welcomed dead spirits that one time I went to Mama's grave with my mouth uncovered.

Now he wants nothing of birds or omens.

"Hogwash, that a bird brings portent of death. Do you want to make it so?" Instead, he gives thanks that his grandfather was not deterred from finding this Valley. "Here we have the eye of God," he says and smacks his lips with satisfaction. "Protection. These hills give room to raise adequate stock, enough space for you women to have your orchards."

At that he knows I'll smile; Mama wouldn't believe the large clumps of abundant grapes this year. I cradled them in my hands—fat and round. And now juice enough in the cellar to last us months. Every time I go down the uneven steps, I pause to admire my jars, lined up like Simon's casks, full from elderberries. And apple butter—all has been bountiful this fall.

When I can, I snag one of the boys to help Mary Grace and me with churning. There's no shame with a woman's work. My oldest, Andrew, already sixteen, keeps the fire steady for baking bread. And if I want a new basket, I ask him, for he has the hands, while Peter would be all fumbles. When it rained, I insisted Joseph and William help with tying knots. Same with the garments of linsey after the spinning was done. Dunking wool and stirring with a wooden paddle is very heavy. Tedious, too, with boiling walnut or hickory bark in the big kettle for hours to get browns and dull blues, then lugging cloths onto bushes to dry.

If Simon will not let me pry one of the boys, I need my neighbors, Genevieve or Frances. We go back and forth most every week; last summer I helped Genevieve butcher chickens. I don't mind being the one to administer head cleavings if the boys are busy. She lives close and has a nose for when I need a womanly hug. With Frances—I see her at church—we're more to set up each other's looms. It comes out even: no one gets all the help, and no one has to always be the beggar.

In spite of hate-filled rumors, our family will manage well enough—we daresn't doubt—as long as we keep our health. Mary Grace still fits herself under the wing of my arm, her head on my chest. And Simon is right: a tiny bird in the house is not a thing to be feared. I must trust. When the wind turns blustery and the nights lengthen, we will stay tight together. Our Massanutten Mountain keeps watch.

Jacob Schwartzendruber — Iowa, February 1860

The sun shone brightly on snow-covered fields—such that my eyes averted under the brim of my hat. I sought diversion on a cold winter day and rode Caspar to the inn at Amish, thinking the stagecoach might have delivered a letter from a brother in the East. A conversation had already ensued around the pot-bellied stove, including two men from church.

The innkeeper slapped his hands wide. "Governor wouldn't sign." He has always been overly jovial to my way of thinking. He can describe trapping a coon with such glee you would think it a rare occasion to deserve both a horse laugh and leg slapping.

"Wouldn't sign?" I asked.

"Fellow from Virginia, a Mr. Camp, came to the governor demanding he sign papers to extradite our Barclay Coppoc," the one given to exaggeration explained.

A man with a drooping eye squinted at the innkeeper. "You seem, kind of a different Quaker. Seem awful glad." He held his lighted cigar carelessly, his eyes nearly closed.

"Me? A cussed nothing." The innkeeper slapped him on the back as if he would join in humor. "Never saw need for religion. Stuck in these parts with some mighty strange ones."

John P. and Ioway Joe smiled good-naturedly. "*Quakers* are not the only odd ones," John said. That was how he maintained good relations with others—quick with a snappy reply, even if it reflected poorly on us Amish.

"Still hiding, this Barclay?" I asked. I knew the young man and his brother had gone from their Quaker mother in Springdale, near to West Branch, and gotten mixed up with John Brown's misguided attack at Harpers Ferry. The brother, Edwin, had been executed when he tried to escape from prison, but Barclay, so far as I knew, remained a fugitive, chased by bloodhounds.

"Said to stay tight in his Springdale home, heavily armed," the man with the half-closed eye said. "Sawyers, the name." He reached to shake my hand. "A brother of mine lives in Springdale, tells me what goes. No one hunting this Barclay had the proper papers till this Mr. Camp came. But our Governor Kirkwood found the requisition faulty in four ways. Wouldn't sign. The Camp fellow had to wait for a corrected set of papers from Virginia."

"A sorry case," I said, "the young one straying with his brother."

"Wouldn't you do the same?" the innkeeper asked of me, his jocularity gone. "Protect your own? Even a scalawag?"

I shifted my weight, took in John's sly smile. He had chided me for not giving our people more warning regarding this John Brown; the man had come through our parts after a ruckus in Kansas. "Too vague," John P. had said, "to only repeat, stay apart."

But today he jumped in. "These Quakers make distinction. They helped Brown when freeing slaves in Kansas but now claim no knowledge of his plans for violence."

"Duped. Must have been duped," I said. "Better not to be embroiled at all."

I had been relieved Brown never came to our settlement, never begged for refuge. He and his fugitives, so far as I know, never strayed south of Iowa City.

"How many slaves did he help free?" Ioway Joe asked. "A dozen or so?"

"Oh, more'n that," the innkeeper said. "Only Missouri, that one time. A noble task, for sure, but the man was crazy as a one-eyed biddy. Supposed to been in and out of here three years or more. Called himself 'Divinely appointed.'" The man's guffaw set him to coughing.

"Takes caution, extricate a trapped one," John P. said. "But we are commanded not to ignore the plight." Small in stature, John turned his gaze to me. "You say so yourself."

"A disgrace, this slavery," I said, undoing the bottom hooks on my coat. "Better to stick with churchly matters. Let the New Englanders tend their abolition work."

"Nothing more godly than freeing the slave," John P. said.

I did not want to be drawn in further, expose our differences to a nonbeliever, but could not stay silent. "Not godly when part of an attempt to overthrow the government."

The innkeeper's mouth opened in a grin of gaps and broken teeth. "By all counts, they had their Underground Railroad across Iowa from Tabor to Clinton. Took a bunch of coloreds by boxcar, West Liberty to Chicago, shipped 'em to Canada."

"Which the greater sin?" John P. asked. "Breaking the law or looking away?"

I kept my head down; a pot of water steamed on the stove. "No answer there," I mumbled. I should not need to remind John: Jesus never allowed himself to be trapped.

"Thought all you plain ones called yourselves peaceful." The innkeeper laughed again, as if party to the best prank of the new decade. "They call this John Brown a dried-up prune. Never once laughed. Strange, all right."

"One wrong deserves another," the man Sawyers said. "How many years already, those so-called train engineers prevaricated? All to get past the Fugitive Slave Law. Said they carried wool and hides. Potatoes, that one time. Till the bag sneezed."

"Half-truths," the innkeeper said. "You dern religious types."

John P. stayed turned to me. "What I hear, Quakers knew what went on in Kansas; told Brown they had no use for guns. Made clear they did not approve: him practicing military maneuvers with his men right in the front yard." He pointed a finger at me. "*They* tried not to judge. Fed this Brown all right, but gave no powder or lead. Only helped with slaves."

"But at risk of losing two of their young?" I asked. "The poor mother only knew her boys were meeting Brown in Chambersburg, Pennsylvania. Not the whole of it."

Sawyers puffed smoke toward the stove. "People get caught up in self-righteous living. Could be abolitionists, could be religious folks. Quaker fellows may have thought Brown an honest, trustworthy man. No profanity, no tobacco use, they say."

"The better to stay apart," I said. "Not get hoodwinked. Boys should have known: you don't fight the Lord's enemies with the sword."

Ioway Joe had stayed quiet, save for discarding peanut shells on the floor, munching. "*Ja*, Quakers say they stand for peace. But letting this man do drills and live among them—?" He shook his head gravely. "Better not allow inroads."

"Exactly so," I said. "Not be caught up; not snared by the plots of evil men. Tend instead that which is right; not snoop into the wrongs of owning slaves."

"Still, the young men are to be admired, wanting to free their fellow-men," John P. said. "Misguided, you might say, but not seeking their own advantage."

Nothing was to be gained from staying longer. I secured my long coat again and tardily inquired if any mail had come for me.

The innkeeper made a show of riffling through postings. "Not this time," he called out.

Caspar's tail flicked at my approach, but I rode home with heaviness. Why do men struggle to stand clear? And why do these things happen—seemingly chance meetings, but within the purview of God. Unsettling. And these public rifts with John P.—unseemly.

I do not know why he needs to contradict me. When I have asked in private, he uses the excuse of wanting to amplify the conversation. He is an unusual circumstance. Ten years older than I and a stepson of my dearly departed Barbara; he comes from her first husband's second wife. Early on, a solid friendship grew between John P. and me, both ordained in the Old Country. But I felt a chill when Barbara and I married. Not that angry words passed, only that I was twenty and eager to take up life with the woman he had most recently called Mother. Whatever he thinks, I never fell prey to any deceit in my intentions regarding Barbara.

As a fellow ordained minister, he signed a testimonial for me when I left for America; two years later he came also with his second wife and six children. We both lived in the Glades area of Pennsylvania for a time; they left first for Fairfield County, Ohio. My Barbara always liked his daughter, Helena, the one who married Vill'm Wertz, one of our first settlers in Iowa.

I have tried not to make too much of John's choices, although I recall my surprise when he brought his children here in large prairie schooners; by then he had three married ones and their families. Nine adults and nine children in their party, as I recall, arriving within a week of my family. He made much of the claim they had no problem traversing the Iowa mud. Of course, those Conestoga front wheels are four-and-a-half feet high and the back ones stand six feet. There is something about the way he speaks—not exactly proud, but conveying a whiff of thinking himself advanced. He never mentioned the five horses needed to pull each wagon, but very nearly bragged about the big wheels that protected his tires and added another five inches to the width. From my calculations it took them twenty-two days from Ohio, whereas we made the trip all the way from Maryland in three weeks.

Barbara, of course, never criticized him. But I made clear I would never have subjected my family to that corduroy road that leads across the Black Swamp near Indianapolis. Some have reaped terrible consequences: two entire days to get across and a wheel can easily slip off the narrow track made of eight-foot logs laid side by side transversely. Some say those logs show rot at the ends. Plus, by taking a northerly route and following the main road all the way to St. Louis, John's party required a steam ferry to cross the Mississippi at Burlington. That meant slogging through Henry and Washington Counties to cross the English River.

What matters, of course, the Guengerichs arrived safely. I do not waste my time finding fault but give thanks for traveling mercies, even when folks bring differences.

We are blessed that our settlement grows—at least two new households of Amish in a year's time. But here is the danger: people give themselves over to signs of progress; even a new bridge across the Mississippi can bring rapture to some. And the rail service to Iowa City has given us a boost these past five years; the Mishler family used the cars last year. Three stagecoach routes depart from Iowa City, one coming southwest to our Frank Pierce and Amish, reaching our inn and postal service. But ease of transportation means our people can be attracted to political affiliation and may lose caution in their dealings.

This John Brown is not the only problem. Travelers bring word of conflicts stirring in the East, but also unrest in Kansas. How blessed we are, not to have settled in Missouri where reports of turmoil abound. This matter of slaves portends nothing but trouble. If people are allowed to take them into the new territories, their free labor could hurt our people along the way. We pay wages for competing labor, but we do not want to be infested with unsavory types.

Nor does it fit our beliefs for one man to think he can govern another. Some argue that anyone with dark skin cannot be considered a citizen.

"He is not a man!"

That cannot be right. Does he not have the same human characteristics as any two-legged creature? Is he not given a mind to discern good from evil, as much as any white man?

But when our men gather at the inn or tavern, questions about politics are put to them. We must not succumb to temptation, or say under pressure: the Negro is not worthy. Nor dare we stoop to settling disputes by using force. Some of our people act like they have forgotten how our Anabaptist ancestors had to run from authorities in the Old World. How the Bernese Swiss persecuted our forefathers when they refused to baptize children as infants.

My grandfather was among the fortunate; he fled to Waldeck in the early eighteenth century when it was a principality ruled by Prussia. There he attained a long-term lease as a tenant manager and was given a contract to supply butter, cheese, and such for the large Wetze dairy farm estate. Still subject to the ruler's authority, he had to petition for any privileges. But if a demand came to join a militia, he could pay a fee to the state church and keep himself separate as part of a religious minority.

So far, our government allows us Amish to remain separate and keep to our beliefs. Among immigrants, we are favored, so long as we till more land and supply more grain—in good standing, considered citizens, and holding rights without asking for them. That same courtesy should be afforded anyone.

Yet today, I still need to preach that our first loyalty must always be to God, not nation. Sometimes I have to pound and raise my voice to keep men awake. Maintaining that primary devotion to God—*no other gods!*—is why my beloved Barbara and I came to this wilderness of Iowa. It seemed the only way to avoid the Devil's inroads back East. Already back in the Old Country, Barbara knew we could never be an ordinary family. Yes, back in Waldeck the voice first came: "Jacob, arise." A Minister of the Book all these years. We could never expect to stay put; the call required a readiness.

Our first move happened in that principality of Hesse in the central part of the *Deutscher Bund*. I had to convince Barbara with strong language: things were not going to soften. Her two big boys from her first marriage would continue to be subject to compulsory service in the military. That is when we brought her Daniel and Jacob to this country, along with our own five youngsters, even though it meant perilous days at sea, betrayed by wind. She had more to leave behind in the *Vaterland* than I. Twice she had carried our twins, only to lose the weaker one as an infant. She also had to break from the remains of her first husband and wept to speak farewells to some of her living steps from his first marriages. Sadly, she was one to clutch.

Once in America—early spring of 1833 it was—we liked the Glades area of Somerset County in western Pennsylvania. I give Barbara credit; she made solid effort back then. Very solid. I was only a young man of thirty-three, but I had to be the eyes and ears. From Somerset we moved to Grantsville, Maryland before needing to depart again from evil influences. This time we set our sights on the Promised Land of Iowa.

Barbara said, "Yes, for the welfare of the church."

I took her at her word.

But on the very day the boys and I finished arranging wooden blades on my water wheel, we walked into the cabin to such a flood of tears as we had never seen before. Those two—my woman and Sarah. I had thought we would be met with fresh corn cakes and rejoicing, but such willing service was not to be. They sat near the table, their heads on each other's shoulder.

My son, Frederick, went to his wife, Sarah, his boots clomping. "What is it?"

The women pulled apart—I can see it yet—and dabbed their eyes with smudged aprons. Sarah has always been quick to excess, but my Barbara was known to stay calm and make appeasement. She might soothe: "Frederick will construct a wooden door and replace the quilt at your cabin entrance. He will do it at once before timber wolves come closer."

But on that May day in 1851, almost eight years ago, Barbara withheld. She made no promise that Frederick would remove the family of skunks that had settled under his log house. More troubling, Barbara would not so much as glance at me. Her hair gone white, her eyebrows dark. She had been more to stay apart, ever since she stepped down from the wagon onto the land I had chosen. If I remarked on the cheerful song of warbling birds, she responded, "Only a few cabins, far back from the road."

Barbara knew how much that finished water wheel meant. I had parted with a large overshot wheel in Maryland, buckets on the perimeter that could hold an enormous quantity of water. I knew the springs here in Iowa might not produce the same abundance. But I had showed immediate diligence, securing sufficient water to benefit us all.

Yet, Barbara's comments that first summer came not from a thankful heart but ranged from poverty to the likelihood of massacre. I learned to stifle reply, lest I hear sputterings of, "Mud into bread," or, "Make friends with Mormons?" I did not know this Barbara. It was as if she preferred to stay mired back East with known troubles, rather than seek another location where, to her way of thinking, new difficulties were certain to be worse. She never gave Iowa a fair trial. When she had said, "For the welfare of the church," I did not realize she felt no obligation to find contentment in this wilderness.

I do not mean to disparage. I am neither hard-nosed, nor blind to her virtues. She was a good woman. Often very good. She fed and clothed our children, plus her steps, wherever we settled. The good Lord allowed us to live in holy matrimony for thirty-five years, ten weeks, and a scattering of days. For that I am grateful.

I learned to refrain from excessive talk of our Iowa soil—a fertile, black loam. Barbara said I gloated. She could see well enough the large crops of wheat and corn we grew. I did not need to remind her how much cheaper land was here than in Maryland. I purchased 560 acres in due time, all to make certain my sons could be properly set up. And timber—plentiful to go with sufficient water, as it turned out. Folks back in Grantsville—her Gnagey friends along the Poplar Lick Run—would have shown surprise at how we could use a plow made of sharp steel, the fields free of stones. Of course, it took five or six yoke of oxen to pull the plow and break through roots of hazelbrush—two or three acres a day—here in this hilly Sharon Township.

Here we follow the same tenets of farming used in the Old Country. Some of our neighbors, the Welsh, Irish and such, are solely caught up in cash crops of corn and wheat for the Chicago markets. But I have not strayed from Father's instruction: "Tend all. Crops *and* livestock." I hear his gravelly voice. "Neglect not the use of manure as fertilizer; make certain there is meadow land aplenty for hay growing." From Waldeck on, I have been faithful, establishing my mill with its cog wheels and bevel gears to go with the farm labor.

Frederick and I have learned the hard way, though: sloughs on the sides of hills do not dry out until the hot season fully comes. If we seed the sloughs in grass, it will grow to six or eight feet high. But if we cut it when half that size, it makes a good hay for our horses and cattle; in that manner we have learned to avoid the long wait for drying.

But my greatest grief: Barbara never knew much happiness in her five years here. If I could have stayed her from her suffering, I surely would have. We turned our cabin into a log house, but I could not prevent every adverse situation. "A portion of rats is to be expected, as common as deer." I tried to make up for the burdens. "Look! A feast of blackberries from the timber." Always, I urged her to trust: "With God on our side, troubles will not find us."

But already that first summer the ague struck her. I entreated the Lord mightily. I practically begged Barbara, "I cannot make a go alone."

She recovered, but a broken ankle a year after the fever nearly broke her spirit. I never knew if she stumbled or slipped, but I saw the result right outside my workshop door. My woman sprawled, her skirts awry. Worse yet, she would not let me assist or carry her. She crawled all the way to our house and put herself to bed, as if I were not there. She would not eat. She did not want to hear me read Scripture aloud. Instead, her cries of pain surrounded me.

I rode to Frederick's, my alarm quivering, and asked him to fetch the doctor. Sarah came every day and gave Barbara the consolation she spurned from me.

I said to Frederick over and over, "I did not place that obstacle in her way." He was as baffled as I.

Once the doctor permitted her to maneuver around again, it was clear to the naked eye: the foot had not been set right. She stayed abed yet eleven long weeks. I tried my hand at corn cakes, but my words of tenderness fell as nought. I could not soothe the woman I cherished. Her firstborn, Daniel, here before us, shrugged his shoulders at my distress.

What puzzles more, that first onset of fevers came for Barbara on a Sunday, the Lord's Day. The same timing of adversity came again when I was ordained a bishop—her second bout with fever. It was a Sunday in '53, designated for Communion also; she insisted I not stay away from church. I believe she knew I would be the Lord's chosen. It could have been John P., her stepson. It could have been his hand that drew the correct slip of paper from the *Ausbund,* our song book used as the time-tested method of learning the Lord's will.

That Sunday morning stays firmly planted in my memory. I rode Caspar the dense eight miles to the Wertz's, the fog so thick I had to guess at solid footing for my horse. Yes, he sees better than I, but sometimes I slowed his gait to a walk for *my* sake. The path squeezed with little possibility of seeing ahead. Once at the Wertz's, we delayed our proceedings because others had encountered the same cloud of gray, including Brother Goldschmidt called to oversee. All morning, disorder prevailed. Some wanted to wait longer. I sided with those not convinced the tardy ones would ever arrive. In the end we chose not to delay another week.

I have always carried myself erect, grown to more than average height, nearly six feet. But from that day on, I began to stoop. I cannot say why; I did not trick anyone. But ever since I chose the proper Scripture tucked on paper in our hymnal, the drop in my neck has persisted as if a yoke had been placed. I am willing, already six years a bishop—I cannot deny the call—but the people do not always listen. Men's minds are set on breaking more prairie land.

But I digress from Barbara's demise—the recollection sorely distasteful. It was yet another three years, near the start of 1856, when the dreaded chills came for her once more, this time on a Thursday night. I will admit I lacked diligence at first. She had always made recovery before. On that day she milked the cow as usual but through the night stayed hot and restless. I turned away from the fire in her body. She found no rest, not even on Friday or Saturday. Huddled by the fireplace in her rocker, she threw off her comforter. Her colorless face sagged in the flickering light of the fire, taking on ten years. Finally after midnight on Saturday night, she quieted in bed for more than a thirty-minute interval.

At daybreak I searched her face. When I asked point blank, she only said, "Go."

I finished the chores and proceeded alone to church at the Kemps' house. As bishop, I had to be present for the marriage ceremony that day. To those who inquired, I expressed relief regarding Barbara. But a corner of my mind stayed fitful. Once atop Caspar to return home, my pulse raced; I feared I had misjudged. When I took in Barbara's worsened condition, I knew it was so. Sickness wrenched my stomach as I rushed to Frederick once more, begging him to summon the doctor and take word to her Daniel. Long ago, when at sea, each of them had dreamed of what could not be obtained. For Daniel it was wild plums; for Barbara, water.

The doctor came that evening and stayed through the night, but the medicine brought no improvement. Barbara was much troubled by slime on her lungs, trying again and again to force removal; at times, inward gasps erupted as she tried to draw breath. She remained conscious, although sometimes delirious. When she attempted speech, I rushed to her side but could never make it out. Sometimes I blamed a tree branch scraping an upper log at an inopportune time. Once, though, I am certain I heard, "A human, so far, and no farther." I do not know what to make of it, but heaven must have been on her mind.

The days that followed—over a week—haunt as much as my recurring dreams. Daniel kept vigil, while I left at times to give care to the animals. Her eyes shut, face sinking to the side, she remained with shallow breathing. I bent close to offer encouragement; she gave no recognition. On the evening of January 24 she quietly fell asleep at age sixty-nine, thirteen years my senior. We buried her body two days later under a sheltering tree at the Peter B. Miller burial ground. Younger men than I dug through frozen ground. Oh, that Barbara found joy at last in Paradise, freed from her earthly toils and sorrows.

I stayed at loose ends, tasting the bitter sponge. "A sore disappointment," I whispered.

"Mother? Regarding you?" Frederick asked.

"I failed."

"You cannot say." His hand, scarred by fire since childhood, flicked as if to chase my thoughts away. "Not all your married life." He interceded for me at the Great Mercy Seat.

"There is no slicing it by halves: God's call twixt a woman's heartache."

"You did what you believed right. You saw the need here and responded; now we live with opportunity."

"I have tried to walk humbly."

"The Lord's ways—a mystery."

"I have not been shepherd enough—not my own."

He scowled. "Not ours to say."

My failure still drenches like water spraying outside the wheel. Barbara's death—a punishment I cannot name. Never able to speak to Daniel of my depths, I am a man afflicted with grief. Spurned when she needed me most. My dear help-meet taken from my side, gone already three years this very month. Not a day goes by . . .

What yet is there to do? If I live ten more years—I am nearing sixty—and reach Barbara's age, it will be a goodly span. I have managed alone with help from Anna, my only daughter. Her smile supplies the devotion others lack. She still sends sustenance, even from a distance; her corn cakes are always better than mine. She and her husband, a Daniel Yoder, came two years after us but settled on the Deer Creek. She has her seven to care for but keeps me in butter—I do not have to use as much speck—and insists on shearing my sheep before she does their own. Best of all, she does not badger.

Sarah is the one, quick to say, even with children within hearing distance, "Widows will not come to Iowa without a man. You must go looking."

Barbara only used a voice like that with a child. I have no comeback. Can Sarah not see my reliance on hazelnuts and crab apples? For certain, I can boil potatoes with the jackets on.

She must have nudged Frederick, though, for he has mentioned several times I should go back East and have a look. In this case, he does not have cattle or land in mind. Yes, a woman with virtues would be handy, but I am not a young man.

Here is the truth I dare not say: my lonesome state may be the Lord's chastening. Barbara used to say, "Charity comes to the charitable." I would nod, but now I wipe sweat.

Ever since moving to Iowa, these dreams haunt. The latest: I am hauling manure. Strange, *ja*, in the middle of winter. I have four good horses, so that is not the problem. But as I continue—I cannot say where—the road becomes more and more slanted, and the wagon begins to tilt. I seek to right things with greater firmness, straining my body in the opposite direction. The horses do their best, but the wagon gets stuck in a precarious sideways position. Of course, the slickest mud is on the edges where danger is the greatest. In my dream I seek to lessen the load, even if it means hauling two loads instead of one. To that end, I rise cautiously, wanting to conduct the removal as lightly as possible. But the wagon tips further and I have to jump off. I stand there at a loss, surveying two wheels in the air.

I sleep no more those nights. I cannot bear to think on its meaning. And no woman to take lonesome thoughts from me.

J. Fretz Funk — Chicago, April 1860

I'm of two worlds. In fact, I think it likely two hearts and two minds were given me in my mother's womb. The mind that was twenty-four, on the move with the wind at my back, came to Chicago almost three years ago. I introduced myself—Fretz Funk—and watched people's puzzlement, whether to take me seriously or not. Long ago my family had decided that Mother's maiden name fit me well, better than my staid given name of John. How many men go by John? And how many answer to Fretz? That's all I needed. That youthful certain mind looked to my own interests, first and foremost.

Ambition—that's what works in business. Chicago is such a different world from what I left behind. I had thought leaving home would have little effect on me. But when my mother, Susanna, squeezed my hand and looked me in the eye, hers glistening, I was reduced to follow suit. That softening may have been the start. I'm not the same as when I left. This past winter when I visited back home again, our leave-taking was not as strained, but Mother could see how I straddled. She only said, "Remember where you came from."

Most of the time I want to be the master of my fate: a successful man. I've worked my way up from clerk to being in charge of forty employees at Beidler's two places of business: one at 10 North Canal Street and the other at the corner of Desplaines and North Lake. I like what I've accomplished these years. If I'm to get anywhere, I must continue to put up with the mud and filth of Chicago, not dwell unduly. But inside . . .

I have to push the buzzing away.

Jacob Beidler is the man I work for. He's married to my half-sister, Mary Ann; he invited me to come to Chicago and work for him and his brother, Henry, in their lumber business. I came with sixty dollars in my pocket and two suits of clothing. And expectations. When Jacob bores into me, his blue eyes like ice, I see him as Beidler, the boss who gives orders at J. Beidler and Brother.

The other day he called me into his office to give a report on Mr. Draper, the man who'd been injured at work. "Any evidence our company was negligent?"

"No, Sir," I said.

"No proof at all?" he asked.

"None."

"He can't sue for damages?"

"No, Sir. The man may have caused his own injury."

"Or been injured because of a careless co-worker."

"Correct. No evidence one way or another. Furthermore, he was informed as are all workers: the job of lifting includes inherent hazards."

"Excellent. Then we can drop him without a problem."

I hesitated. "Whatever you're comfortable with, Sir. The man has a family, of course."

"We no longer need his services; he'll have to tend his bad back on his own."

"A letter needs to come from you, Sir. Or Henry."

"I'll post it in the morning. One less troublemaker."

In spite of how that may sound, Beidler's not a hard man—he says so himself—not if you're willing to work. When he makes more money than expected, his eyes brighten at the numbers. He's quick to pass on a small bonus. "On the rebound," he says. Numerous times, he's described how the economic crash of '57 set him back.

I take my lodging with him and Mary Ann. At their house Beidler is Jacob, my brother-in-law. He insisted I live with them, and Mary Ann said I needed to take the largest room upstairs. My fireplace comes with cherry woodwork and has a window placed symmetrically on each side. Their youngsters have separate rooms, although the two girls share one. Each of those rooms is larger than the one where my two brothers and I slept back home. So here I am in this grand house with high ceilings and beautiful oak wood in the foyer. It fits Jacob, the right haven for Beidler to come home to. Sometimes, though, these furnishings mock: *you'll never be polished enough to make something like this your own.*

Mary Ann is perfect for Jacob, with her devotion to the homemaking arts. When I left home, Mother gave me a hand-forged needle. Mary Ann looked at it and put it back in my hand. "Let me know when you have garments that need mending." She washes my clothes, too. And if I develop a head cold, she is quick to ply me with as much hot whiskey as I need. I might not have made it in this city of strange people and unimagined scenes without her kindnesses. She comes from my father's first wife, Margaret, killed in their front yard by a neighbor's angry boar that got loose. Margaret tried to drive the savage beast away, but fell in her hurry. The hog attacked her and bit with a vengeance. Mary Ann was left to do a mother's work at an early age. I've tried talking about books with her, but she shows little interest.

I've been pleasantly surprised, though: Chicago women make themselves available, whether for church socials or magic shows. I've always wanted to be taller, but with these ladies, I seem to cut a good enough figure. They like to flirt, so entertainment comes easily. Very nice-looking women, I must say, and well-dressed in their lovely fullness. It's taken some time, though, to negotiate their hoop skirts and lean in for a kiss. Tight corsets! How they must welcome nighttime freedom. Of course, when I want solid companionship, there's Helen, a schoolteacher; she doesn't pile her hair so high and enjoys a worthwhile lecture. We can go to the lyceum and hear a good speaker on phrenology for twenty-five cents.

Sometimes Jacob helps me pass the time when he invites me into the parlor for brandy in the evening. His liquor cabinet is well-stocked—two kinds of rum, a bottle of vodka, always whiskey—a welcome reward from the day's labor. The Temperance Movement has made no headway in this house, and I'm the beneficiary. Jacob has given me tips on handling Irishmen—the tough lot they come from as immigrants. At first, I could hardly understand what they were saying, and they're bull-headed at taking instructions. There's no question, though, they work hard cleaning the docks of mud, dredged from the Chicago River, that stinking collection of offal. If the river's at a depth of thirteen feet or more, ships can go in and out of the harbor with lumber. Those men do the heavy loading and unloading.

I'll never forget the time, though, I came upon teamsters in distress. I was driving a wagonload of lumber to the dock when I saw men standing in mud, swearing and repeatedly pulling hard on the reins, as if they could jerk their horses forward. My situation was no better, but I soon realized the only solution was to unload half my lumber. I didn't want Beidler's horses damaging their legs—easy to stretch tendons or a ligament—from pulling in mud like that. I heaved half the boards to drier ground on the side and hoped the pile would still be there when I returned. After I accomplished that removal, I clucked and tapped lightly with the whip. Burt and Sugar made grudging progress before stopping again. No budging.

I blamed Sugar—she can be very lazy and Burt follows suit. We were fairly close to the dock, and yet not nearly close enough. The only way to proceed was to unload half the remaining half. In the process, I had to jump off but tried to step lightly. I was wretched with anger at my pants and boots. Still, I refrained from mindlessly lashing out.

"Come on, come on," I coaxed.

Eventually, I managed the entire maneuver, hauling quarter loads to the dock and onto the boat. It took three hours longer than it should have, but I never lost control.

Taking the Lord's name in vain isn't foreign to me—my friends back home always said any use of language came naturally for me—but I've noticed Beidler refrains at work. I try to follow his example. Of course, my father taught us boys to respect horses, so that part came easily. I learned how to work from him, a Jacob also—Jacob Funk, stonemason and bricklayer by trade, along with being a farmer. Hard work and economy of means—that's part of my heritage. My father learned it from his father, John, buried at Deep Run; that John learned it from Abraham, the offspring of our immigrant Heinrich, who lived near Franconia.

But when I debated about going to Chicago, Father had encouraged me. "Give it a once about. You're young and strong. There's money to be had."

He was progressive for his generation. Whenever he went to an auction, he brought home a wooden crate of books. We could all read English and German. He took me along in the farm wagon, too, when he'd go to market in Philadelphia. That was a thirty-mile trip, but it gave me a chance to see a great city and see how business was transacted. We marveled at locomotives of the Philadelphia & Reading Railroad with names like Comet and Spitfire.

Father knew Beidler had done exceedingly well for himself in Illinois; he'd started as a carpenter in Pennsylvania before he moved to Springfield and opened a grocery store. But Beidler wasn't satisfied there, even though he met higher-ups, including a lawyer, Abraham Lincoln. I was only nine when Beidler moved to Chicago and put his efforts into a sash and door business before turning solely to lumber. Father liked to tell others of his son-in-law in Chicago; I wanted to make him equally proud of a son.

I give Father credit: he taught me to think for myself.

"Don't be like the crowd."

He wanted formal schooling for me, so I read Shakespeare and Longfellow at Freeland Seminary, a men's school. "*There are no birds in last year's nest!*" What a magnificent line from Henry Wadsworth Longfellow. I was sitting in class, daydreaming about Jennibel's golden hair at the nearby school for women, when my teacher called on me.

There are no—

"How would you recite those words, Master Funk?"

I stumbled at first, pouncing on *birds*, then on *nest*, before seeing the importance of *last year's*. I hurriedly sat down, altogether dissatisfied with myself.

Freeland is twenty-five miles from my home, so being a scholar there entailed the excitement of packing shirts, towels, and soap. The second time I had to beg from friends because I forgot to take candles! Freeland offers a Normal Course—what my brother Abe wants to study this fall—after which I took an exam and received an official teaching certificate. At first I studied grammar, algebra, elocution, and the like, but the second time I moved on to geometry and philosophy, plus the theory and practice of teaching. Freeland is where my use of language became more ornate, my handwriting more Spenserian.

I never doubted I was ready for Chicago, but I discovered I couldn't lapse into so much floweriness when at work. The Irishmen still make no attempt to hide their laughter.

"Tushy, tushy," they mutter to my back side.

My cheeks burn—that strange word with its soft, squishy sounds; I hate the whole lot of them. My rear end isn't excessively large, but I'm shorter than most, and the men like to irritate.

Reading gave me my longing to venture out from familiar scenes. But even before my delight in words and ideas, my love began with the *feel* of books. I doted on leather bindings of sheepskin or calf, preserved with the tannic acid from tree bark. Our new family Bible from Philadelphia was light brown with a marble effect on the leather and a spine that had five gold lines. I ran my hand over the raised parts, turned its beauty from front to side.

The binder man intrigued me also. He wandered around our area, often barefoot in the summer. We never knew his name—a strange one, all by himself. He ate no meat but chewed on plants as he walked. I wanted to be as mysterious as he. Did he have a home at some distant place? Where did his ideas come from—the designs of flowers and hearts that decorated his book covers? I knew he relied on heated brass tools, but Mother pointed out the orderliness of his art, a balance that was uncommon. I have a distant relative in Virginia, a Funk named Joseph, who publishes church music books. Wherever we Funks settle, some of us have demonstrated a streak for doing the unexpected, and books are often involved.

So it seemed natural that I went from being attracted to books to teaching. But I only earned twenty to thirty dollars a month at Chestnut Ridge. I look back on those days with fondness, but a term was only for five months—no way to get ahead. Sure, it was rewarding, moving students beyond being in a blab school where everyone recited their lessons at the same time. I introduced new studies like map drawing to go with the usual reading, writing, and ciphering. Exciting, too, the challenge of coaxing the older parents for permission to teach geography. They thought it worldly and not of much use. What value, studying South America? I finally lit on the idea of saying a geography class would offer better knowledge of the Holy Land. How could I not feel a little smug about that?

Freeland Seminary took me beyond my upbringing when it came to politics, too. The men I'd known best only voted and held lower-level township offices. Now Father has had to align himself with Republicans, but he only expresses enthusiasm when he tells about his father's brother serving the Whig Party in the Pennsylvania legislature years ago. Other Mennonites back home think people sully themselves if they dip too far into politics.

As a lad, my ears perked up when I heard the names Abraham Hunsicker or John Oberholtzer. They caused great turbulence when they started their separate group of Mennonites, mostly because Hunsicker became heavily involved in politics and supported education. But he completely riled feathers when he said *charity* was the essence of Christianity—more important than preserving Mennonite forms and creeds. I never understood why Father didn't join up with him, a fellow Whig, except Father never liked to have *anyone* tell him what to think.

Still, he considered it safe to send me to Freeland where I often heard Henry Hunsicker, the principal and son of this Abraham, speak about "The Land of the Free and Home of the Brave." It made a big impression on me when Abraham thanked God and our country for the opportunity to be wealthy. Everything about Freeland rang with the thrill of liberty, taking pride in our stars and stripes. I liked to say, "Free soil, free schools, and Fremont." That was in the fall of 1856 when I wrote a letter to the local newspaper and encouraged everyone to vote for John C. Fremont. I was outraged at reports of Border Ruffians and their horrible crimes on the faraway plains of Kansas.

I brought my beginner's interest in politics to Chicago where I stated my firm belief: the star-spangled banner flies for everyone, not just the white man. I'd studied enough to believe the founders of our nation couldn't possibly have wanted the perpetuation of this dreadful curse of slavery. It was understood at Freeland that we might have to actively rid ourselves of this blight. But it would be a worthy fight, and I was on board, so long as people relied on reasonable means to effect change.

In spite of my family line being Mennonite, I also brought to Chicago my aloofness from religion. I preferred to reason things out. Ralph Waldo Emerson and his transcendentalism had impressed me most: the questioning mind, able to discern truth. When I was nineteen and knew everything I needed to know, I stayed skeptical as my friends joined the church. I snickered at their enthusiasm for protracted meetings. Even Salome fell in with that crowd. I could see right through the excess—weeping bodies falling to the floor, only to rise an hour later in an ecstatic stupor they called conversion. I refused to sit on any anxious bench, as if I were agitated to receive release from sin. Oh, there'd been a time—I might have been nine—when I was more pious. But that wore off, and I decided religion was for sissies.

I was unprepared for Chicago to give me a severe taste of loneliness. I brooded and spilled the poetry of my emptiness.

"No one to love, no one to cheer / Sad and lonely here I stand."

Yes, I missed Salome, my best girl. But mostly, I was dissatisfied with myself. I came to Chicago not knowing anything about lumber. Had I thought I'd fall in love with boards? Once I'd been happy in the arms of my Dulcinea, only to spurn that contentment in order to gratify the ambitious spleen of my restless nature. I wanted to get ahead, be somebody.

But one time I was brought up short by a dream; I wrote down part of it in a poem. I saw my loved one *"Attired in all her simple beauty"*—exactly what my heart wished for—only to see her visage turn sour when *"in her eye there beamed a look of cold disdain"* and *"on her lips there was a headless smile."* No matter what beautiful lady I've courted here, my fears have never disappeared. Was there truth? Had I been wrong to ask Salome to wait? Some other enterprising fellow might grab hold.

Through the loneliness I've persevered by writing letters to friends faraway. And I pass the time by walking. When I'm restless on a Saturday, I go to Dearborn Park. That would have been unheard of back home—to walk for no apparent reason. Of course, we walked in the woods to pick up chestnuts; that was purposeful. But here whenever I've stooped to entertain myself again with an artificial circus, or ride an elephant for a fee—drinking lager beer in abundance afterwards, a lady with all her charms on my lap—I ask still later: For what end? Nothing comes to mind, no matter how long I walk, other than some fleeting pleasure.

My nagging dissatisfaction was compounded by a strange thing that happened my first long winter in Chicago—no colder place on earth where a raw wind cuts to the core right through my overcoat. During that winter of 1858, this filthy city was swept by a revival. While mud sat under the surface of melting snow, people from all walks of life were caught up in religious fervor. Even Third Presbyterian—where I go with Jacob's family—had frequent evening meetings. And almost every noon I found myself leaving the lumber yard and praying at Metropolitan Hall with up to 5,000 others. Yes, me.

Still, I resisted.

Do not make a fool of yourself, Fretz.

I didn't want to merely follow the herd, so at night I took to the streets, lighted by gas lamps, wrestling with my inner turmoil. What did I miss?

When would this longing and grasping after something I didn't have, ever let go its hold? Salome used to speak of a light burning inside her; I had no name for *my* desire.

A psychologist might not be surprised—I've been to enough lectures—that I considered this turbulence the pull of God. One January night in particular, out walking with no one to confide in, I desperately wanted to escape the limits of my human vision and see everything. I wanted to grasp the beauty *and* deformity of the whole world. But I couldn't get past my humanness. I couldn't see what my future held. I came up against a dismal choice: stay mired in despair, or ask like Saul, "Lord, what wilt thou have me do?" I pushed against the absurdity and went home. I hadn't come to Chicago to place my dreams in some fictitious, unviewable presence. That was beneath me.

But that same month, on yet another night, the image of pilgrim, traveler, follower came to me. What shook me more, it appeared in the form of the binder man, the one with ragged clothes who couldn't have known where he'd spend most nights. Yet, I sensed some faint assurance, thinking of the man's doggedness: there must be something better ahead. Even finer than the sweetness of Salome? At what cost? I finally determined I'd have to set aside my reliance on myself. But that was an obstacle, too: reassuring and unfair at the same time. Throw aside my philosophy of the self? Place it alongside what God would show me? Not likely!

I can't explain how I came to peace. Perhaps it was a state of exhaustion. Anyone could see through my decision and say it wasn't conversion. I didn't completely let go. I still wanted some say; for sure, I didn't want to be a nomad. I'm surrounded by people who see financial success as a correlate of spiritual worth. So if a questioner says I wasn't fully cleansed within, I'd be the last to argue. A year and a half later, I know some bargaining was involved. Isn't that true of any change that matters? But for a time, my soul put aside its excessive wrestling. I relaxed, thinking I'd surrendered a portion. As an outward sign of some change within—away from *only* self-reliance—I decided to be baptized. Give up my vanity and follow the example of Jesus, that strange itinerant who didn't put himself above God. I convinced myself I could follow my own inclinations, so long as they weren't contrary to God's command to love my neighbor as much as I loved myself.

That turned out to be the easy part, thinking through to some kind of resolution. Acting on those principles, however, has turned out to be far more difficult. Sometimes I still listen to my baser instincts. I waste time chasing after a sweet fragrance; I lose wagers with fickle friends and drink too much whiskey. I seek advantage by conversing with Jacob at home, so I can put myself ahead of others at work. At the same time it's not unusual for me to go to church meetings three times on Sunday; I avail myself of endless weekly prayer groups. Anything that might nudge me toward less selfishness and more contentment, whether pretense or not. I no longer walk past the poor on the streets as easily; I'm a little less critical at work. Some of the men probably have no place to go but to the taverns.

But I dilly-dallied over baptism. My first thought was to join Third Presbyterian where Jacob and Mary Ann are highly respected. Their preacher, Rev. A. L. Brooks, would make a good lawyer with his well-thought-out remarks, even entertaining at times. But he gives little personal welcome. There I was, a stranger in their midst: not overly large, only five feet, five inches, but carrying myself with a strong bearing. Often as not, though, people avoided my outstretched hand, made no inquiry as to my well-being. They must have seen my struggling self, hiding beneath composure.

As I studied the doctrines of the Presbyterian Church, my dilemma about church membership worsened. For the most part, they do things with decency and order; in that regard they're like Episcopalians. But they're not at all nonresistant with regard to warfare, and I was raised by people who preached turning the other cheek. In addition, the Calvinist belief in predestination still baffles me. I can't balance their emphasis on doing good works, while speaking of assured salvation. I suppose any denomination has inconsistencies in the eyes of an outsider, but I couldn't get past the hurdles.

The gravest stumbling block surprised me even more: their practice of infant baptism. My great-great-grandfather Heinrich Funk's books had stuck with me from back before I could fully understand the words on the page. I hadn't cared one whit about my relative being an ordained minister or bishop, but the thought of him putting words on paper in an organized manner had captured me.

One of his books, *Spiegel der Taufe*, had a plain brown binding; his ideas about baptism fit with the teaching I'd heard from my youth. We're to be as children in innocence and trust, but we can best come to God when we're men and women who understand the trials of sticking with a weighty decision. For years I'd observed the cup of water being poured on the head of a young adult; that seemed right, too. Some Baptist friends had tried to convince me about immersion, but I never fell for their line.

Perhaps it was inevitable. This past January, long months after my partial conversion, I went from Chicago's streets that crossed each other at right angles—almost always exactly north and south, east and west—back to the winding, hilly roads in Hilltown Township, Bucks County. But what had once been familiar seemed as strange as my stumbling moves toward religious commitment. To be at home, but not fully so. Already when traveling there, I had wondered if the place would still look beautiful, if I'd gravitate again to my poker-playing friends in Doylestown. Then of a sudden, Abe was singing along with his zitter, and I was sitting at the table with my mother and father who still speak Pennsylvania Dutch to each other. Father took great pleasure in the cigars I brought from Chicago, something I didn't think possible with the way he'd always exclaimed about tobacco from Philadelphia.

I followed through and became a member of the Line Lexington Mennonite church; they still meet in their plain stone building. I was instructed by John Geil, the preacher of my youth, and handed a second chance. The man's become tottery and has long white hair—things I would have poked fun at—but he's still well-versed in the traditional doctrines of the Mennonites. He still draws on ancient history to support his use of logic. I like the man.

I can't hide my other strong motivation for traveling to Pennsylvania: Salome still lives there. Only a night had passed before I rode Father's trusty mare to see her. From Skunk Hollow Road, to Stump Road, to Naces Corner. I wore my best clothes, including my new blue neckpiece. Like always, Salome's smile melted my nonchalance. I nearly knocked her backward with my embrace; Chicago's women faded.

Salome had first caught my eye when she was one of my students at Chestnut Ridge School. Tall for her age, she was sharper than most. When I classified students in reading groups—and insisted each pupil needed a reader—I saw how advanced she was, far ahead of those her age in reading, superior even to some of the older ones. When I left for Chicago, I hadn't wanted her to forget me, so I'd given her a little book, *The Language of Flowers*, bound in red and gold. I was ecstatic to learn she still treasured it.

I don't know why I resorted to bragging. I spoke too much of Chicago and its 120,000 inhabitants. "It's every bit as magnificent as Philadelphia. The architecture, commerce, and of course, Lake Michigan with its connection to harbors back here in the East. Fortunes are there for the taking."

"But you wrote that you hated Chicago."

"Yes, it can be cold—more ways than one. And dirty. Sewage drains into the Chicago River."

She shrank back. "You said, 'magnificent.' Just now."

"It's like everything, not all good, not all bad." I laughed. "I've had near-disasters. Once I was unloading lumber and slipped into the river. I had to swim dog-fashion to get out."

"That's awful. Why do you laugh?"

"You're right. Many people—" I hesitated. "The children. Some of them live a hard life. Like parts of Philadelphia, I suppose. One little girl—bright golden locks and dimples." I grabbed Salome's arm. "We could help, the two of us. The girl stood barefoot outside a tavern." Salome's dark eyes widened. "A goblet of lager beer in one little hand, cake in the other."

"Oh." She might as well have said "No" to everything right then.

"I'm sorry," I said. "Sorry I mentioned it. Sorry for the child. The image haunts."

Much as I tried, I couldn't win Salome's full affection. I take small consolation: she hasn't found another. I'm not sure why. When I touch her soft hands, my heart thumps like that of a youthful boy. She remains the object of my devotion, like Quixote's unrequited love for his Dulcinea, his unseen lady. Salome's nearing her twentieth birthday and I'm four years older, but that's not insurmountable. Yet, I made no progress. No promise came. We're second cousins, but I'm fairly certain that's not it. She says she must help her parents with their younger ones.

I had my chance, and I failed miserably. Oh, to have the companionship of one so sweet. I've written more sentimental poems, and yet, I doubt death will be the cause of breaking our "silken bonds." I torture myself: she doesn't love me as I love her.

"Please write more often." I must have sounded pathetic. "That would alleviate some of my lonesome nights."

"I wouldn't mind coming to visit."

I cheered up, but that's the best I could get. I don't know how a visit will ever work out. She's too good for me, and she knows it. She could guess: I've been loose.

I fared little better at impressing my younger brothers. "The Chicago River can be fifty to seventy-five yards wide. But dead dogs and cats float. Sewers empty into some parts. Slaughter houses, tanneries, whiskey distilleries—all along its banks. It's like a farmer made liquid manure from his dung yard and unloaded it."

Jakie spat. "Men wash themselves in that?"

"Not the general rule, not anymore. Some parts of the river, much better; companies take large quantities of ice to cool beverages. The water's clean there."

"A western city, huh?" Jakie muttered.

Abe steered me away, wanting to know about drawbridges. He still wants to move here someday, but I don't know if he has the temperament to deal in this city.

"Seventeen in all; two of them built entirely of iron. Spectacular. Railroads can use three; the rest are for teams and foot passengers."

Abe smacked a fist into his other hand. "I must see that for myself."

"A man stands on the bridge and turns a horizontal lever attached to a key—looks like an auger. That's how the wheels of the drawbridge turn, so a vessel can pass through."

"I must," Abe said again, rubbing his arms, scratching his thin hairline.

I nodded. "Something to see all right. Wheels sit on a single, circular stone pier, right in the middle of the river."

With all my inflated talk, I said nothing to my brothers of loneliness, nor of my doubts whether I'm meant for business. Instead, I turned to my mother. As a child, she'd taught me prayers from *The Book of Common Prayer*. I recited one of her favorite lines: "*We have left undone those things which we ought to have done, and we have done those things which we ought not to have done.*" She waited, so I added, "*And there is no health in us.*"

She smiled. "Do you worship with Episcopalians?"

"I'd like to more often, but my friends don't care for the cadence of their prayers and hymns, the way I do." I shook my head. "It wouldn't help anyway. They're taken up with infant baptism, too."

I credit my parents: allowing me exposure to other denominations in my youth. Already when I was eight, my father let me attend a Welsh Baptist Sunday school. That's when I was so proud to learn 1,600 Bible verses and win a Testament for my achievement. Later I attended Dunker and Reformed churches, not that I was serious about either. It was a chance to ride my horse, Diamond, and get away with friends in the evenings.

Salome's never had that. She gave no indication, but her father, Jacob Kratz, is the conservative type and might add to her reluctance about Chicago. I suspect he has a low view of change, especially when it comes to something like a Sunday school. I went to his singing school, though, the year before I moved to Chicago. He knew I was tone deaf but didn't seem to hold my bad ear against me. He likely knew why I attended. As his oldest child, Salome would be the first to leave home. One day she let it slip; they used to live in a one-room log cabin and ate from a common bowl. My face must have fallen, for she was quick to add that they had individual spoons.

So here I am—three months since my return from the East. Back in the new, away from the old nest. The Presbyterians at Third have completed and paid $60,000 for a new edifice to their low wooden building. I was shocked at the pomp and show. Of course, Jacob calls the improvements "first-rate," and Mary Ann offers nothing contrary. My discord deepened so much, I thought I couldn't attend anymore. Then a greater truth sank in: God can be worshipped anywhere. It's my attitude that counts. As long as I'm not made to stand fawning at the entrance, I can enter in the right spirit.

But politics among Presbyterians—I'm surprised at how freely it comes up. After the Sunday service, it's not unusual for men to stand around, debating whether the Dred Scott case was unconstitutional and whether the Chief Justice was right to rule that Scott couldn't sue for his freedom. I overheard someone say, "As a Negro, the man wasn't a United States citizen," followed by an awkward silence.

Something similar happened last year when Lincoln gave his acceptance speech for the nomination by Illinois Republicans to the United States Senate. That time I heard a church member call it radical when Lincoln quoted from the Bible: "*A house divided against itself cannot stand.*" I fiddled with my overcoat buttons but didn't have the nerve to interrupt and call it bold that Lincoln was the first Republican leader to *say* those words publicly.

Nothing fascinated me more than the seven Lincoln-Douglas debates almost two years ago; from August through October the *Chicago Press and Tribune* did the best at keeping me abreast. I've only studied debate a short while, but Stephen Douglas was by far the better orator, even though he tried to paint Abe Lincoln as a dangerous radical, a lover of Negroes and such. But Lincoln showed a clearer grasp of facts and logic; he expressed belief in the humanity of black folks, insisting they stood before God as equal with whites. If only Lincoln weren't so tall. I never thought I'd say that about a person's height. The time I saw him, he looked awful—even his own people said he looked cadaverous—black, wrinkled clothes that didn't fit, deep-set eyes, a large Adam's apple.

I couldn't help but tell Mary Ann, "If I looked that bad, I'd have stayed inside." But then I added, "When Lincoln opens his mouth, everything changes; he makes sense."

I couldn't believe it when Douglas won election to the Senate with his fifty-four votes to Lincoln's forty-six. From what I've seen, Republican meetings are much more civil, compared with the rowdiness of Democrats. Such filthy slang and slander as I've heard from the latter. One meeting sickened me so much, I thought I'd have nothing more to do with politics. But as time passes, my resolve lessens. This fall could be even more exciting; I may get involved again.

Ugly as this city can be, I've learned I still have to put myself forward at work; I no longer try to escape the worlds of politics or religion. I can't. In fact, I've developed a disdain for those who try to hide from the world, whether they live in a Catholic convent or on a Mennonite farm. Much as I'm ambivalent about excess money, it makes a difference in my pocket. I'm determined to fit in here, even without Salome. And when I'm tempted to fall back to brooding over unanswerable questions, I remember the words I studied so idly as a student. Shakespeare's Hamlet said: "*There's a divinity that shapes our ends, / Rough-hew them how we will.*" I used to think that attitude was fatalistic; now it seems realistic.

BETSEY PETERSHEIM — western Virginia, July 1860

"Run, Viney!"

Momma's voice left no doubt. It came again.

"Run, Viney, run!"

I would show how fast I was. Then she would hug me to her—Tobias, too, unless he had flopped himself on the ground to catch his breath.

But I woke up and went from happy to sad. I was not Lovina. Momma was not fixing corn mush at the stove. Mother was.

It has been over two years, and we are used to the new one's ways. Things are not so upside down anymore. She wants Poppa to keep his fingernails cleaner and hang his hat on the hook when he comes in. She uses words like "exceedingly" when she means business. She told us her father had to take a second wife, too, but she already had three big sisters from that first woman. We listened like mice because this Mother spoke hushed, almost praying. Poppa wanted to say something, but Mother shushed him like she does. Some days she is sad and goes about weepy.

I have a big brother, Tobias, and two little sisters from my own momma. Lydia is five and Mary is four. Our new mother's name is Lydia, too, but we call her Mother. Last summer she dropped a tiny boy *Bobbli* on us. Momma always told me ahead of time when a new *Bobbli* was going to come. The same day this new boy Levi showed up, we had a terrible frost. That is not supposed to happen in June, for it was already the fifth day. When Poppa and Tobias went out to feed the animals that morning, everything was white. I stuck my nose out, but the air felt cold like winter. Only the day before, Poppa's wheat had been blooming. We never had trouble like that when Momma was here.

Poppa's eyes looked red. "The price of wheat will go right up." His mouth had a twitch. "Wheat had been selling good." He stuck his hand in his hair and grabbed hold. Then he tried to soothe. "A rooster could sit on your bottom lip, Betsey. Changes come. Some we like and some we do not. But we can always replant. And remember: we are blessed with our new baby Levi. Every one of us a Petersheim."

I did not like to hold Levi when he was a squirmy baby. I wanted to call him Left Eye. He has a different chin, squared off, even if Poppa never says so.

Here is another change. Mother calls Poppa: Crist. Grownups always called him Christian. But Mother said, "Too many Christians: Schlabach in Maryland, Selders at Brookside. And too many Daniels and Marys. Lydias, too," she added softly. Then she bounced Levi to make him coo.

"It is no different back in Somerset County," Poppa said.

His mouth twitched when Mother said again, "Too many of the same."

Some of the men at church call Poppa by Crist now, so I guess it is all said and done.

Later I complained to Tobias, "Momma always called Poppa: Poppa. The right way."

He whispered back, "Poppa was not Momma's poppa."

I made a mean face; Tobias likes to say things just to sound smart.

Soon after Momma was gone, but before the new Mother, Poppa had started calling me Betsey because I was a big helper. Everybody followed after him and not one person looked cross-eyed, so I am used to that upside down now. But my momma would not know to call me Betsey.

Whenever I asked Poppa to say more about the change, he only repeated, "Enough, Child. Big ones have doings. Be content—a big helper now."

But one time he added, "Your momma objected to using the name Mary—her mother. Not until—our Mary." Poppa looked far away. "Her father . . . Lovina was not the usual."

I do not like it when he will not tell me full, but I am not to beg. Only one other time he let slip, "There was an Elizabeth who was also your momma's Momma."

"Sarah's mother?" I asked.

"No, no. Goodness, Child! Not Daniel's woman."

Then he was back to mum. I could not make any sense. He would only say again, how it did not go well for Momma. She was not our strong Momma after baby Mary came. She had to stay in bed and left us all silent. But Poppa always shook his head: it is not Mary's fault. Poppa placed a flat stone on the edge of the field where Momma's body is stowed. I wish Momma would come back, but Poppa says she is in the ground and up in heaven. Both. When Momma was strong, she gave us hugs. She never said we had to tuck our covers just so in the daytime. This Mother goes to the loft every morning and checks that we keep order.

She came from a big state called Pennsylvania. Sometimes Poppa calls it only by Somerset. That is my home-home, too. Poppa says we moved to this Virginia country after baby Mary came. She was Momma's last. Poppa says I was three back then. He points to the front door—the side where the sun comes up—and says Virginia is a big state that goes all the way to the ocean. We are far to the west on top of a mountain where there is flatness. And a big cave in back where bears hide. We are not ever to go near. But here we have sky and can raise corn. We have a meadow to run in; I am almost as fast as Tobias. I like summer best when we catch lightning bugs. Once, Poppa let us stay up late and showed us the North Star.

We had to come through dark woods to get here. That was a state called Maryland, but not related to any of the Marys. That is where we go for church once a month. I like to learn my States. It is a long trip to Red House but not as far as Pennsylvania. Poppa says it is a strong ten miles by wagon, but the crow gets there faster. Soon we will have to bundle up extra again to ride on the wagon. Saturday nights before church, Mother makes Tobias and me clean our shoes, plus Mary's and Lydia's. Tobias is allowed to use a knife to get dirt out of cracks; I am to grease and rub the shoes soft. I put them in a row at the door for Mother to inspect.

I want to have church again at our house, but Poppa looks at Mother and says, "Not yet."

She casts her eyes about and says, "Where would we put everyone?" She calls our house a cabin.

We only have church every other Sunday. Poppa showed me the days with numbers that go with a moon's face from thin to fat. Two Sundays every month are marked. That is when we have our Amish church: one time, here in Virginia, then skip a week. The next Sunday over at Red House in Maryland, then skip another week.

On our skips we have visiting Sundays. Sometimes Daniel Beachy brings his family in the afternoon. That is the Daniel who is our Minister of the Book. I get to play with Sarah the whole time. She will always be a year younger than me. Daniel's wife, Elizabeth, and their big girl, Mary—more names!—help Mother with the food. Sometimes Jonas and Tobias let Sarah and me build houses with them in the woods. We drag big sticks. I like Jonas because he does not tease like Tobias does. He has black hair that sits like a cap. Tobias's hair is often on the fritz and does not hide his big ears.

Poppa used to play with us on our off Sundays, if the Beachys could not come. He would lie down on his back in the meadow with Tobias and me. One time he crossed one leg over his other knee and put his hands behind his head. I did the same, but he scolded. "Fix your dress, Betsey, over your knees. A girl must be proper."

I did as he said but turned away. Tobias scrunched his face at me, and I jerked back to look at the clouds.

"What does that one look like?" Poppa asked, pointing to the left.

"A rabbit with ears," I said.

"Not stubby ears," Tobias said.

"Babies have stubbly." I licked my lips a tiny bit, but I did not stick out my tongue.

"And the one to the right?" Poppa asked.

Tobias waved his hand high. "A long, long wagon with only one wheel."

"No wagon can be that big!" I said.

"And what good would it be without more wheels?" Poppa asked. Tobias laughed, too.

"We would have to fetch corn from the field—an armful—not have it in our barn," I said. "That would be silly."

Back then, Poppa explained other things, too. I was five when he showed me how to make buckwheat cakes. He taught me to stand back— only reach with my arm—so the fat could not leap from the kettle and pop into my eye. By then I was bigger and used to Betsey; Auntie Mommie stopped coming through the snow so much to help.

But the big change came that summer when Poppa sent us to stay at Auntie Mommie's. We were there three nights. Auntie Mommie and her man, Christian, have three children. Their Daniel is my age, but their girl, Magdalena, is older. Their Valentine has a case of the freckles. They live not far away at Brookside. That is a prettier name than German Settlement where the Beachys live; their place was once called Mount Carmel, and before that, Salem. Our meadow is just a meadow. Poppa says Uncle Christian was the first Amish man here. The Beachy family came next when I was still a baby in my home-home. Now I am seven.

Auntie Mommie's big house was once a stagecoach inn. Poppa says that means travelers could give a coin to stay there at night; they had beds for strangers. But when Auntie and Uncle Christian bought that inn building, they made it into their house. We did not need to pay when we stayed there. Sometimes Poppa lets me touch the coins from his leather pouch. He has coppers and shillings and one gold dollar with an Indian head on it.

I never slept in a stone house before. I was shivery and hot on the floor—both. Auntie Mommie heard me twist and turn and brought me extra cover. She is Poppa's sister and has long fingers. She is a Lydia too, but went from Petersheim to Selders. Poppa says when a woman marries, she gets her man's last name. Our Mother went from being a Lydia Hershberger.

When Poppa returned and came to get us at Auntie Mommie's, he surprised us with this woman. She is bigger than Momma and younger; her face is long and her nose comes rather to a point. She has three dresses hanging in the wardrobe. Poppa says not to put out my lower lip. He rubs my back. "We live near to Backbone Mountain. The bones in your back make a spine to help you stand up straight."

* * *

Mother made each of us girls a new dress. I wanted to give her a hug, but when I stepped close, I felt shy. The dress will be warm for winter, but hot to try on now—the prettiest dark green like a pine tree. I only had gray dresses before like Momma. But Mother surprised us girls even more; she put a tiny lace trim about the neck. I giggled to touch it; I was so happy. Mary clapped her hands. The lace feels softer than I know, and I can rub it without looking. Poppa said nothing, but he did not make Mother take it off. None of the women at church have lace.

Sometimes Mother scolds me after church for being restless when Daniel Beachy preaches. He is slower than our work horses. He speaks low on the same note, whilst Peter Schrock's voice goes up and down. Peter is our new minister in Maryland. He came to visit from my home-home and is a jolly sort, even though his eyes hide under bushy eyebrows. Now he lives near Red House and is our newest chosen. At first his deep voice and laugh frightened me, but now it sounds like music. Solemn and happy—both. Our other Minister of the Book in Maryland is Peter Miller. We have to say both names for both men so as not to be confused.

It is better to hear Daniel's ramble than that old one who visited. Two bishops came to help Daniel with the minister's lot when the big folks chose Peter Schrock. The old one had a tall hunch and hair speckled with white. Mother said he lives in a faraway state called Iowa and will not come again. His name is scarier than Schlabach. I have to spit to say Schwartzendruber. He started the big folks talking about Iowa. But Mother did not approve of the old one traveling all the way here. She whispered to Elizabeth, "What if he took sick?" And then her voice hissed with a hand to cover. "If he wants to move far away, he should stay put, not keep looking back like Lot's wife."

That Jacob pounded on the preacher's table such that Levi was startled awake. Three times I counted "everlasting fires." He said a dwelling place in hell means roasting hot. I know to stay back when Poppa burns tall grass or brush in springtime.

When Jacob talked loud, I tried to do what I tell Mary in summertime. She does not like grasshoppers because they jump of a sudden.

"Keep your eyes fixed," I tell her. "The hopper cannot frighten, if you keep your eyes set square. It is only when you cast your eye to the side and forget to expect."

She insists she does as I say, but she still clings when the grasshopper jumps without so much as a flinch. I try to smooth her hair like Poppa does, but she runs inside to Mother.

It went the same for me when I stared at this preacher's hand trembling on his Bible. His lips seemed not to move, but he still said words.

"The *sins* of the transgressor melt from *brimstone*."

I lurched on the bench and made a bad squeak. I had to sit back fast, so no one would know whence the disturbance. I leaned my head into Mother's side, but she patted Levi squirming on her lap. I straightened to take Mary's hand.

One time another preacher man came right to our cabin. That was before Mother. His name was Johnny, but he was not entirely one of us. If we cannot have church at our place, I want him to come again. He is my favorite visitor. Johnny Kline is his first and last name. He came when we were all poor in spirit with Momma's passing. Auntie Mommie had told him about our lonely family when he came to visit the Tunkers in Brookside. Now Mother says they are called Dunkers or Dunkards. She is much to correct everyone.

This Johnny rode his horse, Nell, two miles up the mountain to our house, and we are not even his kind. But Poppa says the Tunkers come from the same soil as we Amish. We are the same to not wear loud clothes, nor fight with swords. Poppa says we all promise to live in peace, not be angry like the world.

Johnny was the kindest. His face was as round as the moon when it is full. Poppa said Johnny came from a faraway part of Virginia, but not the farthest away ocean part. He came to visit his people and give encouragement. He spoke more tenderly than our Daniel Beachy and not so slow. Johnny could have been talking to our baby bunnies.

He did not even know Momma, but he gathered Tobias and me on his lap and said a prayer just for us. I did not want Johnny to leave. But he did, and Momma was still gone. I wish he would come again, but maybe he knows we have Mother now.

J. Fretz — Chicago, August 1860

"**M**y skin crawls," Joe says, "something bad. Don't know. A feeling. Agitation, this confounded agitation. How long, a kettle hiss?"

"Violence won't bring change," I say. "Not the right kind. Those vigilante groups . . . can't let abolitionists like that take over. Stay tight against the extreme fringe."

Phil nods. "John Brown and his ilk might have set *back* the anti-slavery cause. Their murderous ways. Lincoln never went for it."

"Pure revenge against those *favoring* slavery; the ones, destroyed Lawrence, Kansas four years ago." I shake my head. "Savagery, both sides."

Joe stays hunched over his stein, his brown eyes dull. "Want us to ignore things? That it? Steam won't build forever. That lid'll blow."

"No!" I exclaim. "Not ignore. Better ways. Frederick Douglass tried to warn Brown when he proposed attacking the federal arsenal at Harpers Ferry. Called it pointless."

"That Brown—no freedom fighter," Phil says, his lips tight. "No martyr, that man."

I clap Joe on the shoulder. "I'm telling you: violence doesn't solve. Don't be so bullheaded. Remember those men in California a year ago?"

My friends know the story as well as I. Two men thought they had to defend their honor. The result: Chief Justice David Terry of the California Supreme Court killed an anti-slavery senator, David Broderick. Both men Democrats, but the judge came from Kentucky, took his pro-slavery thoughts all the way to the west coast. Broderick—unusual, but part of an anti-slavery wing of Democrats—first to fire, but missed. Reports said he was shaking from hatred, not fear. He'd left New York City to follow the gold rush. Dead at age thirty-nine.

Joe drains his mug. "Have to choose; not good, this half-slave, half-free."

In spite of our uncertain footing, it's an exciting time for us young men in the city—all kinds of trade and commerce. A primary grain depot, Chicago has new construction everywhere: factories, foundries, ship building. Last year over 459 million feet of lumber came our way. The city built piers to protect the harbor and the shipping industry. Not that lumber is our only available building material, but the quality of the red brick manufactured here isn't as good as what can be brought from Springfield. Milwaukee gives us competition, too, with its buff-colored brick—very smooth and durable. Stone, too, for that matter; only twenty miles south, a beautiful white—some say straw-colored—Athens Marble.

With all that potential for selfish gain, I've used my new commitment to Sunday school work to maintain some balance. I haven't lost the itch to teach! Mr. Thomas Lord—lives two doors away with his family—is one of the few Presbyterians who's taken an interest in me. When he heard about my teaching background, he invited me to go with him. Since then, I've met other young men and women from different denominations, providing instruction for children, helping out at the Reuben Street Mission. This month we started a new one on Erie Street. Some Sundays, over a hundred scholars. Of course, I'm still learning, too; I need evening church services, noontime prayer meetings. I'm no saint.

The way some immigrants have to live! A thin pad on the floor where five youngsters sleep. Some of these fathers remind me of the Irish I work with—a hard lot. Sunday's a day for beer gardens and dance halls. But my use of German comes in handy. Kind of a go-between, as long as I remember not to mix in Pennsylvania Dutch words. Most in the Reuben Street neighborhood come from that part of the Old Country where the German language prevails; some can barely speak English.

I never expected these Sunday school boys to work their way into my thinking. The way they count on me! I told Mary Ann, "I want to enhance the outlook of these lads. Give them 'an inch' as Douglass might say."

We were grubbing for early potatoes in her garden—her children scratching underground to rob from plants while I gently lifted soil with the spade.

"An inch? Who did you say?" she asked.

"Mr. Douglass. I want enough skill at letters for my boys, so they can read the Bible. Open new worlds, like Father did for me; my teachers at Freeland, too. That inch, that start. Maybe there weren't as many books at home when you—"

Mary Ann moved the bucket to the next plant. "The Senator from Illinois?"

"No, no, *Frederick*, not Stephen. Spells his last name with a double 's.' A black man—I told you—came from a slave mother and unknown white father."

Mary Ann looked up with surprise, then scolded Estelle. "Stay back, so Uncle can dig."

"His narrative tells how he's self-taught and escaped to freedom when he was twenty-one. You should read it. Inspiring. He went from being taught the alphabet by his Master's woman to . . . well, he schemed. When the woman stopped, white boys taught him. She'd opened the window but then thought better of it. He wasn't going to let it close."

"Was that legal?"

"Is learning illegal? Would you want Estelle denied?"

Mary Ann hesitated. "Isn't that different? Most dark ones are taken care of, aren't they?"

"Not when slave catchers are everywhere, causing trouble where there needn't be any."

At that Mary Ann reprimanded J. Michael for dragging too much dirt out from under a plant. "Put it back; more potatoes need to grow."

"You should read it," I urged again. "Frederick was very generous to his Master's woman—called her 'a good soul.'"

"Good soul?"

I waited till my sister looked me square in the eye. I spoke softly but she could read my lips, too. "Said it was the Master who had to *train* his wife to think of Frederick as a brute." Mary Ann bent down and brushed a curl from Isabel's forehead. "Douglass saw how injurious that training was *to the woman*. Changed from her good instincts—he called it deplorable—all to squelch a young lad's hunger to read. *Tried* to squelch."

"Enough spuds for now, children," Mary Ann said suddenly. "You, too, Fretz."

Estelle ran ahead, while Mary Ann took a hand from the other two. I lightly tamped the soil around each disturbed plant. Sheltering her children? She hasn't seen the homes of my boys. I was about to say Douglass had called it *depravity*, the woman's effort to shut him up in mental darkness. I would have stopped myself, though, not said that Douglass believes a slave owner degrades *himself* when he thinks it reasonable for him to take, *as a right*, another's earnings. Still, shouldn't Estelle know some people steal another's dignity when they refuse to see that person's right to be treated as human? Someday J. Michael will have the misfortune of hearing a slave catcher give thanks he was able to return a slave to the role appointed by God.

My Sunday school boys—white boys—understand that kind of mistreatment. I pass along to them some learnings from Douglass, some of the bread I've been so privileged, literally and figuratively, to receive. But some folks in Chicago only show coldness to the poor, thinking *them* depraved, no higher than beasts. I want my boys to see: knowledge can be part of the remedy. They don't have to accept a dismal life—being some wealthy man's slave. Oh, they wouldn't understand that. My favorite class liked the idea of having a motto, but they chose "The True Soldiers." I had to caution them: we want to march with Jesus.

Marching—now that's a frenzy that surprises me even more than my boys. But I've told myself, if I'm going to stay in Chicago, I must do what's right in front of me. Yes, I've joined the Wide-Awakes. We're in all the big cities in the North and will do whatever we can to make sure Lincoln is elected president. Enough of these Buchanan years! I'm officially a Lincoln man. When I'm not at church or teaching my boys, my evenings go to political affairs. It's become a badge of honor to be called a Black Republican of the darkest kind.

We Wide-Awakes march in the streets at night; Phil or Joe and I often go together. The excitement in our club infects us all. Most of us wear black oilcloth capes and hats, although these hot August nights have been too oppressive for some. We carry our torches high overhead with the tar barrels flaming. Sometimes, I admit, we've made fools of ourselves—there's no good reason to be disorderly—but we also hear solid lectures and attend rallies. I've been privileged to hear abolitionists like Cassius M. Clay hold forth a clear message regarding the plight of our dark brother. Over four million Negroes who don't have the opportunity to move at will! How can this be the United States? These people eat and breathe as we do, bear the image of God, and yet they're treated as little better than four-legged animals.

With two presidential candidates coming from Illinois, there's been a lot of reading to keep up with, too. My friends and I share copies of William Lloyd Garrison's national paper, *The Liberator*; I read Frederick Douglass's *North Star*, too. I'd be lost without these voices, but some of Garrison's writings surprise me. He claims Southern planters practice "unbridled lust and filthy *amalgamation*." Now there's a word to behold. No doubt, some slave owners demand inappropriate relations and produce children with mixed racial heritage, but Garrison should be more careful not to overgeneralize. Emotional language like that feeds fear.

But sometimes Joe surprises me, too; he'll even take the side of the South! "They'll need to adjust their ledgers if slavery's done away with."

"That doesn't make it right to keep people in bondage. You support getting ahead by taking advantage?" I had to slow myself. "Listen, there's an old man back home, old Isaiah. I was shocked—just a lad—when I met him. A former slave living in Bucks County. It wasn't his skin color." Joe looked straight ahead. "You don't see, do you?"

"Not fair, either side."

"But what kind of life would that be? Isaiah had overcome his shackles, like Douglass, but not nearly as fortunate." Joe's eyes could have been those of a statue. "Some say, we have as many as 1,000 here in Chicago who've escaped bondage. Think about it. They can stand in bright sunlight and breathe free air, but . . . they *always* keep an eye on the shadows. Could you? How would you ever feel safe, dreaded slave catchers out roaming?"

Joe's my friend, but he acted unconvinced. It's not uncommon, running up against people who see things differently. Recently, I had a worse go-round with a Mr. William Thomson; it happened so quickly I scarcely knew what transpired. He's a business acquaintance and I considered him a friend. He lives in Michigan now, but he was back here talking with Beidler. We men had enjoyed Mary Ann's delicious fare of roasted goose and had retired to the parlor for after-dinner drinks. Beidler chose his favorite wing-back chair, covered with a deep red and gold velvet, and Thomson and I shared the settee. That man has a way of assuming the right to more than half the space, but I crossed one leg away from him and squeezed against the arm of the settee.

We'd been talking amiably enough of national affairs, how Lincoln had been wise to spread his ideas by publishing his debates with Stephen Douglas. And his effort to secure the Republican Party's nomination had been helped by having the convention here in Chicago. But as we conversed, Thomson's loyalty to Democrats trickled out. He said one of their usual lines, "To reject slavery categorically in the territories is to open the door to civil war." I didn't like the way he pounced on the word *categorically*, but I still wasn't overly alarmed—the brandy may have lulled me—until he looked at me and said, "Reckless. Your Rail Splitter invites social disorder." Thomson says all his *s* sounds like a plump woman with too much spit. "Reckless!" he said again—still talking to *me*—and ended with a long hiss. Then he asked, "How does *social disorder* find a place with Christian virtues?"

I've heard these arguments before, but I paused, trying to push his irritating quirks to the back of my mind. Some of Lincoln's remarks have been taken to mean the Republican Party is ready to make war on slavery.

In my hesitation, Thomson spoke again. "You cannot be an abolitionist and a Christian!" His red cheeks blazed; his loose jowls flopped.

Now I was stunned. But I wasn't going to cower or pass it off as nothing. The Irishmen at the lumber yard can be crude, but they don't attack my political beliefs. Not to my face. "How can you claim to be a Christian and look the other way when you see oppression?" popped out of my mouth. I half-smiled. "Or don't you see?"

Just as swiftly, he countered, "An abolitionist is no better than an infidel. What are you, a universalist? You people sicken me; you act like you know more than God."

At that Beidler got up and made a show of tightening stoppers and putting bottles back in the cabinet. With great deliberation he pocketed the key, propped an elbow on the mantel, and pulled his watch piece from his breast pocket. I was loath to let such rank charges go uncontested, but I couldn't forget my surroundings. I busied myself with a last swirl in my glass.

As quickly as the animosity leaped out, Thomson drew himself up and became the perfect gentleman, expressing thanks to Beidler but declining the offer of an escort to his nearby hotel. He didn't reach to shake hands with me, although I adopted nonchalance nearby, leaning against the oak door frame in the foyer. As the door closed, I retreated up the stairs. My beliefs had been *categorically* placed outside of Christianity. *Absolutely, without exception.*

The next morning Jacob and I faced each other across our cooked wheat, but neither of us said a word about Mr. Thomson. I could only hope my boss had put aside my indignation at the end of last night's conversation. Beidler claims to be a Lincoln man, going back to when they met in Springfield some years ago, but he doesn't follow politics as closely as I do. He might not know Thomson was spouting the same line Stephen Douglas has put forward about popular sovereignty: locals in western territories should decide for themselves whether to encourage or prohibit slavery.

For me, I'm solidly with Lincoln, thinking Congress has the right to ban slavery in the western lands and should do so without delay. Indeed, *not* to do so is to ignore the moral imperative. How could anyone claim slavery is morally neutral? Our Declaration of Independence makes clear: "All men are created equal." But those on the other side hide behind the first naturalization law in 1790 with its guidelines for how immigrants could become American citizens. Most notably, that process was limited to white people. That's the ugly truth. I can't conclude anymore that it must have been a mistake.

On this, I'm with abolitionists: anyone born in this country is a citizen, and every citizen is equal before the law. Lincoln's distinction may be useful—not everyone is equal in intellect, or size, or social capacity—but whatever the case, a man should have the right to improve himself. Equality has to apply to those inalienable rights our early leaders identified: life, liberty, and the pursuit of happiness. It has to!

While Thomson's attacks forced me to think through my ideas again, what lingered was his bluster. But then I remembered the kind of sympathy Frederick Douglass wrote about. Why couldn't I apply the same? Thomson's attitudes harm *him*. At that, I regretted my anger; my words had served no useful purpose. He might not be as false as Northerners who oppose slavery only because they think it gives unfair economic advantage to slave owners—the opposite of Joe's line. At least Joe cares about more than the interests of the *northern white* man.

Beidler's never told me he's completely committed to Free Soil principles; that's what the Republican Party stands for: "Free Soil, Free Labor, Free Men." Sometimes, though, Beidler sounds like Father.

All would be fine if we could still be Whigs.

If only Beidler would say he cares first and foremost about the welfare of enslaved people. I know he won't say that at work; he might lose a sale. But when I've offered to loan him Frederick Douglass's narrative, he shrugs. The book's full of stirring stories of downtrodden suffering: a man separated from his wife, a mother from her child. But Douglass never accepts wretchedness. He comes up with his own solutions. There's something of the spiritual in that man. I like him.

One good thing about all that's pressing here: I've been able to push Father's offer to the back of my mind. Late in the winter, his question reared itself. "Might you have interest in taking over the farm?"

I was stunned—an opportunity like that at the very time my interest in Chicago had deepened! As the eldest son, I might have known the offer was coming, but I thought when I left home I was forsaking any claim to property. Much as I've known bouts of discontent here for three years and begged Salome to join me, I've never seriously considered moving back.

Oh, I've pined for the familiar—homesick for those rolling, green hills of Bucks County, a meadow nearby for our running contests and games of stick ball. Four acres of forest with magnificent oak, elm, and hickory. I can picture the main entrance facing the rising sun, with its little portico and round pillars, the white fence surrounding the small yard. I can close my eyes and smell honeysuckle, feel it burst in my mouth. I see the branches of the viney yellow jessamine reaching all the way to my second-story bedroom window. Mother was partial to the four old pear trees, but the quince were my favorite.

But all of that's related to *Fernweh*, that longing for far off places. Strange. When I lived in Pennsylvania, I dreamed of life in Chicago. Now that I'm here, I romanticize my faraway home. Father built that stone farmhouse in 1838 when I was three. He's a clever man, devising a system of wooden pipes running from one of the springs to the house, then rigging up a hydraulic ram to pump the water. Sure, I still keep my ear to the ground, reading the *Bucks County Intelligencer*. That connection goes back to when my brothers and I used to cut cord wood and haul it to the newspaper's office in Doylestown; our work paid for a subscription for Father.

But this offer for me to take over . . .

Everything I could want is on that property: a smokehouse, a milk cave that goes twenty-seven feet deep, a stairway down to the springhouse where Mother keeps food, especially during the hot summer. Some of our neighbors—the more plain Mennonites—criticized Father for too much fanciness. He put in a beautiful winding stairway with walnut railing to the upper story. And drawers. My father loves drawers—under each windowsill, under the hand-carved mantel, each with a wooden knob.

Everything wholesome is back there. But here, I've traded an excellent water supply—how many pails of water did I carry to the horses?—for Chicago's dysentery. This place of cold strangers where a sharp wind blows in from Lake Michigan. Impersonal by any count, this city where people love anything that makes a display, whether clothes, a horse, or a second corner lot. The flamboyance often becomes distasteful. I'd rather look out on Mother's dahlias and Rose of Sharon, take in the fragrance from her yellow rose bush and hear the dinner bell calling me. Oh, I know: that's nostalgia carrying me away again.

When the offer first came, I wrote back and asked Father how much I could make off the farm in a year. I try to guard against the smell of money, but I reminded him I've moved ahead by graduating from Bell and Stratton Commercial College. Father was gracious, knowing full well I could do better for myself in this city, putting my new business skills to use. He didn't press for a decision by a certain date; he only wrote of feeling old and tired some days.

"Make money and get rich, Son. But do it honestly."

When Beidler got wind—I'd told Mary Ann of my dilemma—he started talking about a partnership. But he's not offered specifics. A month has passed, and I think Father's question may have been a formality, some obligation to ask the eldest son. Abe is twenty already and Jakie, only two years younger, might be the best suited of us all—stocky and taller than I.

Nothing has improved for me with Salome. She says she'll never forget me, but she warns me not to stay in Chicago too long if the temptations are as plentiful as they sound. Sometimes I read the closing of her letter first. So far, she still signs: "Yours in True Love." Her letters are always kind and attentive, and I hear her gentle, unassuming ways. That's when I know I don't want to lose her! And yet, I'm not willing to return to a farmer's life in Pennsylvania in order to obtain her hand. My head spins. One part knows I should let her go. The other part tempts me to hold out longer; she hasn't given any indication of wanting her freedom.

In my weaker moments I compare it to driving a business contract. Time and again, I've seen Beidler know when to walk away, when to strike a bargain. I'm too soft, though, for his tactics. But I despair: will I ever fully become my own man? I'm twenty-five, but I remain dependent on Mary Ann and Jacob. I can come and go as I like, but living here doesn't advance my desire to be under obligation to no one. Most of the time, the taste of family life is fine—sharing meals and such—but the children sometimes bother with their noise. Estelle's voice is shrill, and I don't have Mary Ann's patience. Still, I like it when J. Michael shows me his schoolwork; I've given him a start of geometry—only the basic concepts.

To be sure, I'm borrowing on Jacob's good will. I'm too frugal to locate a place of residence by my lonesome. It would take far too much of my limited resources, compared with the meager monthly rent I pay. And coming home to an empty house? Phil tells me I shouldn't be sleeping alone all the time. I laugh him off, but it rankles. I can only dream of a woman's body beside me, breathing together and turning as one. I dabble as a suitor, but I'm too timid for serious moves.

Instead, I waste time, thinking of the silliest things. If I returned to Pennsylvania, I might have to give up my taste for liquor! I'm not prone to overconsumption, but neither do I see any need for the other extreme. I was surprised when Father and Mother were some of the first to abstain back home. (How can *they* make decisions and solve problems so effortlessly?) People shook their heads when Father refused to serve alcohol for the hired men working in his fields; they said he'd soon have to do all the work himself. As it turned out, though, Mother made a tasty root beer that laborers found to be entirely refreshing.

And something even more trifling happened recently: a large woman at Third Presbyterian sat on my silk hat. How could she not look? I'd placed it on the spot beside me and looked away. That quickly, she sat on it full square! The same hat Father gave me when I was fourteen. I know it's foolish, but I was sick at heart. I always felt taller and grown up when I wore it—a man! I could replace it, but I haven't. A minor comeuppance, but I see no humor. Instead, I feel defensive. Does it matter if I like the way I look in my vest and long-sleeved shirts at the office? If I went back to wearing work clothes on the farm, I'd be a different person.

ESTHER — Shenandoah Valley, Virginia, September 1860

Simon frowns and says, "'Tis only speculation and will come to nothing." His bottom teeth jut out crosswise.

I grab his arm and put my head on his shoulder. I don't like it when he's cross. "But Andrew—already seventeen? And Peter looks to be eighteen. Even Joseph and William—Mary Grace!—may not be safe."

"You're too excitable, like your women friends. Think not on it."

I take the measure of my words. "We can't be entirely apart. Genevieve knew to spread lard and egg whites on a cloth with mustard last winter. That deep cold that latched on, plaster didn't burn my chest as much."

"Too much fraternizing," he mutters.

I make myself count to ten. He never objected when Genevieve's boys went swimming in the creek with our boys. "You, you're the one, said people were whipped into a fury over the raid."

"Say nothing more to me or anyone of this John Brown and his lunatics. Full of notions. That was long ago and has nothing to do with me. None of us. The man was hanged."

I don't like public disputes any more than Simon, but I need to know what's what, not be left in the dark. He could say what he hears in town, not make me ask. Our boys have seen slaves walk in large groups southward on the Pike.

"Driven like cattle," Andrew says.

Simon wouldn't need to pinch his lips. Nor withdraw himself of a sudden. Either time, I'm left bereft.

Frances knows, folks still in an uproar. That John Brown planned to head right up the valley from Harpers Ferry and kill white people. Simon will only speak of that area as beautiful: a huge gash in the mountains dividing peaceful waters. But Genevieve says there may be others who think like that Brown, hankering after revolution.

We've been fortunate; when the state militia calls Simon to their drills—a muster of four days already this fall—he pays a small fee to be exempt. Come another year, we'll need to pay the same for Andrew, equivalency for military demands. We don't object: the state has the right to require something.

Most of those surrounding us, the English, hold a different conscience, but we're taught not to be swayed by common thought. We can't say why Jehovah drowned Pharoah's men in the Red Sea. But we know that's no longer God's way. We're to live in peace like Jesus said. Stay separate from the rough-and-tumble, from people who clamored for Brown's blood because he tried to turn slaves against their owners. That's the way with violence: it begets more. One mob, no better than another.

Simon's right about Methodists, though; some in the Valley have slipped. Genevieve admitted her George used several of the dark ones for harvest.

"We can't lose wheat to rain," she said, her lips atremble. I wanted to steady her—no one wants ripe grain to fall from the stalk—but she kept her eyes cast down.

Frances was bolder. Her voice went deep when she asked Genevieve point blank, "Did George pay wages to the rented slaves?"

Genevieve's thin arms flailed with extra force at carpet draped on bushes. Finally, she said, "Only to the owner." But she added, "George and the boys worked right alongside the Negroes. He calls them family." Frances pressed no further.

Much has changed since I was a little girl; the Methodists used to be plainer like us. Sobering, what can happen if we allow the world to squeeze us into its mold. Only the Primitive Baptists and Dunkers stay firm like us, separate in garb. Mama never once paraded in silk and velvet or wore fancy pins. But Genevieve's not uppity, even if she puts up with the encumbrance of a hoop skirt on occasion. She's always been partial to Mary Grace, tender to our boys. She's like as not to talk about saving souls for heaven, more so than our own preachers.

But Frances poked at far more than clothes when she came to help me spade this fall. She knows I want to get a head start as soon as the garden vines curl their brown edges. She brought it up.

"Some of our own will hire from the black men when short on help."

I raised my head sharply. Did she think Simon—? She knows whereof she speaks, for her husband, Samuel Coffman, is our minister and stays alert. He was strong to denounce that Brown's claim that he and his violent ways would bring salvation to the poor.

Frances pushed the spade again with a sharp thrust. "Temptation sits heavily this time of year. Our men can't be sure what a Master will do with a worker's money."

The Dunkers in our Valley are said to be stronger on troubling matters like this. They make it clear: *you cannot use a slave and be one of us.* But I don't think Simon will stoop, not so long as our boys stay healthy.

Our bishop, Martin, is faithful, too. "All men are free in Christ, not for sale like horses."

We darest not hold anyone in bondage. Mama used to speak of Martin's father, Peter Burkholder, how he preached against slavery way back: "Not to exalt over or claim to own." That Peter's the one, wrote our *Mennonite Confession of Faith* and still is revered.

"Men stealers. Those who buy men; nothing but men stealers," Mama said.

Samuel's the one reminds us at Weavers church of our heritage. Not long ago he told of a Mennonite preacher before him, a Rodes, killed in these parts along with most in his family. Mary Grace snuggled into me on the bench.

But Simon scoffed on the way home, as if the past has no bearing.

"Why bring up skirmishes with the Indian? A hundred years ago and more." He clicked his tongue at the horses. "Supposed to look ahead, not be backward." He only wants to talk of his new riding horse, Midnight, his finest black one; the browns are for work.

"Our children need to hear; not all is ease." But then I clamp my mouth. I dare not dwell on the Rodes woman who died also, their house and barn burned. Three or four of their boys killed, too. One of them hid in a pear tree but was shot right out. And two girls taken, only to be killed later when they couldn't keep up with their captors. Another girl fled—running with her baby sister in her arms—twelve miles to safety.

Simon won't admit, but our times are rowdy with people astir over this year's election. Rancor against the Republicans. Even Simon's brother, Gabriel, when we went for a visit that Sunday a month ago, called it the Black Republican John Brown Party of the North! Afterwards, Simon only repeated his usual: "Not for women. Keep to your orchard."

I didn't tell him what Gabriel's wife put to me. Hushed-like, Harriet asked regarding Simon and me. (She didn't mean warts or stomachache.) I insisted nothing ailed the two of us; we didn't need another start of ginseng. Nor did we need a baby every year for twenty years. Harriet has her pack of eight, but just because Mary Grace is nine, doesn't mean there's a problem. Of course, I would welcome another girl, but it's not entirely needful. Our grandmothers wore themselves out—Mama birthed ten—what with wilderness living and rustling grub for a hungry brood. It's not for me, and no verse requires it. Only a nosy sister-in-law.

Like usual, Gabriel and Simon made sport of preachers that day—always called them a stubborn lot. Gabriel mentioned this Shank, a Mennonite who had to be removed as bishop in their Lower District because he fell out with his neighbor over ownership of a spring. The man wouldn't see it any other way, so the conference leaders put him out.

"'Course, we're not all related, the Shanks around here." But then Gabriel changed his tune. "Our bloodline goes back—the original Michael, the one who settled in the Linville Creek area." But Simon wouldn't respect that either: no regard for the first bishop in our Virginia Mennonite churches.

Now we hear of yet another dissension amidst our Valley's Middle District. A Joseph Funk carries on a dispute with an Elder among the German Baptists, a John Kline, who lives in the same Broadway area as Gabriel. This Joseph, over eighty years old and given to his ups and downs. But such pettiness over baptism.

Frances surprised me to call it worthy. "We may be swallowed by the Dunkers if we don't make our position known."

Of course, we Mennonites only sprinkle, while they insist three dips are needed. But Frances's square face, with her hair pulled back tight, took on a severity. "No indication a bath is better than a touch of water, though some try to make it so."

I didn't want to argue, but such enmity between leaders! First, one man published his view; then the other sent forth a reply. More harmful things said since. This Kline man is said to be godly, not a troublemaker, but for him to say, "To pour or sprinkle is not to baptize at all"— how does that *not* contribute to ill will?

Our Funk man made clear he didn't mean to stir controversy; he only sought the true meaning when translating his grandfather Heinrich's German writings on baptism. But it doesn't square. He'd do better to be satisfied with his translation of Burkholder's *Confession of Faith* from German to English. That's for our children who have picked up the rudiments of reading. This Joseph's done plenty of good. No need to stir up over church matters. A singing teacher for years. Now he's come up with a book of songs called *Harmonia Sacra*. Andrew wants to see the man's print shop—he lives not far away in Singers Glen—but Simon scoffs and calls that easy work. What could be the harm?

With all that inflames amidst public authorities, how dare we drift to dispute in our churches? Same could go for me, I suppose, with Simon. Yes, he could be more forthright, and not insist on only doing one way or the other with the youngsters. But he's not mean-spirited, just set in his ways. His work—plus Midnight—is all. When he needs me to bind wheat in the field, I'm expected and darest not complain. He won't be jovial until the fall work is done. Only come winter, he'll allow himself a second cinnamon bun and squeeze me about the waist.

For my part, I will make sure our boys go to school again this winter. Last spring, I benefited from William's croup, for he had to stay inside. I asked him to teach me his letters—rather on the sly—but I didn't want to settle for an X as Mama had. Mary Grace took a turn at the slate, too, and through it all Simon never missed a solid meal. No harm done, my being able to write my name.

Jacob — Iowa, November 1860

All has changed. Everything she does is done quickly, even her assessments. I never thought this would happen. Of course, I never anticipated being a widower, not fully.

"Do you ever contemplate?" I asked.

"What would be the use?" she replied, her dark eyes flashing. "I do what is in front of me. I say my mind."

"Might there not be regret? A word too hastily spoken?"

"Yes, there can be times to speak remorse."

I want to ask if it was always that easy with her Daniel, but I refrain. I wonder how she can rattle needlessly at times, then mince words.

An idea began forming last spring for me to make a trip East, come warmer weather. One thing led to the next, as they say. I had long wanted to visit again in the Glades settlement of Somerset County and secure copies of the early disciplines and ministers' manuals. I only brought disciplines of 1809 and 1837 where we ministers outlined the procedure regarding temptations to pride in showy furniture and such. I failed to anticipate the extent in Iowa: mothers given to making high collars for their children's shirts, men attracted to silken neckcloths.

My trip came about with careful planning and the Lord's blessing. I traveled East by train with my grandson Samuel, the one who wants to be a teacher. He made possible the start of my journey by providing companionship to Indiana, sitting by the window and sparing me from the worst of flying dirt. These trains can damage clothes with their sparks from coal firing. Such exposure to wind and soot was disagreeable, but we saved ourselves considerable time by using modern transportation. When we disembarked, however, it took time to be assured of my legs. The jerking and unevenness of the ride adversely affected my innards as well.

Altogether, I was absent from Iowa six weeks. Now Frederick has filled me in on what was preached in my absence. And Jakob accomplished much field work for me—most of my corn shucked. How can I not look on my grown grandsons with favor?

Plus, now I possess the desired copy of the Unzicker and Nafziger manuscripts. The thrill of touching old letters, the *Ordnungsbriefe* going back to Strasbourg in 1568! I, Jacob Schwartzendruber, called to be a part of this blessed chain. Come winter, I will ask young Jakob to handwrite another copy of each precious document—one for the keeping of my son, Joseph. He has recently been chosen in the lot as a minister to serve with me and the others: John P., Peter, Benjamin, and Keim. I do not want the responsibility of preserving the only copy in the West. Jakob has a steady hand, and I will remind him to refrain from excessive swirls.

The Hans Nafziger manuscript from the eighteenth century gives much helpful detail regarding the ceremonies of baptism and marriage. It is just as I thought! The young man is *not* to propose marriage on his own; he is to make known his request of the young lady through the deacon or minister. We dare not stray from the example of Eleazer, Abraham's servant, when Abraham sought a wife for his son Isaac.

But I am brought up short by Joseph Unzicker's tender feeling toward the erring member. Some among us, lacking charity themselves, have been emboldened to say that *I* live to chastise.

But yes, the trip East—to think I completed it in my sixtieth year! I had come around on the matter of a woman, as some in my family kept urging. Our Reber brother knew of this Mary, living with her daughter in Indiana. Where better to find a new mate than one with roots in Grantsville, the same place my Joseph found his Barbara? Mary is the widow of Daniel Miller who was once a deacon in Pennsylvania and made his untimely departure at age forty-three.

She is still a young one, only forty-seven; I make no effort to keep up with her pace. But size-wise, I have advantage, for she barely comes to my chest. Her face, round and pleasing, remains unblemished by fierce winds. Barbara and I knew of the Millers when we lived in the Glades, although my only recollection of Mary centered on her quick movements, darting rather like a mouse. I have given her my troth and trust, for she is grounded in Bishop Benedict's instruction. She has requested that she be buried with her first husband, and I have made clear to my sons: those wishes must be carried out. Of course, we do not know which of us will go first, but as she says, "You do not lack for lines on your face."

I will admit, some suddenness was involved in the transaction, but there was little other way, what with the vagaries of travel and winter coming on. I first renewed acquaintance on my way to Pennsylvania. I do not think her daughter, Nancy, was entirely pleased. Mary and I had opportunity for several conversations, and I put forward the question regarding her willingness to move to Iowa. I exerted no pressure but asked that she seek the Lord's will. I made the same earnest request for prayer from Brother Joseph Oesch, who traveled with me through Ohio and beyond.

Finally, when returning west to Iowa, I stopped again—nearly a month had passed—and learned the direction of Mary's thoughts. We did not have time to discuss every difference, but I made clear my desire for companionship. She seemed to understand and knew my call from God was of utmost importance. One small thing almost tripped us up. She had heard tales of Iowa timber rattlers, that one of them filled a half bushel. Of course, I thought of the rattler that had wound itself around George's newborn's cradle, but I did not need to tell that whole tale—George's Mary throwing a tin cup to waken him from his Sunday afternoon snooze.

Instead, I squelched the new Mary's fear by saying, "Many newcomers bring a dog with them for protection."

"A dog," she said. "I have no plans to bring a dog."

We had ourselves a good chuckle and after that, all proceeded smoothly. We were united in Indiana by Bishop Joseph Miller on the eleventh of September.

I tried as best I could to describe the condition of my log house, including the new cook stove I had purchased in the summer. She understood that Barbara and I had moved from a small chest, to a store box, to a table with four legs. But she says I did not adequately explain the setup.

Of course, I have not made improvements as do some, for I believe we are blessed when we live simply. But when I told her about this Diogenes fellow, she all but snorted and said, "I doubt he had a woman."

"No, we do not need to imitate his extreme example."

Then she put her hand on my thigh and said, "I want to put a gleam in your eye again." That seemed harmless enough.

She reminds me periodically, the northern settlement in Indiana began five years before ours in Iowa. I am quick to offer admiration for the highly suitable prairie land in Elkhart County and have only briefly cautioned her about the dangers of a haughty spirit. When we disagree, she is more to sniff than harrumph. Her snort has not been frequent, so I have held my tongue. She is accustomed to the work of dipping candles and has used lard lamps before, but she has been slow to warm to our rye coffee.

"Your beans. Where are your beans?"

But when I saw her glass dishes—the colored ones—alarm flashed. I did not want to cause upset so soon but said, "Wooden and pewter bowls were adequate for Barbara and me."

At that, she paused. "Then take your tin ones to the woodshed for when you add on a summer kitchen. I will put my family pottery from the Old Country in a box under the bed."

I have no plans to build on, but her solution got us past that bump. I do not know what she writes to her daughter, but I do not want her packing up.

She seems more satisfied with the arrangement in the other room: the bedstead in the corner, the big chest with drawers, all in relation to the fireplace at the gable end. But one item that crowds our living is Mary's sewing chair. Yes, she brought it by rail, declaring she was certain Barbara's would be too big and likely straight-backed. We have kept both chairs, thinking a grandchild may have need of Barbara's. Mary has not found fault with Barbara's spinning wheel or flax wheel. But other what-nots have appeared that I was not aware of in advance. A small pin cushion, covered in bright red cloth, sits on the window ledge by her sewing chair. I had not thought it necessary to inspect all of Mary's boxes when they were being readied.

She likes to say she is not one to go overboard. But she still planted flower bulbs, even after I showed her where abundant patches of lady slippers, violets, and jack-in-the pulpits show up in the spring. She sniffed, so I decided to let the squirrels have their say.

Frederick's Sarah is more agreeable now that Mary has put meat on my bones. Sarah was the one, said my clothes no longer fit my frame. Some of that was due to the wear of years—Anna had done my mending—but the other part was the hump developing in my upper back. I do not see it, of course, but Mary harps: "Straighten yourself." I have learned to turn away when she says I stretch my chin forward unnecessarily, "Like a rooster pecking."

Rather than dwell on such stumblings, I recall the pleasant nature of my visits in Pennsylvania. Things looked much as I remember in the Glades, despite being there twenty years ago. The main difference: reduced stands of timber. But what a blessing to see old friends again! And I had occasion to visit my brother Christian's grave, gone but a few months after we moved West.

One topic, especially in Somerset County, sprang from what some call a fever—interest in Iowa. Everywhere I went, eagerness abounded to hear of our soil and creeks. I was glad to answer questions, but I also added caution about the rigors of settling anew. How can I ever forget my dear Barbara?

"Tell your eager ones: do not jump at adventure or higher grain prices." My eyes may have reddened. "The women may not take to primitive conditions."

Some families from Pennsylvania have avoided the long journey to Iowa by taking up residence in western Maryland where land remains cheaper. The Somerset County brethren asked me to make the extra trek to preach with a young church at Red House. It is always an honor to be looked on with favor and asked to give oversight, so I traveled with Abner Yoder, a young bishop, the Sunday they were choosing an extra minister. They have a large gaggle of children, mostly from Beachy and Petersheim families that come across the border from Preston County in Virginia. I did not shirk from giving warnings, even though a visitor.

How could I, when my dreams persist? Already several years ago when I helped my stepson, Daniel, prepare his fields and stayed with him three nights, the dream came of an enemy with arrows and bullets. I had to use both hands to yank him from fiery danger.

"*Komm, du!*" I shouted.

But Daniel—sorely heavy against my pull—sensed nothing of danger; his eyes stayed blind to fierce devouring flames.

Afterwards, I had to speak to him with sharpness. "Do not associate with Wagler and Plank. They are troublemakers! *Ja*, removed to Henry County—I am sorry for Brother Goldschmidt—but that does not mean the threat is gone from right here."

Daniel kept his head down and picked at his teeth with a thin reed.

I wanted to jerk his arm, but he is my grown step.

"This back and forth among our members . . . " Not so much as a flicker crossed his eyebrows. "Those swamps to the south, that treeless Washington County you have to traverse—not nearly barrier enough."

"The Dunkards residing in Henry County are good people," he mumbled.

"*Ja*, given to earnestness. But their preachers are prone to entice people with excessive show of emotion."

He did not lift his head nor give any satisfaction. I have never said he runs at the mouth.

"Some may have given aid in your first years here," I said. "But now, the gravity. Do not be hoodwinked by the Amish there. Remarkable, *ja*, the first of our people to make it to Iowa, all the way from France and Alsace-Lorraine after the Napoleonic Wars. But now, Daniel, do you hear? Stay away!"

Daniel had moved to Iowa five years before me in 1846—the same year Iowa was admitted as a state into the Union—having found his bride in Pennsylvania, then moving to Ohio before coming the rest of the way. How quickly nonchalance had taken hold.

My other recurring dream—even more frightful—came more recently in springtime. Two opposing forces made ready to do battle. I stationed myself to the side with clouded view but spied a church member only a quarter mile away, mingling in the midst of strangers. I cannot say who, only that I recognized the plain garb. No long beard, though, like that of a Dunker. I stayed partially hidden, but as I strained to see, more than one man looked familiar, mixed up with those armed ones. I do not think it was Frederick or

Joseph, nor Christian. One of them had the youthful stature of my George, but not the sandy hair. No, none of my sons, I am almost for certain. No battle ensued, but I slept no more that night.

I would be remiss not to give attention and pass along warnings wherever I speak. This talk in the East of approaching war! Far more than a random comment here and there. *Ja*, another reason for people's itch to move West. And agitation regarding Abraham Lincoln being elected. It seems John Brown's disturbance has petered out, and preachers no longer hear questions about hiring extra hands. But too many have allowed themselves to be caught up.

Since returning home, I have not delayed, but have advised others on The Bench: we *must* warn our young regarding state militias. We must hold forth the Sermon on the Mount: "Love your enemies, bless them that curse you." Some of our young may not know their fathers and grandfathers were forced to leave Europe because it was nearly impossible to avoid compulsory military training. This Nafziger who wrote so well about the ordinances made sure *The Martyrs Mirror* was available for his people in the Palatinate and Alsace. But not all of ours have brought along these stories of Anabaptist forefathers suffering in the sixteenth century; others seem in the dark about accepting persecution rather than fighting.

I also have renewed my vigilance regarding the looseness of tacking on nicknames for newcomers, particularly these folks from Ohio. I make no exceptions for my family. My Joseph maintains his eyes fell on land with a beautiful stand of hickory trees that first time he came walking from Maryland to make his claim in this Iowa Territory. I have tried, but I cannot root out his moniker of Hickory Joe. And Ioway Joe is not to blame that his name, Joseph C. Schwarzendruber, is the same in essence as my son, Joseph J. The other Joseph became Ioway Joe as the first of our Amish to live in Iowa County, his land on the *west* side of the county line. But the nickname is unnecessary. What is needful is respect for the past by passing along family names—a father's initial—even if the women say too many Barbaras crop up.

And yes, another development threatens our unity: people build larger and better. Some of that is to be expected as families push out at the seams. But if excess pride follows, it becomes a sore difficulty. Even my children may be tempted. Two years ago, George moved his family to the Deer Creek area, that early campsite favored by Indians, when he finished his new house—twenty-by-twenty-six feet and a story-and-a-half high. He hewed the frame with a broad axe, made and split all the studdings, joists, rafters, shingles, what-have-you—all from hard wood. I have never seen siding planed so smooth, even in his large shed where he keeps his horses and cattle. And now it beats all: his Mary has a box stove with four lids on top, much advanced from my fireplace.

Frederick has stayed here in Sharon Township—close enough to holler—but he also has built a frame house. Theirs has *three* rooms both upstairs and down. I do not mean to find fault with Sarah—four living children now—but with such a large house and a full basement, others in the church sit up and take notice. Soon they also want bigger. Sarah comes from solid stock—very solid. But her parents died already back East, and she brought substantial inheritance to help Frederick make his start here. What more can I say?

Some of the murmurings from church folks—sharp as the reach of daggers—have been passed to me through Mary, especially the charge of haughtiness regarding education. It is true: I enjoy reading, but I never fail to advise moderation. We must always test whether book learning is of the spirit. Daniel's big boys have both gone to the log schoolhouse—open two months in the winter and only a mile from their home. But my grandsons do not exhibit excess pride. Rather, Jakob speaks fondly of his teacher, Miss Emaline King, and the way she begins each day with Scripture reading and prayer.

And Samuel, the more talkative one, asks many questions. But he also listens beyond his years. He is the one who told me of this Diogenes who lived in Greece some 300 or 400 years before Christ. But Samuel's recounting manifested genuine concern, not inflated views. That man stressed the simple life so much, he lived in a tub. (More likely, a barrel of some kind.) As the tale goes, he had only one possession, a cup, from which he ate and drank. The story sounds farfetched, though, when the man is said to have thrown away that one possession upon seeing a shepherd boy use his hand to dip fresh water at a spring.

Yet, Samuel asked with no trace of mockery, "Should we not also simplify?"

Another time as we traveled, he asked, "Where do you consider your home to be?"

My first thought, of course—right here in Iowa with Barbara. But I could not succumb to wishful thinking. "I have been blessed with many homes where my heart stays planted."

He waited but cracked all his knuckles.

"My home of seasoning with Barbara and the Amish churches in western Pennsylvania and Maryland. Very precious, learning to keep watch."

He rubbed his chin like an oldster.

"Sometimes a homesickness shrouds me—those days when all seemed possible. But now—a gear wheel may have slipped; cascading water falls every-which-way." I cleared my throat of excess, but his eyes wavered not. "I will never forget my dear childhood home—the town of Mengeringhausen, with its landmark Lutheran church. Some say the crooked steeple was built from uncured lumber; others claim the steeple was subjected during the building to winds at cross purposes." I moved my hand to the right, then the left. "One day, a strong wind from the east, followed by a strong wind from the west the next."

Samuel nodded, as if he could picture.

"It is hard to say exactly." I could not dally, lest I manifest doubt. "Of course, our most important home awaits us. That is why we labor faithfully, to be reckoned at last."

Again, he nodded. He may not fully understand, but my earnest words must always point to the greatest goal of all, not be sidetracked by those who find fault.

Now some folks clamor for dividing our settlement into two groups that would meet separately. I shake my head. True enough: forty Amish households make it hard to give an eye everywhere at once, let alone find space enough for meeting in homes. But if we divide, we may not stay true to the *Ordnung*. When I give testimony, I still need to correct some parts of Joseph Keim's sermons. We must stay the course together, lest some drift.

Better not to dwell on those who complain. After four long years of surviving alone, not thinking a woman necessary, I am grateful my way has been made easier. Now when Mary lets down her hair at night, I feel younger again. She has been more forward than I expected, directing in ways I did not know about. But when I acquiesce, it creates harmony, so I do not mind. She says we both sleep better.

David Bowman — Shenandoah Valley, Virginia, March 1861

Abigail says my face grows longer. She tugs on my beard and asks if I cannot see fit to trim an inch or two. "You are past the second button at half a century. Where will this end?"

I tease in return. "Would you rather people see my second button than notice my blue eyes?" She used to say she could see the sky in my eyes, but that was when we were young and had no cares but to give each other sweet sentiments. Now my practical vein comes through. "When my hair disappears on top, I must let it grow down."

She gives another quick tug and I know she means no harm, only a reminder of how we are moving along. Nearly all my brothers are in the same condition. Only Harvey still has a head of hair; the rest of us face a receding every year. I had thought my father an old one at fifty; now I am not so ready to be counted in that number. My back gives out at times—when I stay pinched in one position too long, holding a tautness—but I have nothing physical to complain about. I know full well my lines have fallen on pleasant places.

Our two older girls have gone to their own nests. Mary stayed safe, marrying a German Baptist, but all-too-quickly they moved to Limestone, Tennessee in the east end of that state. We do not hear from her much more than once a year. Emma, though, tore us asunder when she left the fold for a Lutheran and moved farther down the lower Valley, near to Winchester. There they have large plantations; her husband is all for colonization: "Send the freed ones back to Africa."

Abigail would keep our last three at home forever if she could, although she says it is right and good for them to marry. Neither of us wants the day to come when the last one walks out the lane. Delilah seems in no hurry; for that, we are glad. She is our tall solid one, although homely. Abigail does not like me to use that word. "Delilah's long face lacks redeeming features," is how Abigail puts it. Of course, we do not believe in false curling of the hair or the addition of beads as some might do to compensate. Our two young pups, Amos and Joel, remain youthful and not looking to settle. We have sufficient land to maintain our needs, although at times I feel pressed that I have not accumulated extra to set up my boys.

Along with farming I am a cooper, able to supply Abigail and the neighbors with whatever firkin or barrel they might need. The boys have helped me build a work shed where I keep all my carpenter tools. Amos is good to organize, so I have exact places for each hand adze and dowel, each length of stave. We also added a summer porch on the back side of the house for the women; that keeps some of the hot summer's work out of the kitchen. I wish our walls in the upper story were tighter, but wishing does not make it so. I do not have the means to rebuild with bricks as do some; my boys have not complained unduly about mornings when light snow covers their bed and floor. We use the back corner of the loft for storage: Abigail's sweet potatoes, our crocks of apple butter, and such.

"Bait to send the varmints upstairs," Joel jokes.

Our elder, John Kline, is not usually given to gloom, but lately he has repeated warnings. Ever since the start of the year, he speaks of sadness and destruction to come. Some say he sees a wolf behind every rock. There is rampant talk of secession—seven states have given in to the fury—but people get much too worked up. "Threatening clouds," Brother Kline calls it. He is known to have the heart of God, so I cannot dismiss his thoughts as foolishness. He says we must have oil in our lamps, not be caught off guard like the five bridesmaids who did not know the hour of the day and had not trimmed their wicks.

John has been conducting "fast meetings" at the Linville Creek church, but we have not done the same at Flat Rock. Ten years ago prayer meetings were rejected by German Baptists as a foreign religious practice, even though there is no such command from Jesus or the apostles. But two years later the brethren discerned again at the Annual Meeting that such meetings would be tolerated if not identified directly. In keeping with the church's directive, Brother Kline calls members at Linville Church to fast from food and gather to pray.

I could ride the ten miles to their church, but I have not, sometimes claiming snow and ice as a deterrent. In truth, I want my goodly portion of eggs to start the day and do not like to be rushed about it. I make my own supplication at home, although I know it is not the same. Still, I have not pressed to join those who have gathered once a week for over three months already, commencing around ten in the morning and staying the day.

Brother Kline says a shadow hangs over our country that may bring worse tribulation than that experienced by Indians. I was but a young married man in 1834, when we got wind of the Red Man being driven from Georgia to the Oklahoma Territory. That was Andrew Jackson's doing as president. We could scarce believe how his men were stealing land from Indians and forcing them west, their tears ignored. Thousands died during that time of persecution, while we in Virginia knew nothing of the kind. Our prices for crops stayed good.

But now, what confusion John Brown's ruckus caused. That man could not tell the difference between God's will and his own. He professed unselfishness on behalf of the slaves, but in the end his efforts were misguided, based on the belief that a physical attack could overcome evil. He spread unrest among Southerners, too, when they heard of Northerners viewing Brown as a hero. Nor did it help for peace when Abraham Lincoln was elected president last fall; from then on people's hearts seemed set to fight. Now what do we have but a Confederate States of America formed last month in Alabama!

Brother Kline says to be attentive to what our neighbors say. But when I ride past nearby farms and wonder which side each homestead is on—do the Southern-leaners understand what a severed nation would mean?—my judgmental eye only adds more turmoil. Of course, I do not want to offend the common feelings of those surrounding us, but sometimes . . .

My land runs parallel to Winfield's with the creek running between our properties in back. But our minds rarely work in harmony. Yet, because of proximity, I cannot avoid him. Sometimes I have blurted.

Recently, I was leaving Cootes trading store at the same time he arrived to do business. We exchanged greetings, but his tone turned abrupt. "We'll retaliate if Black Republicans try to stop us from our way of doing business."

"Me? Your free labor? I do not—your drift?"

"Nothing is free. Owners feed and clothe. You think a roof is free?"

"Yours do not receive wages." I do not know what makes me bold one time, timid another. I am not naturally a strong-willed person, nor do I cotton to excess emotion. But Abigail says every time I speak of Winfield, I mention his smell of cloves.

He busied himself tying his horse to the post, but his voice rose. "Tired of the North telling us what to do. They started it. Cheap talk. We wouldn't have this Lincoln fellow if the North hadn't decided they could use him against us. No way in hell, immediate emancipation will work. Or should I say, no way in *thunder*, for your tender ears?"

I rubbed Elijah's flank; he senses when I am accosted by someone dishonorable.

"North and South need each other," I said. Winfield knows the cycle as well as I. Northern bankers finance southern planters, especially cotton farmers who raise the crops and ship them to England. Then the English pay the Northern banks, and Southern planters share the profits.

But Winfield had stepped closer, his eyebrows frothy. "Why let the North decide the terms? Kept on the short end here, just 'cause they have capital. Time to shake things up. Damn right, I'm a Breckinridge man." One side of his mouth twisted up. "In case you wonder."

I knew all too well: Breckinridge came in second in our state with his support for secession. John Bell, the compromiser, won Virginia.

"Our state sits between," Winfield continued, "but we've more to gain from the South. In it for the long run, not that it will take long. Once England has to shut its cotton mills, they'll come running to support us."

"A battle will not solve," I said quietly.

"You and your ilk! Why don't you German Baptists come out and announce you're abolitionists? Claim to be above board in your dealings." He spat. "Bunch 'a boot-lickers."

"We are not abolitionists. No contact with the North. Not with officials. I only know, fighting does not solve." My mind scattered, hopeless to explain the New Testament is our church's creed. Why bother to say the command is clear, not to war?

He huffed up the steps to the store, but turned and said, "We'll see about that."

While Winfield and I have often been at odds, so far as I know he does not *own* slaves. But he must hire; I have seen shanties on his property. Nor does he rely on farming entirely, except to keep his family in grain and milk. His livelihood comes from trapping where there is a large market for furs. I know the truth full well: I do not like Winfield Acker. Nothing will be gained from listening to him.

Going back some years, my sons had a run-in with him. I never knew what happened for certain. I had expressed displeasure to Joel and Amos when Winfield set leg-holds for muskrats along the creek. Ever after, we had to put up with a stray dog's whining, until Winfield got around to releasing the animal.

But one time he confronted me and said some of his trap line had been messed with—a stick in a couple of traps. My boys were around twelve and thirteen at the time.

"What is your meaning?" I had asked.

"Those boys of yours. Springing my traps." His sandy red sideburns flashed in the light. "That's not all. Knocked down part of that beaver dam."

"How so?"

"You know what I'm talking about!"

"That wind storm? You put a trap on my side of the creek."

"Where the beaver slide was. Right. Not as dumb as you look. Didn't hurt you, but that dam's been bashed in."

"Yes, it did cause harm. Branches and cornstalks so high, they blocked the water. My cattle barely had a trickle."

"Couldn't have been for long," he mumbled.

When I questioned the boys, they disavowed any mischief. It could have been an animal, true enough, that stepped and snapped a stick into one of his traps. The man exaggerates, so I let it go. But I made clear, "Stay away from Winfield's traps. We do not want trouble."

I could have been taken in by my boys, but if either—more likely Joel—had anything to do with a beaver escaping to freedom, it would not have been the worst thing.

In the years since, I have had to accept an appointment that complicates my life even more—elected to the first degree of ministry among the German Baptist Brethren. We are partly Radical Pietists and partly Anabaptists. Longer ago, our people did not identify leaders, thinking rather that every good Dunker was a preacher of sorts. But now it is customary to name names. Not something I sought, by any count, but church folks at Flat Rock tapped me. More members said my name to the elders than any other from among us. I could not deny having felt some form of call from God—does not every man? But like a gust of wind against which there is no defense, my election was made unanimous and sealed with a handshake and the Kiss of Peace.

In spite of others' confidence, my inner assurance stays weak. I am not a strong reader, nor do I care to memorize Scripture. To progress to the second degree of ministry, I would need to devote myself much more to prayer and study. And to be in full authority—an ordained elder such as John Kline—I would have to evidence much greater wisdom; that last step is a ministry of housekeeping, supervising conditions and relations among the members. Brother Kline is held in such high regard, we often refer to him as Johnny, the tenderness we feel.

But as for me, let me sow crops and fashion another barrel; that is contentment. I have no aptness for explaining mysteries—water into wine? Washed in the blood of the lamb? I do not hanker after complicated thought. Of course, I care about the adversities we all face, but that does not mean I want to provide the opening or closing devotions when we meet for church. Nor does it mean I want to rise and speak after our Flat Rock elders, Jacob Wine and Abraham Neff, have done so. What is left to say? One of Martin Garber's sons would have been a much better choice; I suspect J. M. went to people ahead of time and begged them not to name his name.

Abigail accepts how my simple mind works. When I walk in the house with my morning collection from our fowl-feathered friends, I am at peace and give my wife a kiss. Each of us has our appointed household tasks. Joel and Amos look to the milk cows and sheep—hogs, too, when we have them. I care for Elijah and the work horses and, of course, fix the eggs. Delilah fries potatoes and cooks our mush, while Abigail busies herself with breadmaking or such. Only on Sunday do we rest from all but the necessities.

I do not have to worry about my wife, but some folks think Brother Kline shows the strain of caring for his Anna. She has been sickly almost fifteen years. Reports circulated like wildfire that she had become deranged when he acquired a serious illness while on one of his early mission trips—long before I began making occasional trips into the mountains with him. He was forty-nine when she took her fright; they had been married already a quarter century. But some say her troubles started earlier, when their only child was stillborn. And still others insist she had dreams of a woman in a coffin already when she was a girl. Oh, the stories people tell, as if they know all.

Anna is given to melancholy and silence, but I can attest she is not a wild beast. I always enter at the back of their large brick house that faces south, but I have seen the peace door Johnny crafted at their front entrance, using the wood pattern of a cross over an open Bible. He is always gentle with Anna, as unto a child. She dresses in a heavy gray but moves with no swishing of garments.

On one of our journeys—I still wonder why Brother Kline asks me to ride with him—he and I stopped to rest our horses. Perhaps he doubts my being grounded in the faith and wants extra time to instruct. Others have traveled with him much farther in Virginia and beyond. He speaks of the beautiful Rocks of Seneca, but he has not taken me that far.

Whatever the case, we stood with our hats off on that rest stop, our backs braced to trees while partaking of bread and dried apple. I did not bring up the subject, but Johnny's voice turned soft, as if answering unspoken questions. I could scarce hear amidst the rustle of squirrels nearby.

"It was a trip to Pennsylvania and Ohio when I became sick. As it turned out—typhoid fever. Two full months passed before I could return home. Friends said I lay near death. Anna feared she had been abandoned for good when my recovery took more time than expected."

I held my body still. My jaws scarce moved in swallowing the last of the bread.

"Her fear was for my safety, but also . . ." He took a long drink of water. "She trembled from a dream that had bothered—fiery destruction in the Valley. She reported hearing hymns sung, along with weeping and the rush of animals escaping burning barns."

Nell and Elijah fidgeted, whether from flies that bothered or our extended rest.

"Anna did not recognize me when I finally came home. I had lost considerable weight." He sighed, as if depleted again by the telling. "She is still storm-tossed at times, unknowing. I have tried all manner of remedies, even sought the help of Solomon Hinkel's electrifying machine so Dr. Newham could administer an electric charge to stimulate her nerves."

For my part, I have seen Anna stare with her head off to the side, as if she is somewhere else. Johnny's voice always brings soothing—from lines of worry on her face to tranquil rest.

"But she remains in her childlike state." Without further ado he entered into prayer for his Beloved; that is what he calls her. He entreated the Lord to watch over her. Then he put his hat back on and prepared to mount Nell. "The Good Lord has not yet told me to stay home."

I know whereof he speaks. Some have whispered: he should look to his woman, not go on errands of mercy for others. I do not agree with Brother Kline on every count, but I know Anna receives the best of care from their adopted daughter, Betty, and her husband. I have instructed Abigail not to dirty herself with loose talk. "Anna is well cared for. That is all we need to know. Or say."

When I ride on journeys through Brocks Gap with Brother Kline— I on Elijah and he on his Nell—we experience generous hospitality from church members along the way. People in the outposts share their bread and bed, however frugal, knowing the Scriptures' teaching that one man's belongings are for the good of all. For five years already John has taken his mission concerns to the Annual Meeting.

"The fields are white unto harvest," he likes to say.

But some at Meeting thought he overreached with his plans to further spread the Word. It has been a painful setback, but he continues his endeavors of giving aid.

We make a strange looking pair in our long frock-tailed coats, our leggings for travel, sometimes a handkerchief at the neck. He is round and squat, where I am long and thin. It is not uncommon for Johnny to sing, often in German, as we ride. Abigail does not complain if I am gone several nights to visit the young churches along the Lost River. She has our boys and Delilah to tend animals and look to the crops, so there is no undue hardship. Members at Flat Rock have helped at times with planting or harvesting, depending on when I may need to be gone. I pack items dutifully in my saddlebag and affix my broad-brimmed hat. John has an extra saddlebag for the medicines he carries, for he is a physician as well. His medicine cabinet with various concoctions and bottles sits atop his secretary.

The onset of my rides with him began after his ministrations on behalf of Abigail several years ago; she had suffered much from chills and fever, compounded by painful breathing and coughing. He made repeated trips to our door on her behalf, and I paid him the usual three dollars for a course of medicine. But ever after, I felt indebted. Since then, I have observed how he extends the same kindly manner with others distressed, even stoops to remove an offending tooth with pinchers, if called on.

In Abigail's case he first asked her to drink a heavy dose of warm herb tea to induce extensive perspiration on her part. Then he gave more tea with lobelia in it; this emetic brought the most unpleasant retching I have ever witnessed. I feared my bucket would not contain it. After her treatment, she stayed abed more days before her strength returned.

Since Abigail's travail, I have learned more of how Brother Kline is on the forefront when it comes to medicine, a strong advocate of ridding the body of its corruption. He does not use that word; it is Delilah's. I have witnessed him giving an enema also to fully purge. He is convinced the current medical practices of bloodletting and blistering, even starving the body, are not the best ways to rid the body of disease. Instead, he follows the Thomsonian methods he has studied and used for some twenty-five years; he paid $55 for his license from a Dr. Samuel Thomson of Vermont. He also spent six weeks with a Dr. Curtis in Cincinnati; the latter follows the same system, but the patient only vomits for an hour rather than the three- to six-hour regimen of Thomson.

For either man the main line of thought is this: "Remove the cause; then the effect will cease." Recently, Brother Kline said—it was more of a musing—"When disease occurs, there may be a wee something at work in the body." I may have shown surprise, for he repeated: "A very wee creature, invisible to the naked eye, wreaking devastation from the inside out." Of course, I have seen maggots go about their business, but in humans . . . ?

I cannot question, though, for in everything he is much to investigate thoroughly—far advanced beyond my middlin' thinking. It matters not, whether the building of roads and bridges, or the understanding of bodily workings. Nothing is unimportant—not even the structure of an oak leaf. Nothing escapes his attention. His latest pursuit: donating a parcel of land near to Broadway for the building of an academy. Some of our people think common schools are dangerous places, but my three youngest have benefited these winter months, the second year at Cedar Grove. Whether studying arithmetic or biogenics, they are the better for it.

Delilah is twenty and older than the other scholars, but Abigail insisted she go also. Now we benefit at night when Delilah reads to the rest of us; she started with stories of persecution from our *Martyrs Mirror* but takes delight in repeating poetry verses also. One became such a favorite, even I learned part of it. *"Full many a flower is born to blush unseen, / And waste its sweetness on the desert air."* She said it came from an elegy by a man named Gray.

I cannot match the ease of Delilah's voice when reciting words, nor have I achieved Johnny's heartfelt piety. But lately I have become something of a sounding board on our trips. Or a listening board. That I can do. Sometimes he asks that I not repeat what he has ruminated on. He wrote letters in January on behalf of our brotherhood to Governor John Letcher, another to our representative in Congress, Mr. Harris. I have seen Johnny's special writing chair with its large right arm and its little drawer for pens. It always sits in the exact same spot: the southwest side of his bedroom where natural light streams in.

I completely concur with gratitude for our Virginia governor's stand to preserve the Union. He sees that those who seek revolution, whether in the North or South, are of the reckless sort; having no property, they must think they can better themselves by causing the chaos of war to impair others. Of more consequence, Governor Letcher has reassured Brother Kline by return letter: in the event our country gets pushed into battle, those of us with conscientious scruples against war should be able to pay a small fine to be relieved of duties with the militia.

But that has not dampened Johnny's concern for storm clouds spreading across our mountains. In the churches where we visit he says over and over, "We must learn again the words of Christ: 'My kingdom is not of this world.'" His voice gets quieter. "If we do not mend our ways, we may see blood spilled, tears, and even ashes." He does not hold back. "The sin of holding humans in bondage cries out to heaven for vengeance, not unlike the ancient days when the Israelites were kept against their will in Egypt."

My fears cry out: *I do not want it to be so.*

But when Brother Kline relates the story to me of twenty families embarking for America in 1719 and the mighty storm that threatened their voyage, I have to give heed. That was when our forebearers in Europe faced persecution for refusing to take up arms; they had already scattered from Schwarzenau to Friesland and Holland. His voice is tender.

"On that frightful ship the captain all but gave up with sails lowered and merchandise thrown overboard. And yet, David, listen: those worthy pilgrims sang and prayed as though no harm could reach them."

He goes on to tell how ten years later Alexander Mack came with almost three times the initial number and landed also at Philadelphia. By now I know the story well; he would not need to repeat. For nearly half a century, all went well for those early settlers. But then, the Revolutionary War. As German Baptist Brethren, they could not engage in carnal warfare. Worse, when our brothers spoke of overcoming evil with good, they were misunderstood by their neighbors and classed as Tories. They wanted to be peacefully neutral, but that was taken as a sign of loyalty to Britain! Many of our German Baptists had to scatter again, the first ones coming to Virginia.

How many times have I said to Abigail: "There is no more beautiful Valley, no other place on earth I would rather be! How fortunate our ancestors did not move to the east side of the Blue Ridge."

She knows as well, settlers on that side of the mountains were publicly whipped if they dissented from the established Church of England. Sometimes she wails, "And half the population over there in chains, whilst only one in five carries that burden here in our Valley."

"And continual strife with Indians. We are blessed with more open spaces and natives friendlier to us Germanic peoples."

Oh, we both know there are forts to the south. Struggles aplenty, but those happened earlier in the eighteenth century.

Only now it comes up again—no escaping it—not only for Winfield and me: the way our dark brother is subject to being bought and driven to market as a beast of the field. Johnny says many leading citizens of Virginia—George Washington, for one—tried to halt the work of slave traders years ago. But the pattern was too well established: the British government captured Africans and sold them as slaves in this young country. Greed took root also here in the South. Our beloved Shenandoah Valley has not been spared; the Scots-Irish came around the same time we did. Too many still think nothing of contracting with an East Virginia slaveowner for the yearly service of one or more of his slaves. They see it like unto buying merchandise, exactly what Winfield said dare not be changed.

I have seen ads for Negroes; nearby Harrisonburg has its slave breeders. Slaves, handcuffed to a chain, forty to fifty feet long, can be seen walking the main thoroughfare from Winchester, past our area of Timberville and New Market, on south. They trudge as beasts of burden, given little space to walk behind the person directly in front, likely treated the same way Indians were driven like cattle. How can they have room to lie down at night? The colored race viewed as chattel for the white man. Black slaves, separated from their wives and children, as if of no consequence—as if not fully human, not given to feelings.

Only a year ago I stood as one rooted to the ground. I could not pry my eyes from the sight of five young boys being sold to a slave dealer. Each went for over $1,000. I did nothing. But heavyhearted, I trudged home and looked upon my sons with fresh eyes. From then on I lost my zeal to work from sunup to sundown; I no longer expected my boys to labor as if our existence depended on their bare knuckles rubbed raw. Of course, I had never whipped them, but my words had been harsh if I found either boy slacking, especially Joel. Now Abigail says I may have leaned too far the other way; the boys will not understand the meaning of a good day's work. She has not seen what I have seen.

I stand solidly with our church; ever since 1813, slaveholding has been strictly forbidden. We dare not compromise. Our brethren to the south in Augusta County have a harder time holding the line; buyers there seek thousands of slaves, especially in the fall, and the practice is even more common. As if normal! Even at Brother Kline's church, they had to call a council six years ago because some members were not complying. People claimed they had to be part of the system to get ahead. I do not need Johnny telling me: to be part is to be party to evil, paying wages only to the owner, not the slave.

Even Mennonites here may be coming around to see that a man's practice must fit with his professed beliefs. Of course, if a slave is given freedom and wants to stay at work with his Master, that may be arranged. But he must be given clear papers, not botched. When he is a free person at age twenty-one, he must be paid proper wages. That is the law.

But even with our governor standing for the Union, Brother Kline fears our state may yet be swayed regarding this poisonous talk of secession. He takes small comfort: only four of the nineteen delegates from our Valley who went to the state convention in Richmond actually *favored* secession. John's view is no darker than *The Rockingham Register*, where scant hope is offered: our beloved country sits sadly on the brink. How will voices of reason keep the rabble element in check? Last month a so-called peace convention gathered in Washington and deliberated for twenty-three days. But yielded nothing! No representatives attended from the seceded states, so what good was that?

There is much that frightens, far beyond my disputes with Winfield. I do not want conflict with any man or government. I will hide my head with the chickens if I smell a fox outside the pen. How am I to maintain hope in singing and praying when ugly forces gear up?

ESTHER — Shenandoah Valley, June 1861

Now they've come to our church. Two men with their heavy gear. I've never heard boots so loud. Clomping. Their gray uniforms, their badges. I first heard a clatter through the women's door of our log building; I half turned. Some claimed they'd heard horses nickering in the oak grove and knew something was afoot. The visitors sat at the back until the service was almost over. I fidgeted while Samuel finished his message. No ruffling of intent, but he must have wondered at the men's.

He reminded us about God's Kingdom—from John somewhere: "*if my Kingdom were of this world*"—his words trailed off—"*then would my servants fight.*" He cleared his throat and repeated in a stronger voice: "*If . . . then would my servants fight.*" Samuel is now our bishop, only thirty-nine, one year younger than I, ordained last month. Any Scripture carries weight when he says it.

Martin Burkholder, our beloved former bishop, passed from this earth in December of last year. His widow still wears the black and lives with her four surviving children in the brick house he built—blessed to dwell there only six short years. He'd started our Weavers school several years ago and kept up with his shoemaking also. But so soon gone—only forty-three. Twenty years younger than his father, Peter, at his demise. We're much bereft. Our only comfort: Martin was spared more of this world's sorrow. No one dares criticize him now; those voices stilled that thought him too progressive—preaching in English as well as German.

With the same suddenness as death, those two officers sat in our church, revolvers on their hips. When we prepared to sing our closing hymn, "Blest Be the Tie That Binds," the men marched right up to the front without being invited. One of them spoke with a loud bark, like we were hard of hearing. "An order from the Confederate States of America to which the state of Virginia adheres. All able-bodied men in this Weavers church between the ages of eighteen"—he consulted his paper—"eighteen and forty-five, must report to the nearest militia office one week hence."

I don't know what else—he kept wiping with his thumb at the corner of his greasy-looking mustache—or even if those were his exact words. He sounded official—no meddling. By the end of his speech I reached for my handkerchief in the folds of my dress and used it to dab. The room was stifling with early heat and the flood of sniffles. Mary Grace, my eleven-year-old, put her head on my shoulder and worked an arm inside mine. I pulled her to my bosom.

My thought was for Andrew, my firstborn. He's eighteen, three months from nineteen. Simon, of course, is included in the call-up. He's returned to his morose condition. A month ago he had turned inside himself and would not speak, except for the barest of instructions to the boys. I could only guess at the provocation, knowing when the silence began. There was much talk about men being hassled to change their votes. I didn't know if Simon had been spit upon or reviled in some other manner. Nothing could be gained from plying him with questions. He turned his back in bed.

Finally on a Monday night, he said, "I did a terrible thing."

My eyes jumped to the shotgun above the mantel. It told no tales.

His words came after two Sundays in a row when he'd stayed home from church, no explanation. The night he broke his silence, our children stayed quiet in their beds. Some of them too quiet. Simon and I sat at the kitchen table where the lamp provided light for sewing.

I paused in my shortening of pants' legs for William and Joseph; I was tucking up extra material, so they could wear what's now too short for Andrew and Peter. "What do you mean?" I glanced at his hands, his fingers twisting and untwisting.

"I voted for . . ." He wouldn't say the word, but I knew. His silence had started when he came home from Mount Crawford after the vote had been taken. They called it a popular referendum on secession. He said again, "A terrible thing." His hands cupped his face.

My chest thudded, waiting. But there's no pushing Simon. He'd already gone outside that night, checking on the horses. He used to be a sound sleeper, but now he gets out of bed at any hour if he hears noise. Or thinks he hears. I have tiptoed to watch. He steals to the kitchen window, hunches on creaking floorboards, and peers in the direction of the barn.

"I allowed myself to follow the line of thought . . ." He paused so long, I thought he would not finish. "They pushed the line—the war would be over faster." The rest was muffled, as he buried his head and pulled at clumps of dark hair. "If . . . united here—the South—we could avert . . . that is the nonsense . . . dastardly." He wouldn't look at me.

"The Secesh told you voting for Virginia to leave the Union would be the quickest way to bring an end to hostilities?"

"Yes." His voice was barely audible. "I knew as soon as I began riding home I'd been duped. I wanted—"

"You could not stand." I put a fist to my mouth.

His black eyes bore a hole in me. "I wanted it to be true."

"Under duress." I put an arm on his bent back; he flinched. "Did they threaten?"

I hadn't known what to believe about that voting day. Threats of hanging. But stories can worsen in the retelling. Frances said Samuel had been dragged into town; he'd purposely planned to stay home all day. I told her Simon went of his own accord. I remembered, though, his ride out the lane. He always sits straight on Midnight, but that day a grimness weighed him down. He sagged through the chest.

On the night of the telling, he straightened once more but extended his arms on the table, his hair every-which-way—he seldom takes to a comb these days. I reached a hand to his shoulder, but his head jerked as if seized.

I focused on my needle and thread. "Is there more?" Stitches wavered before my eyes.

Slowly he began. "They spoke of my horses. Midnight." He had no color in his voice, until he imitated an ugly one. "'Betcha' that beauty won't make it far on three legs.'" He returned to his monotone. "I'd mounted for my return home, when a man I'd never seen before came up. Others gathered 'round and guffawed. Some were armed. One jerked at the reins; another picked up stones. Big ones. I looked to gallop away but knew I was no match for that crowd. 'Git yer butt in there,' the first man said. 'I got a torch. Makes quick work. Light up that fancy barn of yours.' The men laughed and the crazy one with rocks started running in circles, as if setting fires. 'Inside, you hear? Git it right this time.'"

I placed the pants on the table, took off my thimble, and leaned to look full on what was left of my man.

"I voted a second time," he whispered.

Then he went silent again, as if grief covered him with a sack. That's the way he stayed, sour, until warmer weather came to stay. Not that he ever said much on good days, but he got some appetite back. Like always, he's better when the crops are in.

Now this. The officers stomping inside our church. Everyone in disarray. We never sang "*When we asunder part/ It gives us inward pain.*" I can't sing the words aloud: "*. . . we shall still be joined in heart, / And hope to meet again.*" Not my men, not with crops that need tending. Samuel could barely rise to dismiss us that day.

Andrew's blinking has grown worse; his fingers bleed around the nails from his chewing and ripping at hangnails. He'll do whatever Simon does, not that he admires his father but because we teach obedience. Andrew was the usual one we sent into Harrisonburg to get the county's weekly newspaper. We scarce could keep up. In less than one full week in April a Jefferson Davis attacked a fort, our President Lincoln called for 75,000 men, and Governor Letcher refused to send troops. But now, Virginia has voted to secede.

Simon reminds me with a scowl: "Lincoln's not *our president*. Davis—our man in the Confederacy. Capitol's in Richmond. A hundred miles from Washington."

Worse yet, when I spoke with Genevieve, she said, "We naturally belong—the South. Our location."

I couldn't say: We're Union people.

I couldn't say: Our ties go back to Pennsylvania, not South Carolina.

I had to look away. Now I haven't seen her, over a month. But she squinted when I said, "We're betwixt. Not rebels. We don't want to disobey our government."

"The North will take advantage," she said. "George says nothing good can come from this Lincoln. Can't get our own shipping lines to trade with Europe." She took in my face but briefly. "Our children, slaves of Negroes, come ten years."

My legs weakened; I made exit, some womanly excuse. Tears clouded my sight as I trudged home. I'd heard those fears all last summer when no rains came, last fall when harvests were poor.

"If Lincoln's elected, disorder to follow."

"Slaves, freed."

"Social disorder. The South, no power."

Simon would not talk of it—"save your breath"—but I needed to know.

And yet, a few short months ago—before Lincoln asked for troops—we still thought ourselves safe. Even before that, our newspaper, *The Rockingham Register*, had asked people to use reason, not jump in headfirst. The editor, a Mr. Wartmann, had voiced caution. If there was to be a war, we here in the Valley might be caught between East and West, North and South. He'd praised the Dunkers and us Mennonites, respecting the law and paying our taxes to the government. I'd asked Andrew to read that part twice. Some people didn't like it, though. This Wartmann pointed out that paying taxes protects slaveholders as well as ourselves.

"Lumped with bad ones," Frances had said.

Only a handful of our men—Mennonites and some Dunkers—voted *against* secession. The paper said only twenty-two in our county—now calling them traitors. When Andrew read that, I told him to stop. We knew some were successful, refusing to go that day. Some professed fevers; others, I don't know what for what.

That night of the telling, I said to Simon, "It's for each man: know his own conscience." He shook his head, but I urged him, "Confess your failing. The bishop."

He made no reply. He might have had to shake Samuel's hand when he went back to church. I can't say for sure. Simon still lacks trust in any man of God. Stays stubborn; won't say what's what. Only says, "Collect yourself."

When Lincoln asked for troops, our newspaper's caution changed. Everyone faced about, as if Lincoln had started the war. No, not everyone. But the rebellious ones forgot; those troops wouldn't have been necessary if Jefferson Davis hadn't fired at that fort. Frances said the same. Too many people—right here in Rockingham County where Lincoln's great-grandfather once owned 600 acres—think Virginia must defend its right to slavery. They blame Lincoln for dissolving the Union.

What are we to do? Rumors said about the Upper District of Mennonites in Augusta County to the south. Twice as many slaves there as we have in Rockingham County. Even fewer of ours voted against secession there, led by two Hildebrands—said to have obtained much land over the years—cousins with the same name of Jacob. I've seen the one, a Mennonite bishop; he came to fill our need when Martin died and we had no bishop of our own. Sometimes he brought the other Jacob's boys as travel companions; Peter mentioned a Gideon. Reports swirl: both Jacobs voted to secede. Willingly. Others say, only one or the other. I wouldn't want people whispering what Simon did or didn't do. Frances knows for certain: when Jeff Davis called for a day of fasting and prayer, Mennonites in Augusta County fell in line.

Our men are to report this week; Simon might go. He makes no response when I ask regarding Andrew. Scattered to pieces. I want to press my arms around him, but Simon turns from comfort. At night he goes out to check the horses. Then he goes out again, as if to meet someone. Or check again. His sleep fitful. I want him to hold me—I'm aggrieved, too—but I hear him whispering. One night he barked, "Halt!" Soon he stumbled outside.

No place to hide, only a half-cellar. If the men desert, they face court-martial. Or worse. They have to report. But to go against conscience? How can any authority think it right? Take my first fruit? Execute for treason? No, I tell myself. A thousand times, no. It won't come to that. Our loving God protects. I stay on the lookout, ever since those officers came to church. No black cat crossed the road, right to left in front of our wagon. No more birds inside.

A bad time, though, a few days after the order to report. The newspaper put forth a long plea—some made-up writing name—to those of us opposed to war. We'd sent Peter for a paper; no good way to send anyone.

Peter looks as old as Andrew, but he's only seventeen. When he returned safely—we had to know something—we sat at the table with him reading. This made-up person wrote how defending ourselves is a law of nature, one the Bible doesn't deny. But the writer poked fun at the idea of turning the other cheek. To the North!

"If peace people want to go the extra mile, they should volunteer to fight for *twice* the length of time as a drafted summons would require. Or"— Peter paused in the reading—"if one son is conscripted, then a father ought to send a second son as well."

No one dared say a word. Not till Peter broke the silence, "I would go."

Simon and I turned to him sharply, then stared at each other. Andrew got up and went outside, letting the door slam. I made haste to shoo the young ones outdoors, too.

But Mary Grace clung. "They won't make a soldier of Peter, will they?"

"No!" I said. "He only pretends."

"And Andrew?" she whispered.

"Of course not. Andrew is strong and will prevail."

In spite of my words, she cried again at bedtime and would not release her grip. I held to her, as much as she to me. "Father?" she asked. "Must he?"

"Think no further on it. We stay safe in this house." I held her cheek tight to mine and pushed back a bristly braid. "God has promised to love us always. Tomorrow we'll go out in the fresh dew; the wet grass will tickle our bare feet. Strawberries aplenty."

I don't like to say things for certain. Not when they're up in the air. I don't like to be muddled. If only Simon would speak his mind, not stay bottled up.

J. Fretz — Chicago, September 1861

I had to let her go. I had to set her free. Almost three months now, my life has been much the poorer, my torment heightened. But I couldn't insist on her promise. Not when I've been negligent. First, I laid family, and now my bosom friend, on the altar of fickle fortune. I'd been so taken with my new business and the furor of war, I fell off on my correspondence. It didn't help that Jakie failed to deliver one of my letters to Salome, back in early April. But later that month she wrote, inquiring as to my silence. Her comment, *better for those single to remain thus during times of warfare*, roused me.

I had no excuse. It must have sounded pitiful to say I hadn't written in my diary during that time either. I asked her forgiveness, but I couldn't forgive myself. What if I'd been the one, counting on her, only to receive no evidence of ongoing affection? I don't know if she expects me to enlist or what. Nothing can be counted on these days. Or little, I should say. I must have sounded like one of Shakespeare's swains, bidding adieu to my fair one. My heart despairs, left to wrestle alone—more weighty decisions than I can bear.

Mary Ann tried to comfort. "Everyone's distressed. People can't think straight."

I still believe I'm meant to be in this restless city. But where will it end? Where will *I* end? Or why? Mired in keeping a lumber ledger clean? Lost on a battlefield? Joe's right: the lid's blown. My mind wanders to Herman Melville's story of Bartleby and his stock answer, "*I would prefer not to.*" That's how I feel about most options. Nothing appeals. Even Salome's promise, "I will remember you in my prayers," seems hollow. She means well, but loose talk of God echoes everywhere. And calls for manliness. Last week, two comely women made clear to Joe and me, if we want to be men, we must go to war. "Conquer or die" rolls off lips.

Soldiers practice their drills in the streets before they proudly march off. Huge spectacles right and left. Banners unfurled on street corners, flags flying, including out my upstairs window. Right now, the Union has more volunteers than it needs—over 100,000 men. Ross says this war can be over by December; we'll celebrate a proper Christmas. But blood revenge is in the air, ever since Bull Run. Not long after that, President Lincoln called for a national day of humiliation and prayer. All one breath—religion and killing. I go to countless meetings at National Hall and Metropolitan Hall. I hear sermons on Christian patriotism. One Sunday I sang "My Country Tis of Thee, Sweet Land of Liberty" five times at various gatherings.

Most of what I hear rings true: a necessary war for the sake of preserving our national unity *and* freeing the slaves. But those two goals must stay together. If the South were allowed to break away, we could face anarchy. We can't have outlaws defying the Constitution and acting like states' rights are more important than our Union. But righting the injustice of slavery *must* be part of our effort.

Men reduced to fighting each other as savages, face-to-face combat like the Greeks and Romans? Is there no alternative, no recourse in honest debate? Why can't people be reasonable about disputes? These slave hunters, relentless. A constant reminder of how low people will stoop. They prowl our city, hunting for fugitive slaves as if they're animals. Some of the captured slaves have been treated so unfairly in trials, I can't stomach the proceedings. Does our country not stand for honesty and fairness? I can't admit to Ross I'm glad when I read of a slave's escape to Canada.

He came to our new company this summer as a bookkeeper. We work closely, so I have to put up with his comments.

"We should colonize those slaves—the freed ones, for sure. Send 'em to St. Domingo or Central America."

"That's ridiculous," I say. "How are we going to transport four million slaves?"

Ross's thick, sandy hair sticks up straight; his freckles multiply when he's contradicted. "That's what our president wants."

"He doesn't always think clearly." I like Lincoln when he quotes Shakespeare and Robert Burns, but he's too ready to compromise on slavery. "His Kentucky roots show; afraid to talk of emancipation."

"He's cagey; he knows not to push too hard." Ross moves his ink bottle toward me, dips his pen, and holds it up. "You only moisten the tip, right? You dip it again when needed. You don't pour the whole contents of the bottle all over the page."

"Of course not, but a president needs to stand for something."

"He's going to preserve the Union; individual freedom will follow. Count on it."

"Miraculous," I mutter. "No, he needs to stop slavery where it exists *now*. It won't die by itself, not by saving the Union. I don't understand that man. All he promises is to keep slavery from expanding into the territories. Not enough."

"He doesn't have constitutional authority to abolish slavery."

"Poppycock! That's cowardice, and he knows it. He's too timid; tries to appease his Southern friends."

"Aren't you the strong one!" Ross's eyes twinkle like he's the superior mastermind. "The most important fight—the *first dip*—not letting more states secede. One step at a time." He dips his pen once more with a dramatic flourish, as if he's sealed the deal.

I'm left stewing; the terms of a new business contract blur in front of me. Lincoln seems to think the West is some kind of utopia where poor people can go to make a better life for themselves. How can we count on him when he shows shoddy thinking like that? Ross knows how to hit every sore spot—my chief tormenter. Last week, he argued the North can't afford to make this look like it's a war against slavery. That would make the South more united and divide us Northerners even more. At that, another clerk asked Ross if he was going to accept a bounty and enlist. Ross said he has an unsound liver. I had to leave the room.

When I calm down, I admit the North's not united. At first, Lincoln had seemed relieved that the Confederates fired the first shot, as if that would unify us. But we're certainly not all abolitionists as some in the South think. Some Northerners want compromise; some want force. Some say it's good riddance for the South to secede with its awful slavery. Some of my workers say Republicans are only good for pitting capital against labor, the rich man against the poor.

Ross is a Republican, but likely as not to side with someone like Reverend Horace Bushnell in Hartford, Connecticut; that man muddied things, saying we must have a Constitutional Amendment to *include God*. As if we don't have enough to be divided over. He accused Lincoln and others of only using natural law or the secular ideas of Thomas Jefferson to justify war and suppress secession. *Include God!*

I'm tired of hearing people—either party—say America is God's Chosen Nation.

Empty words.

When I try to relax at night, it helps to read Thomas Aquinas. But then who should appear in my sleep but Salome's sweet face! I can feel her hand on my cheek.

"Your gray eyes have a bottomless depth."

It's not like I've lost a spouse in death, as some are experiencing prematurely in this war. But I've lost my best companion through my own choices. My light and life—I gave her up.

"... better ... those single to remain thus ..."

I can't get back to sleep. Over a year ago, I said *I want to make my mark.* Salome smiled. Even when my ego was out of control, she believed in me.

"There's much you can do with your life, Fretz."

Now what have I done? I'd been so certain regarding my future with her.

Oh, sure, I've enjoyed Chicago ladies—what man wouldn't? They latch onto my arm and entice me closer with their womanly charms. But no one stands out. No one compares. They flit and twitter, offer false praise for Queen Victoria's modesty, flash their seductive smiles. How can I undo my failure? I have to release Salome again. I have to accept it: my life revolves around politics and business. Even my Sunday school boys have had to take a back seat. I still teach regularly, but my attention's divided. I say the right words, but my fervor fades.

Early this year I took the plunge. Before the war excitement broke out in April, I entered into a business partnership with Beidler and James McMullen. We met in Beidler's office to sign our agreement. A cold rain pounded against the windows that reach almost as high as the ceiling. Chilled, I kept up a good front. Age twenty-six and I've reached an important step in my climb toward success: McMullen, Funk, and Co. Beidler has his own established business interests to tend, but his shrewdness in decision-making is invaluable. And he's our main funding partner, putting down $8,000 to start with.

All three of us share equally in the profits and losses. I manage the lumberyard, oversee the books, and order materials. I've contributed $1,500, but I have to admit, two-thirds of that came as a loan from my father. I agonized before asking him—would I ever pay him back? From my previous salary I'd only saved $600. But Father hasn't held it against me for not moving back to take over the farm. McMullen, with twelve years of bookkeeping experience in a different lumber enterprise, gave $500 plus his labor. He's taken on the tasks of making sales and collecting payments—things I'd never be good at.

When I signed the agreement, I had to blot my excess squiggle.

"Your hand's a block of ice," Beidler said, when we shook all around. He hasn't stopped ribbing me. Jim and I work very well together; he's very particular, and I'm of the same mind—I can't stand inaccuracy. But he brought Ross along, so I'm stuck with his chatter in the office.

We started at a bad time, a slowed economy, but even so, we can pay $5 for 1,000 feet of lumber and sell the same for $7. Enough profit already to buy a schooner for transporting lumber from other Great Lakes ports this coming winter. And we have a horse and buggy solely for transactions within Chicago. My exuberance at starting was so great, I gave $100 to the

Presbyterian Church—a sign of thankfulness to God. I can't begin to say how satisfying it is to have a better start at wealth. It's what our country stands for: if a person works hard and overcomes obstacles, success will follow. Oh, sure, there are limits; I've seen plenty of greed. But I won't let money lead to my ruin.

Jim puts me to shame at times: kindhearted but firm when he needs to be. His long face—no facial hair—gives him a trustworthy look. It's an excellent setup to have added his connections because of our accounts with Catholics in the city. His brother, John, is a priest here and president of the University of St. Mary of the Lake. Out of the blue he gave me a short biography of Saint Francis of Assisi. Deeply touching, but some of it made me uncomfortable. A prayer that reflects his spirit: "*Lord, make me an instrument of Thy peace. Where there is hatred, let me show love.*"

I'm not sure I believe that. I don't know anyone in the North who doesn't despise Southerners. And the other opposites from Francis don't make any business sense either: show pardon instead of injury; faith rather than doubt. How does hope replace despair, or light supplant darkness? Joy is supposed to wipe away my sadness? As illogical as colonizing slaves. Absurd, like expecting Chicago to live by human decency. Only my mother would agree with every line: *console*, rather than be consoled. I don't begin to measure up. I'll never *understand* Ross—not sure I want to. I don't expect him to ask *pardon* for his derogatory views of black-skinned folks. And Salome? I want her for *my* benefit, not to *give* her unlimited love.

Warfare. Enlistment. Those are the words on every tongue. What will my country ask of me? *Die*, so I can be born to eternal life? I don't believe that. My close friends—not Andy or Phil, not Joe—no one's made the plunge. We all pretend to stay above the fray.

But my blood brothers back home write about some of the lads I taught at Chestnut Ridge—among the enlistees. Abe said folks got excited when Virginia broke away from the Union. "It started to seem real that the South could capture our capitol."

Before that, even when Fort Sumter was fired upon, he said things had stayed ho-hum. But enlistments from eastern Pennsylvania men shot up at the prospect of railroads and rivers, even bridges and roads, needing protection around Washington.

Another letter from a boyhood friend, Randolph Smith, upset me dreadfully: he's joined the 91st Pennsylvania volunteers. A lieutenant! He wrote from camp about wanting to murder "every cussed traitor" in this country. And somewhere he'd heard about people in Chicago chasing seceders into the river. How glad he was! I could barely finish reading. We'd been good chums! Now he says army life suits him fine—"a feistiness in camp." Does he mean heavy drinking and gambling? Eagerness to kill?

But Bull Run gave the biggest jolt of all. The Rebels prevailed. We Northerners had no reason to expect a terrible result like that. For one thing, we had over 30,000 troops and the Confederates only 20,000. And then to read that Rebels mindlessly killed our *wounded* men. It was sickening. When my brother, mild-voiced Abe, referred to the Rebels as "wicked and lawless," I knew our country had taken a terrible turn.

Crowds of spectators with their picnic lunches—Northerners!—lined the hillsides at Bull Run, a stream near the critical rail junction at Manassas, Virginia. I still don't understand how the South could use the telegraph and railroads so successfully. Ross was livid—red cheeks under his freckles—about our General Patterson. How could the South rush in reinforcements and move their infantry almost effortlessly? Wasn't anyone paying attention? For once I agreed with Ross.

"They outsmarted us—plain and simple."

I've taken to reading editorials in *The New York Times*. Some writers say we shouldn't have attacked on a Sunday. Others say too much profanity and drinking took place among our men. Plus, soldiers were confused with men on *both* sides wearing *both* blue and gray uniforms. This Rebel general named Jackson—they call him Stonewall—gets a lot of credit. Our troops panicked along with scared picnickers; some of our men, crushed under the wheels of heavy chariots rushing to escape. Even small buggies—like mine!—carrying members of Congress were dashed to pieces in the confusion. Only thirty miles from Washington! How can it be anything but poor effort? We're fortunate the Confederates were as disorganized and exhausted in victory as we were in defeat.

But what I've heard since from the pulpits unsettles me just as much: "Our recent defeats show God chastising the North before He can grant us deliverance."

What? If *God* was involved at all, it might have been in the heavy rain that came the next day. Mud confounded everyone.

I say to Ross—well, I say it to anyone who'll listen—"These reverses show the moral inadequacy of having only one goal: preserving the Union."

He's quick to set me straight. "You know the ways of the Almighty?"

I'm dumbfounded. "Well, no, but—" *Next time, I won't sound presumptuous.*

Reading about Missouri is almost as disturbing, especially because I'd considered moving there to raise beef cattle, back before I decided to come to Chicago. Thank the Lord I let go that idea. But deaths! Last month over 2,000 men, counting both sides, expired in that state—directly south of us!

What's going on? This was supposed to be a short war; the first enlistments were for only ninety days. The South sounds like a ragtag group, compared with our soldiers, but they keep bragging and threatening. How were we supposed to take them seriously? We were going to put them on their heels and restore our country to its rightful unity.

The whole affair makes me queasy; nothing's going as we expected. We can't afford to keep on losing valuable manpower, dragging our economy down. The only advantage I see is business in the South must be even more stagnant. Nowhere to sell their cotton, because we're blockading the East Coast and our banks won't do business with them. And yet, they claim some glorified scheme of appealing to England directly for support.

"You get too worked up," Jacob says over our evening brandy.

"Stop reading so much," Mary Ann says at breakfast.

My own words come back to haunt me—that time I visited Salome back East. *I don't want to go through life like so many others, working myself to death, only to be forgotten.* Now I want to tell her: *I didn't leave the sweet enjoyments of home only for adventure. Nor solely to make money. Certainly not to go to war.* I can't even pretend she hears my cry.

Death has always given me pause; two siblings gone already. The first was long ago when I was only four. My younger sister and I had gone to the fields to watch our father plow. Little Sarah and I sat on the top rail of the fence. I should have given heed. She pointed afar and showed she didn't need to hold on. Just that quickly, she fell and hit her head on a stone. The picture of Father carrying her broken body to the house, cradling and holding her close, stays in my head. I stumbled along behind like a wayward child, but she died that night. Of a sudden, my play companion of almost two years, gone. My world caved.

The case with my oldest full sister, Margaret, was different. She'd already married Benjamin Frick and left home, but suddenly she was dead of galloping consumption at age twenty-six—my exact age now! A stunned husband and son left behind. That happened my first year in Chicago. I've always been glad I stopped with Margaret and her husband in Philadelphia on my first trip to Chicago. I picture her inside their brick house—stone steps up to the front porch—there in the full enjoyment of all she could desire. Even when illness first struck her that fall, she rallied. In fact, I'd received word that the danger for her had passed. I was so relieved, I wrote her a letter—that dreary month of November—my exuberance at her recovery. Imagine my dismay! I'd sealed the letter the very hour her spirit departed. Oh, my youthful haste! I didn't know I could lose a second sister.

How beautiful she looked in her silk dresses when young men came calling. Yes, back home. I was but a smart-mouthed lad, taking in everything, hearing Father defend her against the church deacons who came asking questions, all because she wore a bow on her bonnet. I can still hear Father's disgust—"*Was sin Schlipp?*"—his disdain for attention to such a piffle.

How short life is for some. How quickly it passes for many. Reports abound of young men and old, taken in the full bloom of life, called away from their frail clay tenements, only to be carried back, clothed in glory. I once thought my life was my own.

BETSEY — western Virginia, December 1861

Poppa wants everything to settle down; he says that is what winter is for. "Too much goings on," he says. "Nature needs to sleep and then a man can rest his bones."

"Do you mean Jack?" I ask. Since late summer we have a dog. Poppa called him a mongrel, but we named him Jack. One day we heard a scratchy barking outside the chicken pen. A stray dog was snarling and digging his front feet; then he arched his back and jumped to scare a fox away.

Lydia and I were frightened to touch at first, but Poppa talked soothing and the dog quieted its racket. Tobias says it is gray with black spots; I say brown with black. Now Lydia loves him; she gets him to sit still. He blinks up at us when we pat and brush his coat. When we stop, he follows us.

For a while, though, Mother and Mary stayed back. But Poppa said, "He saved our hens and chicks and eggs." We only have hens and a rooster, but I explained it to Mary.

Soon after, Poppa said, "We are going to be a new state. Our big state of Virginia goes all the way to the ocean. Too big. People in the East are uppity about the rest of us. We will have a new name, too."

"Tomorrow?" I asked.

"*Ach, mein Kind.*"

Now when Tobias talks big, I tell him he is uppity. Last summer when he was about to turn ten, Poppa let him hold the reins on Frank and Tom, our work horses. Ever since, he acts like I am a little girl. When he takes off his shirt at night, he makes a big arm muscle and wants me to touch how hard it is.

But I am the one who gets to hold and rock our new baby Gideon. We have had him almost nine months; he has extra big ears like Tobias but a rounded chin, not squared off like Levi's. I am getting better at spying when Mother is hiding another one under her smock. I am almost nine and can tell when she walks from side to side like a wagon load. Her face gets rounder, and her fingers have the fat.

Tobias is all fumbles with the little ones, except for roughhousing with Levi. All Tobias knows to do is let Levi climb on him and muss his hair like a haystack. Then Poppa has to shout, "*Schtopp!*"

We were milking Goldie and Tillie late one afternoon when Tobias said, "Our new state is about a big fat war and something called slavery. Men will ride their horses and throw spears at each other like Indians."

I do not believe everything he says. Once he said it never snows until November, but we had snows in October and had a poor corn crop.

"Know what else?"

I do not have to ask more; he will say.

"The new state is not about East and West. It is North and South and we are South."

North is where my home-home is, but Poppa's mouth twitched that time he told us about the big trains in a north place called Oakland.

Mother says Poppa's nerves are bad because of talk about people fighting. Poppa says his nerves are not bad. Mother clicks her tongue. She says it is foot traffic on the road; the Northwestern Turnpike goes by our house.

This fall a man walked in our lane from the road. He did not have white skin like we do, but he saw our smoke and came to the door. He was cold and hungry and had no shoes. At first, I kept an arm around Mary and we took peeks, but Poppa spoke softly and did not seem one bit nervous. The man would not say his name, so Poppa called him Mister. Later, Poppa said people with dark skin are a different race; they come from Africa. That is a country, not a state. We can call them Negroes but not darkies.

Mister had walked a long way and was going to find his kin. He was skinny like Jack when he came, but not near to dead. Tobias said the bottoms of his feet had bad cuts and were a light color. Poppa applied our stinky salve and wrapped an old cloth around each foot, but Mister did not like the smell and said it made a burning.

Poppa told him what he tells us. "The smell helps heal."

Mister stayed three nights. He would not sleep in our house—he said he needed to stay alert. He kept to the barn—we tied Jack to a woodshed stake—but Mister ate with us. He bowed his head when we did, but he did not know any German words. We always start with "*Unser Vater,*" but he would not make attempt.

Mister said he had to get to a place called Wheeling. We made a double batch of bread, and Poppa helped me reach the extras on a long board to coals way at the back of the oven. Mister hummed and mumbled when he put the loaves in his knapsack. It sounded like a song, "*Let my people go,*" but Mother said he was crying about Moses on a mountaintop.

Poppa gave him a pair of warm socks, too. Mister tried to hand them back, but Poppa said, "Yours to keep." But Poppa was strict: "Stay away from Rich Mountain. Bad fighting last summer. Very bad." His eyes looked crossed. "Men from the North surprised men from the South." I stopped in my tracks. But then Poppa's eyes let go their sparks. "One of the prettiest—the Cheat River Valley. Snow-white lilacs and redbud in the spring—more than here. Frightful, though, the mud."

I would not want men trampling our mountain laurel or stomping on trillium. Not North or South. I know right where to take Lydia and Mary to look in the woods come springtime.

The next Sunday after Mister left, our Peter Miller told about being a slave in the Old Country. Poppa had called it Indian summer weather when we rode to church in Maryland. Jack does not get to come along. But church was not the usual. When Daniel Beachy stood to preach he said all of God's children are precious. Then he bowed his head full of white hair and said nothing more. Precious minutes went by. The old men sighed in their naps and looked up to see what was the matter.

Later Mother said it was too soon for Daniel to be preaching again; Poppa did not say one way or another. But I know it is a sad time; the Beachys lost another *Bobbli* last month. They kept this one, a girl baby, three months, but she cried and cried. Little Susan's tiny body rests now beside little Moses in their family cemetery. I put my arm around Sarah when sniffles bubbled out of her nose. Tobias told me I would be all bones one day.

But that Sunday afternoon of church going, we children were called in from playing hide-and-seek. This was long hours after Daniel got stoppered up. We sat on the usual benches again, but I was allowed to sit beside Sarah. None of the big folks looked jolly. They had been praying extra after our noon meal.

What Peter Miller told about was when he lived far across the ocean and was a serf. He was not permitted to enter inside the big house of his Master. He said it was very bad to have a Master; he had to sleep in the sheep stable. When it was cold, he used fresh sheep manure to warm his bed of hay. Sarah and I put our hands over our noses, but we did not giggle.

The scary part came when Peter told about escaping; he said it had been twenty years ago. He raised his hand high above his head to show how high the fence was that he climbed. That happened at night. He said the fence had sharp iron points on top, but he pulled himself up high—rather like climbing a tree—and draped his coat over the spikes, so he could scale the top and jump to the ground.

Then he ran like a boy; he looked right at Tobias and Jonas. Peter does not know how fast I am. He said the Lord was with him, and he found his way to a boat that brought him to America, to a big city called New York. But his eyes looked sick when he told about being on the ocean. He said six months is half a year. I have never seen an ocean, but Tobias says it has deep water that could drown me—deeper than the Cheat River.

We children did not get to play anymore that day, because everyone went home long before dark. The big folks hustled us when Peter Miller was done talking. After we tended our horses and milked the cows—Lydia got to run Jack a while—we finished our supper of apple butter on bread. Then Mother made ready the little boys for bedtime. They sleep downstairs where they are close to Poppa and Mother.

But Poppa told us big ones to stay at the table. "You need to know, your Uncle Christian Selders had a hard time of it, too. Not a slave, but indentured to his uncle. When Uncle Christian came to this country, he had to work hard for his uncle. Like a servant."

"What does indentured mean?" I asked.

"Like a slave," Mary said.

"No, I said, *not* a slave," Poppa said. "You must listen with both ears. Slaves have owners like Peter Miller's Master. Do not frown, Betsey; it makes for a bad spirit."

I put my arm around Mary. She does not mean to be *unbekimmert*. But her dress was still damp at the elbow where she dragged in the apple butter dish.

"Your Uncle Christian's parents were very poor in the Old Country," Poppa said. "Food was not easy to be had, so they had to send their boy all the way across the ocean to America. Not much older than you, Tobias."

We girls all swiveled to look at our brother. His hair was on the fritz.

"Was he bad?" Mary asked, but I put my finger to my lips.

"Why did Uncle Christian not stay where he was and work to be a servant?" I asked. Tobias would not get on a big boat and travel across the big fat ocean by his lonesome. Nor would Jonas Beachy, almost twelve and shooting up; he would not be brave enough either.

"You will be an old woman before you are twenty, Betsey, if you keep frowning so much," Poppa said.

"You said—"

"Do not be impatient, you nor Mary. I will get to that. Indentured could be passed on. You see? A different uncle met Christian here in the city of Baltimore. The new uncle paid for Christian's trip on the big boat; that gave him the right to have Christian work for him. For free."

"Forever?" Tobias asked.

"No, only till twenty-one. We call that 'of age.' If Christian had tried to run away before twenty-one, he would have been in trouble with the authorities." Poppa looked long at Tobias. "Very hard work."

"What was the new uncle's name?" I asked.

Poppa studied hard. "I do not remember."

"Eleven years." Tobias sat hunched over like he had a belly ache.

"But here, Uncle Christian had a chance to get ahead. Here we have fairness."

"Not everyone." Mother called in her loud voice from tending the boys. "Not fairness."

"That is so. People like Mister—with dark skin—never get to be free. Not many. Never get their own horse or land." Poppa scooped up Mary to his lap and held her tight. Lydia crawled into the curve of Poppa's other arm; she still sucks her thumb.

"Will our skin turn dark some day?" I asked.

"No," Poppa said. "Skin is skin."

"My face gets dark in summertime," Tobias said. "My nose and chin."

"That is so, but only for a time," Poppa said.

"But why is there not fairness?" I asked.

"That is a hard question." Poppa frowned. "Some white people think those with dark skin are not as good, not as worthy. We do not want to ever think that way."

Mother had brought Gideon to the rocking chair for his last feeding. "Not every *white* person gets *good* land either. Some scrape on rocky ground where they do not have meadows."

"That is so," Poppa said.

"But why?" I covered my mouth to hide my shrillness.

"It is hard to explain," Poppa said. "This will have to be the last question. Some people make laws that help people make money." He looked at Mother like she would know better how to say. But he only repeated, "Sometimes there are laws."

"*Extra* money," Mother said, "*some* folks." She frowned, too, like at church that day.

"Yes, not everyone has the same. Not money nor land." Poppa closed his eyes like he did not want his sad spirit to show. He kissed Mary and Lydia atop each head. "We have white skin, but we do not want to take advantage. Some people are afraid . . ." He stood slowly with his load of girls. "Mister was a good man."

"Are we rich or poor?" I asked, but Poppa shook his head.

"We have two sleepy girls," he said. "We must save something—another day."

Mary and Lydia dropped right off to sleep, but I twisted about. Tomorrow I would ask if I was a servant when I shucked corn. Poppa says we have to work hard to make a go of it. I do not think we are poor, but maybe sometimes.

Now that I know Peter Miller's story, I will not complain when Mother sends me off to Auntie Mommie's. I do not think I am a serf, but one time, Mother said my work was to pay Auntie for when she helped Mother drag the big rag carpet out for a beating. That was the day Poppa put new straw down and helped tack carpet to the floor again. Mother could not go along to Auntie's because of the new boy baby.

But that time I did not have to stay overnight in the stone house. Or stay eleven years. Auntie Mommie put me to work with her girl, Magdalena; we are cousins, but I like Sarah better. The hardest part was standing on chairs to reach every cobweb in the high corners. Magdalena gave me the long stick because I am shorter. We wore big bandanas. When we were done, I was *ausgfeegt*, but Auntie Mommie had to inspect, before we could play with their new dog. He is more of a rascal than Jack; he is a young pup.

* * *

Tobias and I only had to wait another week until we got to stay up late again. It was our skip Sunday, but the Beachys had not come to visit. After our evening prayer at the table, Mother took Mary and Lydia up to the loft where we have new straw ticks for sleep. The little boys had been tucked early.

Poppa said in a low voice to Tobias and me, "This is only for the two of you. *Verschtehnt dihr?* Your mother wants me to explain."

We solemnly nodded, but I did not know what more might be understood.

"There are people in the south part of our country—our state, too— who do not want to be here," Poppa said. "Well, they want to be here but separate. Your mother and I—all our church—stick with the North. We are thankful for our government."

He stopped, but his head stayed down and I knew not to interrupt.

"It is wrong to treat someone as second class." Poppa's mouth twitched extra fast; Mother is right about his nerves. "Mister was trying to get away from chains, much like Peter Miller from his Master."

"All the way across the ocean?" I asked, barely above a whisper.

"No!" Tobias said right away.

Poppa gave Tobias a look but said, "No, Mister comes from one of the states far to the south. It is time for geography. But before that, always remember: it is not right to fight. Our church—we promise not to kill another. Not with rifles or other else."

Tobias piped up fast. "I know."

Poppa almost shouted, "Listen to me!" He looked like he had found a hog rooting in a tender row of corn. "You do not know the evil. Not the extent. *Verschtehscht?*"

Tobias was quick to nod, and I did, too, but slow and long. Poppa does not allow us to touch his rifle. Not even Tobias, not that I know. When they come back from hunting rabbits—or get a deer—Poppa waits until nighttime to clean his gun. We children have gone to bed, but I peek from the loft. The next morning the rifle is all shiny, right where it belongs above the hearth.

Poppa started rearranging dirty plates on the table. I did not know what was what.

"Crist?" Mother said. She had come down from the loft and stood staring. A pewter plate banged into a tin cup. "What?"

"You said to explain the lay of the land." Poppa paid Mother no more heed, but spoke in a voice, hushed and sharp. "All right now. This is easterly. Stand on this side with me." He stretched his arm toward the far end of the table where he had thunked a plate. "Eastern Virginia—that plate. No, I am wrong." He walked to that end and said, "We will call this plate *the ocean.* The Atlantic." He swiped his finger on a plate and licked a tiny drop of apple butter. Then he placed a spoon to the left of the plate. "This big spoon is Virginia—the eastern part." He took two steps farther back from the end of the table. "Out here, on the other side of the Atlantic Ocean is the Old Country, where our forefathers came from."

"And mothers," Mother said.

"Yes, our people." Poppa quietly placed more spoons on the table. "Each spoon is a different state. You see? Here is Maryland. And here is Pennsylvania. And here is a spoon for where our new state will be. We are west, remember?"

"Where is Wheeling?" I asked. "Mister's family?"

"Be patient. Forks are for towns. Wheeling is west of our meadow, beyond the Cheat River, at the edge of our state touching Ohio, another state. The great big West goes far beyond." He walked toward the door. "Way, way out beyond Iowa where that Schwartzendruber man came from."

"Farthest to the west is California—an enormous state," Mother said.

"We have *nothing* to do with California." But then Poppa's voice softened. "This is not exact, mind you. Not for measurement."

"Put forks inside spoons for towns," Mother said.

"Touching," Poppa said. "We are to imagine. The tines touch the spoons. Towns are inside states."

"Where is Oakland?" Tobias asked.

"Yes, Oakland is where your mother and I saw the train. The state of Maryland." Poppa gathered up more spoons.

"You said, writing on the side and lots of smoke," Tobias said.

"And big wheels that went clackety," I added. I know now that Mother was Poppa's bride when they came through that town.

"We do not need to go over that again," Poppa said. "This is geography. A lesson. One fork for Wheeling, touching the spoon of our new state. One fork for Oakland, touching the Maryland spoon. Mary's tiny fork for German Settlement, Lydia's tiny one for Red House. See how close to Oakland?"

"What about Brookside?" I asked.

He gave no attention but said, "Watch." He made an imaginary line on the table with the edge of his hand. The line wobbled above some of the spoons and forks and below others. He pointed one way: "The North side." He stared at us and pointed the other way from his line. "The South. See? States to the south where Mister came from. Above the line, people want everyone—all states—to be one country. Mostly everyone. Now look where we are." He pounded with a fist and the forks jumped. His mouth twitched.

"You confuse them," Mother said. "Too many lines. Too much wiggle waggle."

"We are right in the middle," Poppa said. "That is my point. We stand between two parts, North and South. But the two want to have a fist fight. See?" He rubbed to stop the twitching. "Worse—we do not always know who is on which side. When people have a cannon and swords—"

"Enough, Crist," Mother said, grabbing plates and spoons. "Do not go on and on. You should talk about miracles, not give nightmares."

"The children need to know." Poppa's voice wobbled.

"Tell the rest of Peter Miller's story. A serf in the Old Country; yes, but after Baltimore. Go on." Mother paused as Poppa looked at his table gone awry. "When Peter was legal age—he made his way *west*." She pointed the right way, but then she talked faster and her hands went *alliwwerrum*. "From the *eastern* side of Maryland to the *west* part, but still *north* of us. A miracle: Peter found his old friends, the Gortners. Walking, walking on sore feet. To know in the Old Country; then to find them again, living near to Oakland. Lost and found."

"Not so rare," Poppa said slowly, a grin covering his jiggling mouth. "We Amish run into each other"—he put his arm around Mother—"whether we come across the ocean or from Somerset." He blinked his eyes extra fast at her. "We end up where we are to be."

Tobias and I giggled, but Mother shook her head. "We are talking about Peter. Half a year on the ocean, eleven years of work for an uncle with no back talk. Then miles and miles to find old friends. Near to dropping: *ausgfeegt.*" Poppa said nothing to contradict, but he held on tight. "And now Peter's old friends, the Gortners, are *our* friends, too."

"Yes, Baltimore to Oakland in the state of Maryland is like unto going from the eastern part of Virginia to the western part," Poppa said. "But a difference: Maryland is going to stay together. They are Northerners. Most all."

"Enough of geography," Mother said. "Even Betsey yawns."

Before I went to sleep, though, I thought more on slaves and serfs and servants. I wondered what it would be like to walk from cities to towns like Peter Miller or Mister. I can still run fast but I have never walked to Sarah's place or Magdalena's. I do not think Poppa will make us walk to that Iowa state, or move there like he said Peter Schrock's sister did. She might hear more stories of everlasting fire.

I was close to drooping, but of a sudden an owl startled. What would it be like to sleep in a dark forest—even if we had our wagon—and not know what lurked? Poppa said some animals move about at night; he called them nocturnal.

The next night I heard an owl again very close, but this time I caught on. I did not say peeps about it coming from Tobias under his covers, but we giggled. Almost real—a whooo that stopped a long time, then started again. But Poppa heard us and told us not to frighten Mary.

JACOB — Iowa, December 1861

How can there be such bickering and quarrels over President Lincoln? Such obstinacy. One man provoking others to think they cannot live together in the same country? My grandson Samuel admitted he *voted* for the man. I do not think more of my offspring voted—my sons dare not deviate—unless Anna's Daniel fell prey. He does not always look me in the eye.

All we know for certain: we are to pray for our leaders, not set up a competing government. When our president set aside a day for fasting and prayer this past September, that is what we did here in Iowa. *Oh, God, keep us in your care.*

Already a year ago when I stayed with the brother in Ohio, he said the *Holmes County Farmer* had nothing good to say about Republicans anywhere. I reminded him, God established government to have authority in the public affairs of men. He only nodded, the same response he gave when his woman told him not to burp so loud at the table.

"We are to obey the rules of the land," I said, fixing my eyes on him. "Unless, of course, the rules contradict the laws of God."

"You do not understand how things are in Ohio," he said and belched again.

I cannot attest to everything about this Lincoln's character—some say his language is coarse—but he knows his Bible. When he gave his acceptance speech at one of those big Republican pow-wows, he is said to have quoted from the Gospel of Matthew: *"every city or house divided against itself shall not stand."* How true!

The same kind of tumult occurs with the Amish in Davis County. Back in the fall they asked me to help organize a church. They should not have waited, having settled south of us already seven years ago. How could they neglect the gathering of God's people? Nearly fifty families and no pre-eminence given to God's Almighty Hand. Did they not notice something was amiss? Relying on a justice of the peace or a minister from another denomination to perform their marriage ceremonies does not speak well for their serious intent to follow Amish precepts. Any earnestness regarding conscientious scruples at this late hour gives a bad impression: serious only in order to counter coerced military service.

I took heart, though, when they expressed appreciation for my sermons—I did not refrain from the hard teachings of Jesus—but my warning of everlasting fire held no sway. They claimed they did not need to set aside their modern clothes, their mustaches and trimmed beards, their window decorations. One man said, "Mere commandments of men."

I all but wept. Such hardened hearts, their pride and show. Another man referred to some of the *Ordnung* as "hay and stubble."

My voice trembled to say, "The *Ordnung* was given to keep us safe; it does not restrict when we maintain a spirit of humility."

At home again my dismay continued when Mary said, "Do not become disheveled." *Ja*, my hair was awry from my hat. But our house reeked of vinegar—she uses it everywhere—and I caught a whiff of contempt. I am almost certain she muttered, "It is not yours to save." I never pretended to save souls, but neither can I ignore the reins placed in my hands.

Since those trying days, I hear the Davis County folks have turned to Amish ministers from Indiana and Illinois, or used preachers from Lee or Henry County. Such differences among us! We cannot accept this drift toward division. I catch a tremor when I hold a hot drink to my lips. I drop things—a weakness in my wrists. When I bring in more wood—Mary says I shuffle—I no longer take pleasure in watching another log burst into flames. The cold rattles my bones, and winter has only begun.

"Gird yourself," Mary says. "The wicked one may plant doubts."

Yet, she can be very lax. I do not mean that she makes no effort; I would be bereft without her, even when she chides. She knew to rinse my mouth with a mixture of gunpowder and vinegar when I suffered from sore mouth. The borax no longer worked to cleanse, and my gums had become spongy and subject to bleeding. Mary also brought cheer last summer when she raised stately gladiolas. I did not expect such. I walked among them—the yellow and orange, my favorites—unfolding from a tightly drawn start. We stored the bulbs in a heavy wooden box in my woodshed; she promises to plant again.

But Iowa—I cannot bear to think I was wrong about coming here. I pray the Almighty plans a mighty intervention, and we will stay unified. Late this past August and feeling weighed down, I rode Caspar to the Peter B. Miller cemetery, led by a sudden desire to rest at Barbara's gravesite. But I also needed to see what Frederick had mentioned in passing. Two of my children, George and Christian, had placed a larger headstone to mark Barbara's resting spot. Better for us to be uniform in all things, but the work had already been done, unbeknownst to me.

I sat with my head bowed on my arms, my knees propped up, open to hearing instruction. Usually, a late afternoon breeze relaxes me from the stifling summer heat. But the air changed of a sudden, such that I wished for a jacket. A mighty whistle of wind swept through the sheltering tree branches. One menacing gust turned to another, increasingly untoward. I had come to listen, desperate for direction. Of a sudden I scrambled to my feet and came out from the tree's canopy. I spurred Caspar homeward, a hand securing my hat, but casting sideways glances skyward. Once home I watched a hard rain from the shelter of the horse shed and restored my breathing to normal. I said nothing of my whereabouts to Mary.

About a month or so later, before winter fully set in, the Lord laid Emanuel Hochstetler on my heart. "Jacob, arise" came as clearly as my first call to ministry. He has not been in church but once since he moved here five years ago with his parents, the summer after Barbara died.

His father, Henry Hochstetler, is an enterprising one, much looked up to among us. Frederick talks machinery with him. Most of Henry and his wife Susanna's children are married—their Elizabeth to my Christian—but the Hochstetlers brought their younger boys with them. This son, Emanuel, is well into his twenties but stays unattached.

I rode with trepidation to the Hochstetler farm on Stringtown Road, about halfway between my place and the Deer Creek. Emanuel was shucking corn with his father and brothers. Henry and I exchanged greetings, but when I said I wished to speak with Emanuel, the others hurried away. One lad came back, though, to give Caspar some water and offer an ear of corn.

I tried to carry on a congenial conversation, complimenting Emanuel on being a much faster shucker than I. My gnarled fingers and weak wrists do not move as I wish.

"How do you find living in Iowa?" I asked.

"*Zimlich gut*," he replied. My head whipped up to see if he mocked.

"You have made friends, I suppose."

"*Ja, ja.* Plenty." His grin was not diabolical, but neither was it marked by any trace of seriousness.

"I do not mean to pry, but I do not see you at church." I tugged a third and fourth time on the same husk. Pain shot through my wrist. When I was his age, I could rip off a husk with one motion, too.

"Hnnh. Don't give a dern horse's rip," he mumbled, tossing another husked ear onto the wagon. He wiped at his brown hair with his arm, took yet another swipe across his eyes.

I had not expected such a recalcitrant spirit. But before I could speak, he added, "Friends in the *village* of Amish, not the church of Amish."

"You do not come to the singings with our young folks?"

"Not a thing to sing about," he said and laughed without mirth. "Born without a tune."

I do not believe that. The Hochstetlers are known for good singing voices; he would have been taught songs of the faith from cradle up. Most of our young enjoy the Sunday evening singings—a time to socialize—although I hear troublesome reports of rowdy boys on occasion.

As if he knew the direction of my thoughts, he said, "Too tame," and showed again his perfect row of teeth.

I stayed cautious, not that he was surly, but brief in his replies and given to light-heartedness. Judging from the fullness of his mustache, he has grown it for some time: a sign of the world, worn for pride and not at all sanitary.

Then he surprised me. "Peter Swartzendruber. Now there's a good man."

"Peter? South of Deer Creek?"

"The very one. A brother-in-law, but not a stick of a preacher. Doesn't dress me down as if I were sent from the Devil. Knows how to take a joke." Emanuel said more but covered it with the rip of another husk.

On good terms with Peter? He built a frame house with *four* rooms on the main floor and four upstairs, larger than Frederick's. Yes, they needed a bigger house from their cramped cabin. And yes, his father had already changed the spelling of the last name. But Peter always brings his family— seven youngsters—to church. Still, I may need to pay a visit.

I had to be direct. "Do you not know, one day you will face your Maker? Give account?" It is so like the young to think only old men tremble before the Mercy Seat.

Again, I cannot say as to Emanuel's answer, whether due to a hearing or memory failure on my part. But his look of mirth is seared in my memory; nothing satisfactory could have accompanied the glint in his brown eyes. My hands shook.

We worked in silence yet awhile; I could scarce harness my thoughts. I may have commented on the ears, only two-thirds full, but showing few worms. In the distance a lad imitated crows calling back and forth. Finally, Susanna brought us each a tin cup of water. I thanked her and said I would need to be getting on. She nodded but made no attempt to converse. Her lips curled down as if in pity; strands of brown hair pulled away, giving her a loose look. Nor did she wear the usual female garb; it may have been Henry's coat and hat. But living with men does not justify dressing as one. I opened my mouth but thought better of it. I had called to address a problem; I left burdened with two.

I stood slowly and reached for Emanuel's hand. He gave a grudging shake but did not rise in farewell.

"My heart will rejoice to see you find your place among us," I said. He made no response; I half-stumbled to prepare Caspar for departure.

Yet longer, I stalled with the blanket and saddle, thinking Henry might come out, but then turned to Susanna.

"Scripture asks, '*what woman having ten pieces of silver, if she lose one piece, doth not light a candle, and sweep the house, and seek diligently till she find it?*'"

Susanna kept inspecting corn, but I am sure she heard. I wanted to say more, for Luke next describes the joy when the coin is found. The woman asks her friends and neighbors to rejoice with her.

I chose not to waste more words. I fear that woman is spinning black wool.

The next time our church met, I expected Henry to say something. Instead, the whole family was absent. I was completely flummoxed. Mary thought there might have been sickness. But ever since, their attendance has been spotty. I have not kept record, but I doubt the woman has been there more than once since. Emanuel, not at all. I would never have expected Henry to abdicate his role as *Hausvater*.

Now my dreams are only part of what disturbs. What will come next? *O Gott! Halt mich in deiner Hut.*

David — Shenandoah Valley, January 1862

It still shocks to make the statement, "We are a divided country at war." And to think this dreadful state has gone on for over eight months already. Sometimes we are late to learn of developments. Last April, the national flag was torn from the dome of our Virginia Capitol building and trampled on while crowds cheered. Businesses had to close in Richmond. People started bonfires and a Confederate banner was raised. Men deliberated in secret. "What difference, had we known?" Abigail asks.

Since then, some of our young—my own boys—have been dragged off to camp against their will. Every day last fall the persecution mounted: Joel and Amos, expected to go to drills for the purpose of using weapons to destroy human life. John Kline has written another flurry of letters to numerous persons in authority, all on behalf of those of us conscientiously opposed. Any day now we think we should get assurance. I cannot name everyone he wrote to last month. Colonel Lewis, a friend, is one—now an officer in the Confederate army—but known by Johnny much longer than this rebellious Southern union has existed.

Brother Kline reminded authorities, whether John H. Hopkins or John C. Woodson, both delegates from Rockingham County, we Brethren pay our taxes and fines. The Bible is clear: give Caesar what is Caesar's; give God what is God's. We respect civil authority, but we cannot live contrary to God's principles. Brother Kline knows the Constitution well—Christian liberty, the spirit of Washington and Jefferson—and quotes often from the fifteenth section: "*Nor shall any man be enforced, restrained, molested, or burdened in his body or goods, or otherwise suffer on account of his religious opinion or belief.*" Even I have learned that part by heart. I tell Abigail, my sons and I are not to be compelled to kill another human being.

In spite of such clarity, the law and precedents have been set aside in this current rush to war. Delilah calls it madness. Overnight and in the dark, people changed their minds. Men thought it a grand adventure. Everything changed when President Lincoln—now he wears a beard—wanted to resupply that fort. The truth of it sank in for us the first day after our Annual

Meeting concluded last May. We had met here in Rockingham County from the 19th to the 22nd at the Beaver Creek meetinghouse. A blessed time, but then to come home and learn Virginia had voted to secede.

From the time war first broke out, our meeting planned for the time of Pentecost was in jeopardy. Some brothers in the north said there was too much danger to travel south. What strong persuasion Brother Kline had to use, pointing out that no less evil lurked if we went their way.

"We must not let this war cause disunity in our church," he said, then added, "other denominations divide, North and South."

In the end, not as many came from Ohio and Pennsylvania. But only one brother from Ohio reported seeing Southern soldiers at Harpers Ferry; nowhere did our visitors find their progress impeded. We were able to conduct church business, having set up a large tent and making use of a grove of trees for informal gatherings.

Disagreement persisted among us, though. Several older brethren from Pennsylvania dragged their feet, as in the past, about the propriety of establishing a treasury for the expenses of our German Baptist evangelists. Action had to be postponed yet another year.

Later I said to Brother Kline, "We will never make progress, if new light is not allowed. Consensus is good, but we rehash too much. Why close the door?"

He looked on me with sad eyes. "It is much more important that we stay united."

This is not entirely unusual for me to think I know his mind and heart, only to be reprimanded. Why can he not see the outdated vision of our church as a spotless virgin holds us back? This new Minute Book with oral understandings written down has become a rule book.

I mumble to Abigail, "Our rules—too much form, not enough substance. Why is it wrong to state displeasure with those who cling?"

She raises one eyebrow higher than the other.

"There is no comparison: the plea that gleaming spears be beaten into pruning hooks, placed on the same page with insisting a man's hair be parted in the middle."

"Did you speak up?" she asks.

"Only later."

"You must say at the time. Or not complain."

"You do not understand."

The truth is: there is much *I* do not understand. No question, not even warfare, seems straightforward. We pray for peace, but we are not to pray for the success of either side. I see that governments must at times fight wars, but this is partly a rebellion *against* government! Then these recruiting officers come along and confuse more with their relentless view that warfare is a worthy sacrifice for the love of country. The questions are too complicated; I end up settling with our church's position of asking for equivalency: taxes or fines as sacrifice, as in the past.

I trust my nineteen-year-old Amos, for he has made his solemn vow to the Almighty. When he was taken away to camp on a wagon last fall and forced to shoot, he fired into the air. The man goaded him about his poor aim, but Amos stayed brave.

"We do not shoot people, nor will we practice such."

But Joel, a year younger, has not yet sealed his vow; he has less to say. He had to prove his worthlessness as a soldier, though, before he was allowed to come home and help bring in our crops. We do not know what will happen when spring comes.

That is what spurs Johnny to write more letters. Well, it is part. When Colonel Lewis wrote back, all he promised was to do whatever was in his power. Johnny redoubled his efforts: a letter to General Jackson, another to Colonel Lewis's brother, Charles. I get the Lewis men mixed up, but one is thought to be more inclined to the Union. I am not convinced we can persuade, but Johnny remains steadfast.

"If we carefully explain the doctrine of peace and show how it is based on Scripture, those of us with conscientious scruples will receive a fitting exemption."

Our devout Brother Moomaw lives to the south in Botetourt County and takes the same approach with authorities.

They should listen to my neighbor, Winfield. He calls me a traitor to the Southern cause, while I think he is a traitor to our government in Washington. So far, though, I have refrained from spouting: *Nor shall any man be enforced, restrained, molested, or burdened in his body or goods.*

The last time he came, I was working on a barrel in my shed—my roosters are quick to warn of any approaching stranger. His shadow fell before I saw him. I did not want to be drawn into words, but I could think of no pretext to leave.

He wasted no time. "This talk about the black man wanting to be free—not what I hear from mine. Any darkie works for me, shows respect."

Winfield is a large man, wide through the shoulders and chest. He stands tall with a broad stance and booms out his words. I do not have to be a slave to know I do not want to be drawn into a physical altercation.

"You're a godly man, right, Bowman?" Winfield's voice thundered in my shed.

I shook my head. "Far from perfect."

He knows nothing of my refusal to fast, my insistence on eating eggs to start my day, my discontent with official church business.

"All I know is what others say about you people with the funny hats and pious looks." My hens squabbled. "Let me tell you something, man. My ancestors fought for the right of slavery, God's plan to Christianize these Africans."

I steadied my hands on the rim of the unfinished barrel. Words skittered away. We German Baptists do not expect the world to share our views.

"My slaves'll do anything for me. Ask 'em yourself. That old one, 'the Shuffler,' stays the year now. He wouldn't have the first idea how to get through the day if I didn't tell him. When he forgets an order, I give him the strap; it comes back fast. Carefree, that fella'—the whole lot of 'em! No worries about the next meal. Do what I say—that's all. Then they can sing their songs"—Winfield paused to smooth his reddish sideburns—"be raised up for the possibility of salvation, or whatever you religious ones say." His guffaw stopped abruptly. "Never been inclined that way myself. Only the missus says pious things. But I have it on authority: the Bible favors slavery, far back in time."

I had to stand, or the crick in my back would get worse and I would have to spend nights on the floor. "Not the Golden Rule," I said quietly. I stretched and turned my torso from side to side, bent to touch my toes. "And as ye would that men should do to you, do ye also to them likewise."

"That's what I'm saying! You got cotton stuck in your ears?" Winfield ripped off his coat from the heat of the stove. "No starving, no begging. If I grew up in some primitive hut, I'd jump at the chance to come to this country, too. Get outta' that hell hole."

I chose another length of stave but put it back. I could not risk more bending forward at the waist, but I leaned my back against the work counter, folded my arms in front of me.

"These Northerners and their self-righteous talk about abolition! More of your Golden Goose, I suppose. My slaves—two regulars—my property. Would Northerners come steal my traps? Would you?" His voice matched the heat in his voice. "Should have prosecuted your sons long ago, but let it go. Now Feds dare come on southern soil, as if they own everything. My property is not to be touched by another. You hear? None of it. I do what I want on my land."

I wanted to remind him: the Feds were not the instigators. He'd disagree, and it would only prolong things. I said instead, "I believe it is so; the North also benefits from slavery."

"Believe it is so! Where've you been? Hiding under that big hat of yours in some made-up world? Get those tomatoes outta' your eyes! 'Course, it's so. The North wouldn't be where it is without our slaves. Yet, they act like they can tell *us* what to do."

I know how Johnny keeps his voice low when someone questions him. "The black man is our brother," I said.

"Brother? You're that simple? He's little more 'n an animal. We take *care* of him. Give him a place to live—he's satisfied. Doesn't mean we're equal. He's a different race! You hear? Hot shots in the North accuse us of having no conscience. Hypocrites, the whole lot! Tell us we can't defend our property. We showed 'em—Manassas!"

His face changed to a snarly grin. "Our Stonewall and his men showed 'em." Winfield rustled through my staves—a fitful racket—but removed nothing. "Outsmarted those smart ones. Thought they'd march in here and whip us stupid, Southern oafs. We showed 'em. Two thousand of 'em, never gonna' take another step. Or only step with one leg."

His laugh started again, but my words slipped out. "How can that be victory?"

"What's that?" He moved closer, towering, blocking my exit. He smelled of cloves.

"We are taught not to avenge ourselves."

He backed up and made a show of assessing me, as if he could see through my clothes. "Foolishness—a white man at that. You *are* a Northerner, you rat! Have you forgotten our motto? 'God will vindicate.'" He smacked a hand against an upright. "Our man, Jeff Davis, knows how to lead us back. Our founding principles start with the right to operate in our own best interests." He poked around, held up one of my hand saws. "Yup, great victory that was. Manassas." His voice quieted as he ran a finger and jagged nail along the edge of a saw. "Gonna' take back those western parts, too. Our state and on. Traitors there, too." His voice came back full force. "Finish the American Revolution. Finish God's work!" Then as an afterthought, "Mighty fine tools you have." He ran his hand over the smooth wood of an ax handle.

I had nothing to say to one trapped in the vengeance of the Old Testament. True glory replaced by animal lust. No point, telling him to read the Sermon on the Mount. On that I was certain.

"Cat got your tongue?" he yelled. "Shirking your duty, Bowman. You know that. 'Course you do. A coward—that's what you are—slinking into a corner. Protecting your sons, I bet. No better 'n that fellow, Goodman—says he has a weak heart. And Smothers down the road—all of a sudden, walks like he's lame. Pathetic!"

Winfield left as suddenly as he had come. My only gratitude: my sons had gone to help my friend, J. M., cut timber; Abigail and Delilah stayed inside with their weaving. Only my fowl friends heard his outburst.

Before his shouts I might have blamed women for doing the most to stoke the war. I have learned not to go to the post office—Timberville nor New Market—unless I absolutely must. Women have posted signs, calling on the men of Virginia to render service to state and country. One sign referred in large letters to the words of Virginia's famous orator: "Give me Liberty or give me Death." Proud white women sending their men.

My hopes of last summer look foolish now; I had thought we might face a short series of battles. But now, winter sits upon us—one gray day after another, broken only by a stormy shade of blue. We all have time to reassess what is wishful thinking and what is more likely. If we have only begun . . .

Oh, Lord!

Thousands more will return to our Virginia soil. Dragging a leg, missing an eye. In a box.

And this other scourge, like a plague sent from God—diphtheria! Last fall when Brother Kline and I made only a few mission trips into the mountains—train and road travel sometimes closed to the North—John's skills as physician commanded the greater need. Medicines were, and still are, scarce, but Johnny makes his bottled remedies. Even if herbs do little good, they do no harm. Last summer, I helped him gather sumac and witch hazel. He has moved still closer to practicing what he learned from Doctor Curtis in Cincinnati: heavy reliance on herb tea, but the patient only vomits once or twice, no more than twenty minutes. John also follows through now with steaming and sweating routines before rubbing the patient down with whiskey; he eliminates dousing the patient in cold water.

But why this siege of bodily infirmity, pressing on us now? Nothing has stemmed the tide. The few medical doctors who remain—many have gone to aid the military—report no success against diphtheria. (Even after studying with another physician for a year, they are still learning on the go, too.) Sometimes I think John's greatest skill is in never showing alarm, not his face nor hands. His whole demeanor stays calm. When Sadie Harshbarger was gasping for breath, he took her hand, read aloud a passage from the Bible, and assured her the worst would soon be over. Even I found comfort, hearing her say she was ready to go.

I have lost count of the funerals. Those for the children are the hardest, if I am called on for opening devotions. The little white shrouds and tiny caskets unnerve me. I sweat so much, I could be receiving a steam treatment unawares, or made to lie on a rock-warmed bed for half an hour. Others in attendance pull their wool coats tighter, but to lose a child—can anything shatter more? To bring one up in the fear and admonition of the Lord and then have that child ripped away by death's scourge! Some believe diphtheria is the Lord's will; I could never say that. Another family struck *purposely* with sore throats and breathing difficulties? No!

Nor can I see God ever finding the South's claims to be just. Our big boys—the most vulnerable. My soul grieves; Joel may yet waver. He is prone to think he knows all and can be impulsive. If Abigail could, she would restrict both boys to our house and land, not let either out of her sight. They hear these calls to be manly and march in step; when they refuse to cooperate, they face ridicule. Amos is more to think things through; he benefitted the most from another term at Cedar Grove Academy. This teacher, Joseph Salyard, is not German Baptist, but he does not put forth erroneous ideas as some in the common schools who incite to war.

I tell Abigail: we cannot shield our boys. No more than I can decide for anyone in the church. Some of our members have resorted to paying from $800 to $1500 to secure a substitute to go in their place. Of course, our people did that already during the American Revolution. But such a large sum now! I could not see my way clear with two boys. Not that kind of money. We do not want for material goods, but neither do we have extra.

My inner fretting spills out when I least expect. What if Johnny's wife, Anna, knows more than those of us who claim full faculties? Back in November before John again took up writing letters, I could not help myself. This dark cloud of illness and death put such heaviness. As usual, Johnny and I stopped at a stream to let our horses recover. He gave apples to both Nell and Elijah; we sat nearby on a large boulder, munching as well.

I had been cogitating all trip and could not keep silent. I made mention of Anna's prediction of fiery destruction. "The burden of loose ends must press on you as well."

"This is not Armageddon," Johnny replied, sucking juice from the apple core.

I bit my lip at his words; he seemed to know my thoughts.

"She asked once if it might be a vision of Armageddon." He paused as a black crow took flight through the trees. "She had dreamed of much weeping. Haystacks blazing, huge balls of fire racing across brown meadows. Frantic people, driving their cattle and sheep from burning barns." He twirled the brim of his hat through his thumb and finger.

I held my body still; I dared not swing my legs. He spoke as if reporting reimbursement a man had received for grain at the market.

"She has dreamed this same dream over a period of some twenty-five years."

I was as one astounded. A quarter of a century! "How can you keep your wits?"

"One time—it was 1842—she went with me in the carriage to Hardy County for church meetings. During the night she began to cry in her sleep; I could not waken her. I applied wet towels to her head and gave her a sedative so she could sleep. By morning she was better and we spoke no more of it. She would tell me, though, whenever the dream of fire came back."

I would not be able to sleep with Abigail, if that were the case.

"Four years later is when I became ill with typhoid fever while in Ohio. I told you that before. I may have contracted the disease earlier in Pennsylvania or Maryland where they are not always careful about keeping their water wells covered to prevent contamination. When my grave illness persisted, someone wrote to Anna and explained my absence."

He poked at leaves with a long stick. I am not used to seeing him crush anything, unless it is an herb.

"How I wish the Lord might have intercepted that missive. My condition, described as dire." He tossed the stick aside. "And so it was," he added softly. "But upon receipt of that letter, Anna became disoriented. She refused sustenance and only stared straight ahead, speaking not a word. She viewed me as an apparition."

I could not look at him, lest he disappear. Now whenever I recall this sad tale, I connect it with the time, perhaps a year earlier, when I sat with Johnny at his table, partaking of a hickory nut cake. I take him black walnuts from my trees, but he is partial to his hickory nuts. That time we had returned early from a medical errand, and Johnny wanted to show me a new instrument he had purchased. Later, as we visited over cake, a hand—bony fingers with large knuckles—slowly drew back the curtain to the next room. Below a creased brow, dark eyes fixed on our proceedings. Ever since, I have understood the phrase "emotionless eyes." The face made no murmur but stayed thus until we finished our repast. Then of a sudden, the curtain fell swiftly shut. I never mentioned it.

But on the occasion last fall when the horses began to whinny at our delay, Johnny stood to ready Nell for the last leg of our journey. "When Anna finally saw me, she did not believe it was I, pale and thin, not bothered by this girth which has again accumulated."

I practically tiptoed to my horse, for fear I might miss some of Johnny's words. "Steady now," I whispered to Elijah.

"Her condition since reminds me of how some girls were mistreated in New England. A century before, when false stories were whispered in Salem."

I do not recall what I may have said, whether I managed something about the crush of unfounded rumors or the sorrow I felt for Brother Kline. An infirmity like this in a loved one! I might have stayed silent, knowing how words forsake me.

But I remember the sigh that accompanied his next words, "I have prayed." His head sank momentarily into Nell's side. "If it is not God's will to remove this affliction from her, I have prayed to receive wisdom. Strength to be with her." He straightened and rubbed Nell's flank. She turned a large eye to him. "I have tried physical and spiritual cures. Sometimes Anna is better for a while," he whispered, "until she slips back into her gloom." His voice picked up strength. "The electromagnetic device only brought more pain in the end."

"Sad, very sad," I may have said.

"I have assured Anna, dreams are only fantasies, not prophecies. Her other dream . . ." He paused even longer, but stood as in a trance. I held Elijah's halter tight. "She sees me in a coffin on top of a black catafalque." My breath caught in the mash of leaves under Nell's restless hoofs. "I have a white lily in my folded hands, an open Bible on my chest."

I wanted to place an arm about his shoulder, but he kept his back to me. We are not given to showing affection, beyond the routine Kiss of Peace.

"I have had to reassure her over the years: she is not possessed of a demon." His gaze turned to me. "I know you will say nothing of this to anyone. No one."

I looked him in the eye and nodded.

"I do not know why the Lord does not see fit to heal, remove her misery of melancholy."

I have wondered since if there was a trace of bitterness. I would not have thought that possible for Johnny. But to live daily with an unbalanced one, as he does . . .

Abigail gets wrapped in a frenzy about our boys—but nothing like this.

I will not betray his trust. Anna is not a witch, as some have whispered. But as for clairvoyance, I cannot say. I had never given much credence to the story that she had dreamed of a woman in a coffin, only to have that woman die shortly thereafter. But now I notice more lines on Johnny's forehead. I seek them out; they are still there. I had thought he would never lack stamina. He still gets up at four every morning, eats a large breakfast: bacon or ham, several eggs with biscuits, marmalade or jelly, cold milk or hot tea. But now I see his silver-gray hair; I hear his weariness.

All of that must add to why Johnny renews his efforts with letters. Why he desires that all German Baptists and like-minded people not be "*enforced, restrained, molested, or burdened.*" Why he makes yet another stop to keep the croup and hoarseness from taking root in another household. Why he is determined, the church he loves will carry out the fulfillment of God's will in the midst of this upheaval. It all flows from one stream, even his very life and breath.

ESTHER — Shenandoah Valley, March 1862

All three of my men! Gone to one wilderness or another. Simon and our oldest man-child, Andrew, taking flight to the west. Hiding by day, traveling by night. I don't know where. Ten nights ago, they commenced with others: Simon riding Midnight, Andrew on foot. They had to go. Or else be pursued. But where? Perhaps western Virginia?

But Peter, our second, swayed the opposite. Governor Letcher had called for 40,000 more men, and Peter—brought up in the fear of the Lord—answered. Nothing we could do. Stormed away on foot a month ago; argued with Simon about a horse. Simon feared Peter might steal one. Somewhere he marches, wearing the gray. My son and the 52nd Virginia Infantry. Simon says that means foot soldiers, not horseback. Those others, called cavalry.

Peter has no fear; he laughed at mine. Eighteen years in January and off on an adventure. He would have gone, even without the fifty-dollar bounty. Other men have come home already, weary from eight months of wearing the uniform. They want no more. But Peter thinks he's bigger than any foe, ready to outwit any man. He always outwrestled Andrew, but Andrew is built smaller, like Simon. Peter gets his stature from my side; my brothers, each over six feet. Peter believes he can walk miles and not be weary, sleep on wet ground and jump up refreshed. But thinking to take another's life and not have to give account?

Simon had taken to sending Peter to get a newspaper last fall. Those trips to Harrisonburg—that's when he fell into the hands of acquaintants. The glitter of swords. Genevieve's boy may have been one. Peter spoke of guns with bayonets. He spoke of a Mr. Newblood and called him a "straight shooter." If he saw my shudder, he made no mind. The gruesome has always held appeal. Peter wanted to loiter as a child, peering at the entrails of the bear Simon had shot. Yet in the spring, he'd be the one—just a tyke—bringing me a bouquet of dandelions.

This Mr. Newblood told Peter all manner of things: God was on the side of the South; Northerners were the avengers; we must defend ourselves. Peter claimed they have church services in camp. They make the sinister sound manly, even godly. Peter followed, even after what happened last summer—that awful Sunday when thousands were killed at Manassas.

Andrew, so different—more on the timid side. But Simon wouldn't have a son who couldn't hold his own with a balky horse or handle one end of a cross saw. He'd shame him. Last fall Andrew made his vow with the church, joining five other young ones at Weavers. Brother Samuel made clear to all, young and middle-aged, if they join the military, they can't be church members. You can't destroy someone with one hand and offer supplication to the Almighty with the other. Well, you can; I suppose this Mr. Newblood does. But for us, your pledge to follow God's ways would be marred.

Peter's not the only one of our kind. A Hildebrand boy from Augusta County—a son of one of those Jacobs—joined the same division. But these two boys are in different groups. Companies, they call them. Peter is with Company F. Our bishop, Samuel, always asks kindly if we've heard from Peter. He has relatives far south of here in Greenbrier County; some of those cousins have gone to the military, too. They'd joined the Methodists, but still, Samuel's family. He says to pray God will see fit to bring all the boys safely home.

The danger for Simon and Andrew may be only a little less. They went with others who knew of a pilot to take them safely through the mountains into western Virginia. Simon didn't say what gap, only: "Know nothing."

An officer could come seeking information. I reached for Simon, but his mind was set against tenderness. "Don't make this harder. Gird yourself, woman. Dumb as the sheep."

If the men can slip into Union territory, they'll be safe. But scouts, out and about, looking for men like Simon and Andrew, want to put guns in their hands and hatred in their hearts. They call those who flee deserters. Or slackers. Skedaddlers. But for me, all my big ones gone—Peter deserting us!

They call this "The Brothers' War." I can't think on it. Nothing good between Cain and Abel. Oh, I never thought this would be mine.

Our troubles last fall, bad enough. But that time I had my big boys, when an officer, looking important, came riding to our barn. Insisted Simon go with him. Barking orders. We were caught off guard—no time to prepare. Still thinking we'd be left alone. The officer scoffed when Simon offered extra payment; he wanted muscle.

Simon ended up a teamster, had to take our team and wagon. He hauled booty for two weeks; not one night at home. Trips back and forth on the Valley Pike, hauling stores of goods the Confederate Army had captured from Union men. Others of ours, forced to do the same. Still others made shoes for army men. All of that because Simon and the rest were worthless to train to shoot.

Brother Coffman reminded us: "No man can serve two masters," and encouraged the ones who'd been dragged off, not to return if called again. "Stand your ground."

In January it started up again. Some forced to haul ammunition or clothes through sleet and snow. Frances said others transported sick men to Winchester, using their own conveyances. With spring, the army knocked more often, insisting our men help the cause. Simon decided to get the jump.

Here I am, not used to being the one left in charge of a day's work with three youngsters. We're not supposed to expect the men back in time to plow the fields. Fierce rain and stormy weather settles; no rush for us to push the plow. I fear Simon and Andrew have been drenched as well. Ice hung from trees; long, pointed icicles, six to eight inches, still drip from our house and barn. One day it snowed and thundered at the same time.

Mary Grace shouted above the loud claps, "Ma, it's snowing!"

All has been out of order.

Of my three left, Joseph is fifteen and works almost as hard as his older brothers. Simon taught him to manage the work horses last year. But now he turns glum, the same way Simon was prone. I've never called Joseph the Man of the House, but he goes about as if the burden falls to him, walking with bent shoulders. William stays slight at thirteen, given to sickliness. He wakes to sneeze again and again. That much I can bear, far better than his gasps in great gulps when he shrieks for air.

Twice, Mama has come to the rocking chair my father made. Of a sudden and wearing black, offering neither smile nor frown, she sits silently. I believe her spirit is sent to steady, but the second time my cold shivers ran free. Her lips turned down with dark hairs sprouting from her chin. Fear took hold and I looked away. Then she was gone. She used to say in her gravelly voice, "If you keep your eyes on the viper, it can't get you."

* * *

I heard the horse first, cloppity-cloppity on mucky ground. The bishop came to our farm today. He must have followed our voices; the children and I untangled harnesses and hunted for stored clover and timothy seed in the shed. Simon had said all was in order, but his departure so hasty, he couldn't properly look to everything—burlap helter-skelter on barrels, lids not tight. I took one look at Samuel. My heart sank.

Every day after our morning prayers, one or the other of us—usually Mary Grace—says, "Maybe this will be the day we hear from Father and Andrew." I nod, thinking to encourage but not wanting to plant false hope. Some unexpected courier might bring a letter with word of safe arrival in Ohio. Or Maryland. Andrew could write. But instead I shook hands with Samuel and motioned to a small bench for sitting. My eyes pierced his chest, thinking there might be the bulge of an envelope in an inner pocket.

He stayed standing and kept the pleasantries brief. "I'm sorry to report, Esther: Simon and Andrew are in jail. In Richmond." He ran his fingers through his thick hair.

"Richmond?" I couldn't help but blurt. "They headed north." I looked to Joseph to help set the bishop straight.

Samuel's blue eyes, though sunken, looked on me kindly. "I wanted to tell in person. Your husband and son, safe. But scouts detained the group—seventy-some, intent on fleeing—when they—"

"Seventy?" I interrupted and quickly covered my mouth.

"Near to Petersburg, having crossed the South Branch of the Potomac."

I pulled Mary Grace to me. "Simon only talked of meeting four or five others."

"The number may not be exact," the bishop said, "but we understand more men joined—quite a number—after the first ones left our Weavers church. That is the way with a train such as this. From safe place to safe place they pick up one or two more at each depot. The numbers can grow large."

"A train?" William asked, his eyes momentarily bright. I reached to smooth his unruly hair and pulled him to my other side.

"Not one that belches smoke," Samuel said. "A train of men—mostly ours and Dunkers—seeking to live freely. Each wanting to obey conscience, not follow others' inclination."

"Peter," Mary Grace whispered into the folds of my dress.

I rushed ahead. "Are they together?" My voice turned to a whisper. "My men? One group?"

"We don't know specifics, but their names are both on a list of prisoners at Castle Thunder in Richmond." Samuel's eyes dulled. Rumors swirl that neighbors threaten to kill him.

"They were headed for Ohio," I said, as if the bishop didn't know.

"Yes, over the Shenandoah Mountain, traveling as far north as Petersburg. Thereabouts. Maybe into western Virginia. No doubt our men couldn't refuse when more men asked to join. But Confederate scouts found them, turned them back to Petersburg where they were searched. Hard for a group that size to go undetected."

Now Samuel sat down, teetered on the uneven bench. His breathing loud, his words in bursts. "Safe hideouts. Our Underground. But men, others, on the lookout. Report anything suspicious."

William and Mary Grace stayed close, each with a hand gripping. Joseph had propped his back against a shed post and looked to the hills outside. An awful thought crossed—my stomach lurched—but I shook myself. *Gird yourself. This trouble will be but a short while.*

As if Samuel knew the direction of my thoughts, he said, "We'll do all in our power to convince the authorities. These men meant no harm. Of course, we don't know the exact circumstances. To farm as in the past . . ." His voice wobbled and he swiveled away on the bench, as if he couldn't bear to look on us. We stayed huddled—my youngest sheep, nary a bleat.

At last, the bishop's voice went on, steadied. He repeated what he'd doubtless said to others. "The men were marched back through Franklin and on to Monterey—our understanding—before arriving at the jail in Staunton. Reports vary; one or two may have escaped. But more captives added to their number as they marched. At Staunton, said to be put on a train to Richmond."

"A real one?" William asked again. Somewhere within he imagines an excitement I can't comprehend.

"All the information we have," the bishop said, turning to us again. "Given blankets, now." He looked me in the eye. "I wish we could give more assurance. They have food." Then he added, "Sadly . . . sadly, their horses put into service at Staunton."

Mary Grace burrowed her sniffles in my side, her arms tight about my waist. I raised my free arm and said, "Joseph, come here." I drew him to me. "Here's my big boy," I said. He's slow to show affection, but he put an arm about my shoulder and pressed his head against mine. We stood thus—William clinging also—seeking even breaths. Someone rides Midnight in the Confederate Army. Someone urges him to charge at a blue uniform.

The bishop looked again with reddened eyes. "These are sorely trying days; no one wants unwelcome news. Whether messenger or recipient. Susannah Brunk has illness in her brood. Margaret Rhodes' husband . . ." Samuel shook his head and stood again. "I must . . ." He reached a hand and found mine, his skin warm and rough. "Be of good courage, Esther. And children"—such trembles—"your mother will lean on you." He shook Joseph's hand. "The Lord will see fit . . ." A cow bellowed. "We don't . . . God parted the Red Sea; that much we know."

Then he was gone, saying he would, if at all possible, send us help to sow oats next month. I know not to expect; there aren't extra men among us. If a man hasn't fled, he's living in fear for his life. I've heard that Henry

Brunk, Susannah's husband—some few others—stay close, hiding in the mountains.

The bishop asked nothing regarding Peter. This evening before supper, though, we said our usual prayer. We remembered each one: Peter, first—I can't turn my back—Andrew, Simon. The others hiding. Midnight, too, wherever. I can't sway those in charge. Nor change the minds of prison guards. Not answer William and Mary Grace's every question, or stay Joseph from his moods. We wait for dry days, seeds at the ready. Next week, looking to spread manure.

David — Shenandoah Valley, early April 1862

I had gone to my cellar on this first day of April to retrieve the last of the potatoes for Abigail. With two less mouths to feed, our supply has not dwindled as much as usual, but the quality has declined markedly—wrinkled and sprouting. In another month we will cut up what remains and use them for seed. The thought of a freshly dug potato, piled with butter, allowed my mind to wander when a voice broke in.

"Who's down there?"

I banged my head on the low ceiling as I tried to stand erect too quickly. I stooped again to walk toward the light of the open door. There stood Winfield, hands on his knees, bending to peer into the basement.

"That you, Bowman?" he asked again.

"Yes," I said, "as you might expect."

"Who else?" He started down the steps.

I turned around in my dirt floor cellar, as if someone might be there whose presence I could not account for. "No one else."

"I'll see about that." He came the rest of the way, puffing from exertion. The stone steps are deep, and he took each one carefully, as if anticipating an unstable one.

He held a lantern high to see into corners. His head bent forward; his eyes cunning. He kicked at boards piled under old wooden buckets. "What's under?"

"Dirt. We put our tubers on boards to keep them from collecting moisture. The wife wants the last bucket."

"Hmpf." He kicked at the other end. "So where are they?"

"This bucket . . . We have eaten all else."

"You know what I mean," he yelled. "Those fool boys of yours. Grown men. They're needed."

"Not here."

"I have eyes."

I had not seen Winfield for several months. Nor had I missed him. His loud voice makes me fidgety, his poking . . .

"Where are they?" he asked again.

"Gone to visit relatives."

"Hmpf. What farmer lets his boys take off in the spring?" He spat a stream of tobacco juice. "Relatives, huh? No good. You and your lies."

"Looking for work," I said, "where there is family." That is my prayer.

"You and your kind. No work of your own for those boys? Hardly. Your country needs all of us, but you skunk out. Not worth a fart in a whirlwind."

I picked up my bucket. I needed air.

"You and your exemption." He moved heavily up the steps, calculating again where best to step. "Bunch of blubber before the authorities. Folderol for sissies." He turned to me at the top. "Wait till this is over; those boys of yours want to come back, act like nothing happened. Who's going to buy grain from them then? Huh?" He spat again. "Or barrels from you?"

I set the scrubby potatoes down to close the half-doors to the cellar. I feared he might come snooping inside and hassle my women. But he swung a leg on his horse and left. That is the way we parted in January also, without courtesy of farewell. This time I sat on the back porch steps to collect myself before going through the summer kitchen.

It has been several weeks since Joel and Amos left. No, they are not likely visiting relatives. Not blood family. Their sister Mary's place in Tennessee would not have been safe. My boys likely look for work, but we know not where they sleep, whether they have food. We may not hear for months.

I sent my sons away. It does not seem possible. "Go from this house; do not return until it is safe."

Three days later, the exemption came from our state of Virginia. What glorious news for members of all churches whose creeds prohibit the bearing of arms: exempt from the militia! We have Brother Kline's persistence to thank, making known our stance. Back in February he had written again to our Governor Letcher, as well as a second time to his friend Colonel Lewis, even to a Mr. Judah Benjamin who is the Confederate Secretary of War. We lost hope when the governor had called for *more* men—40,000 more!

That is when I said to Abigail, "It has to be. We must entrust our boys to God's providential care. Find a safer place."

Now with word of the exemption, Abigail has taken to wailing again. "Sent in vain. If only we had waited, not been so hasty." She sends daggers my way.

My boys might still be here, but all would not be well. Not when soldiers march to and fro and practice their maneuvers nearby. Not when my neighbor with no official authority comes poking for my sons like they are criminals.

What a tearful farewell when the boys left! Abigail fled inside the house, rather than watch them trudge out our driveway, past the row of whispering pines. Delilah and I stood steady, till they fully disappeared. Joel, the eager one, made for adventure. Neither boy wanted to be of further assistance to the Confederate army. They both knew coercion would come, fiercer than anything they had yet known. We armed them on their journey with New Testaments—I gave one to Delilah, too—all the gold I saw fit to spare, a flask of whiskey for each, and written directions.

I did not want them heading straight north on the turnpike, nor trying to find Emma at Winchester. Many seek to slip through Union lines, but to do so, a man must get past Confederate lookouts. Two groups of our men have been captured already. I sent my sons heading for *western* Virginia. And not the usual way to Moorefield. They were to go through Brocks Gap and along the Lost River—that much was familiar. But then with Brother Kline's help, I directed them toward mission outposts, out-of-the-way places, where we have ridden to visit outlying churches. Johnny drew maps and gave site markers to look for, where to make proper turns. Joel can get crosswise in his eagerness, but Amos stays clear-headed.

I trust the boys have not been lured into a group. I should have given more warning; it does not lend itself to stealth. I know they have had rain, but I trust enough sun also to lend warmth and dry out their clothes.

"Do not start out in fog," I said repeatedly. "Nothing can disorient like blanketed mountains." And again, "Head toward Seneca Rocks." Johnny has described the area often enough that I know of its difficulty. "No scouts or troops will roam there to molest."

Joel smacked a fist in his other hand. "Like mountain goats."

Delilah has been good to prop up her mother. "The boys will find their way; I know my brothers—sure-footed, they will scramble over boulders."

"But snakes and the deceit of poison berries!" We often do not make it through a meal without Abigail's recital of fears.

For me, the dangers of the mind are the worst. "If only they do not lose heart . . ."

"Amos knows to think through solutions, not plunge wildly ahead," Delilah says.

"If our boys can get to Keyser—that will someday be West Virginia—or even to Oakland . . ." Johnny has told me about our people residing there. "By then they will be near the Baltimore and Ohio Railroad, not far from Ohio."

"Then what?" Abigail breaks into fresh tears. "We do not know."

"That is right; we do not know," I say. "They may trudge on as far as Indiana, even Iowa. They know not to go to Missouri or Kansas; we have been clear."

If only we do not have to wait longer than two months. We will coax Abigail for that long. At the very latest the boys are to send word from Ohio with Brother Kline when he attends our church's Annual Meeting in June. He insists he is going, no matter the rumors. He will pick up correspondence the boys leave behind in hands they trust among our people. Make delivery for us.

"After they get beyond the reach of fighting," Delilah adds, squeezing her mother's arm, "they can be on their own, not need to pay a pilot."

I steady my voice. "People share our beliefs. Ohio and on. They will put the boys up, see that they find work. Give advice, regarding where and when, further."

Abigail's sad eyes persist. "You do not know."

"Not in the absolute. But Johnny agrees. We are to pray, not be consumed by fears."

That is what I and my fellow ministers say to all at Flat Rock; that is the calling. We are to count on a merciful God. What other comfort have we?

Abigail knows as well as I—when not consumed by doubt—there are problems with any choice a man makes, even now. For the boys to be exempt, officially, I would have to pay $500 for each son, plus 2 percent of any property that either owned. I am far from a wealthy man.

Joel still never joined our church, but I did not press him to make a premature decision. He will ask for membership when he is ready to own up to his own waywardness. Last year, when he turned seventeen, I gave him Ruby, a beautiful gray mare with white speckles. I could hardly watch when he parted from her. "I'll be back," he whispered countless times. She was out-of-sorts for days and ate little but is more resigned now to Delilah's care.

For me, I am exempt as a minister of the Word. But other stipulations follow: surrender guns and take an oath of loyalty to the Confederacy. Both are riddled with problems. I do not know how any of our men can truthfully express loyalty to this rebellion; each will have to do as his conscience dictates. Nor is it possible for a man to survive without the means to curb animals that may molest crops. Or live without a rifle to supply sufficient provision of meat, when another winter approaches.

Difficulties crop up also for anyone with scruples who chooses the option of paying for a substitute. One Mennonite is said to have paid as little as fifteen dollars a month, but his substitute did not stay the course. That brought another round of trouble. Others have had to pay up to $600 to hire a man, and that for only six months. When time expires, the one with the summons is like as not to be called again. Yet another round of scrambling. Still others have paid a substitute, only to learn the man was subject to service himself but had not said as much. Or the man was not fully able-bodied. Countless difficulties have come to light, far more than our ancestors encountered when released from duty by providing a proxy in Europe or during the Revolutionary War.

But all these problems pale compared with the trials of those jailed in their attempt to flee. We hear little of substance—rumors are rife!—about the large group, numbering fifty or more, taken to Richmond. But for the smaller group of eighteen, confined nearby in the Harrisonburg Courthouse, more reliable word comes from some of their women who live close by—allowed to take in baskets of food. Some of the men—our Dunkers: Wine, Hollar, and Nisewander, along with a few Mennonites—have been forced to load and unload wagons for the Confederacy. But most spend their days in a large jury room on the second floor. Conditions are cold and damp, but the women have taken blankets.

These eighteen froze in their movement, when they saw pickets near Moorefield over a week ago. Abigail says it has been longer, but I grow weary, arguing about timing. They were trying to go North; that much we know. All their money, taken. Their horses, saddles, bridles, left at Woodstock. Made to walk the next day to Mount Jackson where more waiting ensued before they were walked to Harrisonburg.

According to the women, the men say they could have escaped! Only two or sometimes three guards kept an eye on them en route to jail. Long gaps developed in their line. But when they spread out too much, one of the guards would yell, "Close up the prisoners!" Then a man might feel a guard's bayonet in his back, especially if he was slow to obey the order to bunch up again. Some nearly passed out while being herded, given little to eat.

I sought out Johnny for more word, knowing how people often congregate at his mill. But that day, no one else was there. Traffic slow because of concerns. John said the men were wise to understand, if some had escaped, it would have gone harder for those still captured.

But then he surprised. "This capture was brought to the attention of no less than Stonewall Jackson."

"How do you know?"

"Jackson wrote to an aide of Governor Letcher, saying there must be a better way to put noncombatants to work. My informant reported no disparaging words from Jackson about us."

Color must have drained from my face. "Are we to believe?"

"This Jackson is said to be a religious man himself; that may be why he respects our principles. His headquarters located at Winchester."

"My daughter Emma lives there!" I lowered my head. "Not that it matters."

"Here is what troubles. Jackson wants to form companies—about 100 men each—not using guns. A way to involve us, we suspect, likely working as our men did last summer as teamsters, only more highly organized to serve their purposes."

"What will come, though, now that Virginia has passed its exemption law?"

Johnny lifted empty hands. "No way to know. Perhaps scuttled."

"Would men in a company like that be paid for their labor?"

Again Johnny shrugged. "My fear, these companies—a way to sneak our men into the army, coerce them to drill. Unawares, our men could be caught up, lacking recourse."

I had much to think on as I rode home. Who had brought Brother Kline this word? He sometimes speaks of a friend, Algernon Gray in Harrisonburg, but he knows many others. Ever since, I have made it my business to be more conversant as well. We must learn all we can, especially as dissension and uncertainty mount. Jacob Wine contends strongly we should not entertain any sort of work that would give aid to the war effort—not if we are sincere in our opposition. J. M. Garber, farming near to New Market, talks often with his Quaker neighbor. They hold fast and will have nothing to do with an alternative plan. Nor will any of them buy a substitute; they call it morally wrong to pay someone to kill for you.

* * *

Johnny has been arrested! He and two Mennonite ministers, taken to the jail at Harrisonburg and placed behind bars with those eighteen imprisoned some weeks ago. These latest, captured on Saturday and labeled "men of property and influence," only five days after I had spoken with John at his mill. Since then, a visitor, Benjamin Byerly, brought the Staunton newspaper that applauded these arrests. That was the third time he came to my door, riding from his home in Dayton, seeking gifts of money to help pay the fines of our men in prison.

The first time, I told him I had naught to spare. I had sent what extra I could with my sons. But he came two days later, and again another time.

After Byerly left the last time, I said to Abigail, "I must go visit my dear friend."

"You will do no such thing." She stood in front of the door, as if I might go that very day.

"I am over fifty and exempt as a Minister of the Word."

"The same is true for Brother Kline."

"I have no influence, little property."

"The authorities might keep any man who shows up offering support."

I paced from the stove, to the window, to the fireplace, then around the circuit again. Delilah looked from one to the other of us but offered no suggestion.

"It is the only decent thing," I said. "A brotherly visit."

"Do not stick your nose in." Abigail stood hunched, her voice louder than usual.

"Neither money nor reputation; they do not want me. Brother Kline would come if I—"

"Do *not* get yourself mixed up with that Beery man." Abigail's hair hung loose at her ears. "You have told me."

"You are unreasonable."

"There is no reason in this madness. A month ago we had two sons; now we have none. Do you want Delilah and I to fend alone?"

I looked to Delilah, but she would not insert herself. She sat reading her New Testament, sometimes resting her head on the back of the chair, closing her eyes.

Rumors threaten to swallow us. The latest: these last three are to be executed. Benjamin Byerly whispered it first. "Not Johnny!" I said. "We cannot make do without him."

About the Heatwole man, a Gabriel, we know nothing. But I had told Abigail how this Joseph Beery hired a substitute for his son and then encouraged the substitute to desert. Very poor thinking on Beery's part, for the hired substitute named Beery to the authorities.

Vile sentiments spew from the newspaper; a man spits on the road when I pass by on the way to New Market. Sometimes I avoid going past Winfield's place. Or I settle for keeping to myself at home.

Another rumor says Jackson is preparing his men to do battle in these parts.

"Not our beautiful Valley!" I cry out.

I take consolation; my farm is back from the main thoroughfare—safe from the turnpike where soldiers would likely march. But a wretchedness overtakes me—putting my own welfare first.

In the end I gave Byerly money; I did that much that third time. To aid me, Delilah persisted—I felt badgered—encouraging me to sell the work horses. Sometimes it is easier for a young one to see what must be done.

"What is a horse, compared with a man's release?" she asked.

I could not believe it the first time she suggested it. I argued: "Selling two horses in springtime—like cutting off my hands!"

She stayed relentless. "We must get the men out of jail."

I argued the more. "We have food because of these beasts. We cannot abstain from raising crops; nor can we survive on eggs." She changed not, even when I said, "When the war is over, our circumstances may be worse. A replacement horse could cost even more; we must plan ahead and save."

Nothing held up against her statement: "We must release the men." Not even the farm work I did for one of the brethren in prison.

In the end I gave Byerly the $600 from selling my work horses. We do not know when there may be a conclusion for the men. It is called a commutation fee—the money that goes for the jailed men's exemption. All who sought to flee and were captured. Everyone among us German Baptists has trusted Byerly and given what we can for him to take to authorities. I can read Scripture again before the gathered—even though stumbling—with a clear conscience.

But when I go to my horse shed, only Elijah and Joel's horse greet me. Ruby might have fetched close to $1,000, what with the army's demand for horses. But I could not do that. Ruby must be here when Joel returns. If I sold her, Abigail could say, "I knew all along you did not expect the boys back."

So far, the men still sit in jail. The women faithfully carry in food but report many of the men have taken sick. Conditions sound like unto that of a cold dungeon. Day after day we are drenched with rain, plus three more days of sleet that had the look of snow. Brother Kline is said to preach and provide medical care, but he cannot have the necessary herbs with him. I have taken to slipping chamomile and such into the basket the Showalter woman takes.

She says some of the men still try to sing at night—they had composed a song already while detained at Mount Jackson—but others have become too hoarse. Even Johnny suffers. I *must* go see him. But I do not. I fear for the sentinels at the doors. Rumor says a captured young man was nearly shot one night when he stood too near a window. The ball went up through the ceiling, having filled the man's eyes and face with glass.

Abigail prevails. "First the boys, then the horses. No more."

I am not the man I ought to be. "*I was . . . in prison and ye visited me not.*"

Betsey — western Virginia, April 1862

"*Harrich mol! Des is addlich wichdich!* Mary, you too. Listen! When you hear the sound of drums and horses—dreadful to the ears—come in the house directly."

Mother's face looks pale, her walk slow. She groans when she picks up Gideon. Poppa calls him a chunk.

Soon after those instructions, Tobias dawdled to finish milking Tillie—only to get a few more dribbles in his bucket. He said it was two seconds. He knew better, but I squeezed my lips tight. Poppa frowned but said nothing. He could have been thinking about our balky work horses, Frank and Tom, or the hard rains that washed away precious seeds.

The booms make everyone jumpy. Poppa says it would be easier if the noises did not start up at unexpected times. But when the noises go on ceaselessly, he says it would be easier if they gave us a rest. No one knows why the men practice marching in our mountains.

That is not all. They shot our Jack! We think, but did not see. Poppa found him.

"A bullet to the head," he said.

"What?" we children echoed. "How could—? Not Jack!"

We girls begged and begged to see, but Poppa would only take Tobias to help dig the grave. But we know Jack is separate from Momma's resting place.

"We cannot be sure," Mother said, "about the doer."

"That is so," Poppa said. "No one saw the mischief. But we can be glad we got to keep Jack over a year. A good companion."

"But not this summer!" Lydia said. "My best dog."

"We will lose our chickens," I said, rubbing my eyes. "And eggs."

"Any fox will know to stay far from gunshot," Poppa said. "It does not pay to worry. We do not understand why some do bad. Only remember: obey, when we say to come."

Jack liked to run in our meadow this spring. Once the snow was gone, he would leap again and again to catch a stick. Sometimes Tobias and I took

Levi outside, too, unless it was muddy. "Run his legs," Mother said. But now we are all stuck inside more, because of those soldiers.

"Squeezed again," Poppa mumbled. "In between."

Some of the blue ones—they are called Union—camped in the fields at the Beachys almost two weeks. Sarah said she was scared and the men ate them all out of butter. Some of them—our Mary calls them mens—walked right inside and carried ticks from the loft to the downstairs where they slept cozy by the fire. Sarah's little sister, Leah, was not one bit afraid; she got up from her blankets during the night and tiptoed between the men to get a drink of water. She stumbled on a pair of boots, and one man sat up straight. But Leah did not run.

My sister, Mary, will not go by herself if she needs to use the chamber pot during the night. She does not like critters scampering, so we climb down the ladder together.

But Lydia said she wished the soldiers would come right to our meadow. Poppa let out a big sigh.

"*O, Herr, in Deiner himmlischen Barmherzigkeit!*" He shook his head slowly like the pendulum on our clock. "Soldiers do not do what we want, child."

If the men came up high to our meadow, they could look in all directions. Our trees are only now putting on green leaves; some are feathery light and others look yellow. But Poppa says you cannot tell west from east when fog settles up here. Some days the clock shows near to noon before the fog flies away.

Sarah said the Union men were polite—no rough talk—but they trampled. Poppa and Tobias took our team to help plow ground for the Beachys. The men left something behind—like candy but not. Not sweet and sticky like Christmas taffy. Daniel called it hardtack; the men put it in their coffee to soften. Tobias pulled a piece from his pocket and dared me to chew. I spit it out fast—it was like a pebble—when he said it had been smushed in the dirt. I did not want a bellyache.

Poppa said some gray men—they are called Confederates—got sick last summer in these mountains. I think he means the Cheat River Valley. They had measles and mumps and some got a bad case of the yellow skin. But the Beachys let the men in blue eat whatever they asked for. Poppa and Tobias took from our store of bacon and beef to help replenish. The Beachys have butter now, too.

One time I saw a soldier boy up close. That was after we lost Jack. He walked in from the others marching; he looked sick in the eyes. Mother called it a dreadful cast of yellow, but not on his skin. He asked for water to fill his canteen. Mother motioned for me to fetch the big dipper. I spilled when my hands shook. That boy did not smile once.

Poppa asked if he snooped, but Mother said, "No, he was but a boy." I saw him stare at Levi and Gideon, but he made no move to snatch. He had shiny medals—one said US—and fancy stripes that made a big V on his sleeve. He did not look one bit happy. His cap was partly squashed and had a little round piece on top. When he walked back to the road, he trudged like he was in no hurry. I watched to be sure he was gone.

We do not hear so many booms anymore, so we can go outside a little bit more. But we have had other visitors. Mother says our larder has gone down exceedingly. We sent our last apples—even though shriveled and full of black spots—with the Big Boys. They filled pockets and knapsacks. We do not know their real names—they are on the run from their part of Virginia—but Poppa called the laid-up one Mack, and the one with mud splattered on his ripped pants, Muck. Neither one said for sure what happened—Poppa thought a bad spill—but they were glad for help. And food. Mother scrubbed to get rid of the worst and sewed a big patch.

Mack said he hurt his ankle on big rocks he had to scramble over. His foot was fat like a baby bunny's cheeks. We made straw beds in the barn, the same place where Mister had slept. Mother took catnip and sprinkled salt on the ankle; she bound it with an old piece of cloth. I got to carry meals because Mack would not come inside at all. They ate and ate.

When Poppa heard them speak to each other in German—Tobias heard it, too—he asked, *"Bischt du deitsch?"* It was their turn to be surprised. They are German Baptists, so we did not need to be afraid. We know some of the same songs.

On Sunday morning, Poppa told Muck at the breakfast table where the Dunker church was meeting. But Muck said, "It is better not to be anywhere exactly. Not where expected."

"Then come with us," Poppa said.

"I won't leave my brother."

Poppa frowned. "It is the Lord's Day."

"We almost got caught one time," Muck said. He looked around like someone bad could hear him. I looked, too. "We had to run lickety-split through cold water. Before the big rocks."

"Do you know of Peter Fike, one of the first of your kind, settled in these parts?" Poppa asked. "At Eglon."

"Never heard of him." Muck spoke like Tobias when he does not want to hear.

"Or Benjamin Beeghly—do you know that name?" Poppa asked. "He came from Amish of good repute in Somerset County, but crossed over to yours. We hail from Pennsylvania, too."

"Where we come from our leader is John Kline."

"Johnny?" Tobias asked.

"The man with the round face?" I asked almost as fast.

We could hardly take turns telling Muck about Johnny's visit after our momma died. Poppa smiled broadly, but Mother said nothing.

"A good friend of my father," Muck said. "They go on mission trips together."

Poppa's smile skittered away, but Mother said, "Like us for peace, Crist."

"We Amish are not for missions," Poppa said.

But Mother hastened. "We do not need to criticize." She got up very slowly to fetch more stew.

"Yes," Poppa said, "we are glad to have you Dunker boys."

"And Mister," I said.

"Yes, Mister, too," Poppa said. "But not noisy ones."

Mother sizzled back. "Soldiers are not all bad. They may train to hurt, but we cannot tell about their hearts." She banged the stir spoon extra loud and dipped the last. "Finish it, Muck."

His head had moved fast, back and forth between Mother and Poppa.

"We cannot be sure," Poppa said. "Spies and seedy sorts on the loose, too. Thieves."

"We know," Muck said. "Unsavory peddlers, out and about. Some say stolen goods. Contraband."

Poppa nodded. "They try to sell what we do not need."

"We are to come in when we hear the mens," Mary blurted.

After two more days, we were sad to see our new friends leave. Mack did not look as scary as he had sounded that one time. We do not know how the Big Boys fare. They wanted to ride a train to Ohio, but Poppa warned to watch out for soldiers on the way to Oakland.

Before they left, we stood outside in a circle. Poppa gave Mack his best hickory stick to lean on. The boys sang a song we had never heard before:

> My dearest friends, in bonds of love,
> Our hearts in sweetest union prove,
> Your friendship's like a drawing band,
> Yet we must take the parting hand.

Mary and I had big tears when they sang more. The Big Boys were here four days and five nights; they did not eat us out of butter, but we baked extra bread. Mack did not look like he would steal. They shook hands all around, even with Levi and Gideon. We may not get to see them ever again. Poppa's eyes were red when he thanked Muck for helping put in crops. Mack still had a limp when they walked away, but they left anyway. He waved his new stick from the road; he did not look one bit afraid.

I told Tobias, "If I had to make up a new name for myself, I would pick something pretty like Jezebel, or Princess."

"Princess is not real."

"Is so; Peter Schrock's horse."

Tobias did not say more but practiced mooing loud.

I wanted to ask him about that word conterbad or whatever Muck had said. But Tobias kept on, bent double, then straightening, head back, to moo like a sick cow.

The scary time happened when I took food for Mack. I had halted outside the barn, for I heard low voices.

Then Muck nearly shouted, "We dare not filch! Pillaging in that milk house."

I backed against the barn wall and strained to hear.

"You ate of it, too! The man said easy money for food." Mack's voice came fast. "All we want. Besides, a bonus—home again. Once is all it takes. Only find the right man."

"Crazy talk!" Muck said. "Could be the wrong one. You don't know. No hauling. Worse than a lame leg next time."

"'Take it or leave it.' You heard him. Looking to change up patterns."

"You are sick! Wading in that cold water froze your noggin."

"Girl coming," Mack said. "Food smell."

The stew tilted, but Muck said more. "Not going to Petersburg! Only the shortcut to Oakland. Even that . . . Get yourself hanged next time!"

I heard rustling in the straw and I stepped away quickly, pretending to dawdle.

Muck met me and looked me over extra.

"Mack's food," I said, handing him the pewter bowl. I turned to run. "Dinner!"

* * *

We have another one! Baby Noah came during the night. Mother keeps saying he is early and calls him a noodler. He is tinier than the other boy *Bobblin*. Mother nurses him for long stretches—I spy her napping—but Gideon begs for her yet, too. When I rock Noah to help him sleep, he looks like a bird. His nose is very pointed and his cheeks have no fat. He has his tiny boy-thing like my brothers. I do not want him to end up like the Beachy babies and not make it.

When Gideon was first born, I had asked Tobias if babies come from a mother's belly button. Tobias was mean to laugh. But now I know more; I keep my ears open.

With Noah the night was full of commotion; I wanted to climb down the ladder.

What woke me first was Mother hissing, "Hotter. We must have hot water!" I roused enough to slowly inch, peeking over the rail. Poppa was having a time with orders.

Finally, he brought Levi to the loft and whispered sharp, "Look to him; not a peep." I tucked all but his head under my covers. Levi smacked his lips, but I did not have to shush him. Gideon got to stay below because he sleeps through anything.

But Poppa stayed *dappich*. I knew in an instant, right where the soft blankets were. *Bottom of the chest.* No, no. *Guck nunner!*

Another time Mother said, "*Du musscht!* Where is your courage, man?"

I stuck my head out to peek again. The lantern flickered and a figure hunched—it had to be Poppa—below Mother, at that end of her. She has told me not to touch myself down there; it is a special place for later. She seemed up on the kitchen table, her knees hoisted. I pulled back from the railing.

But with more *rumrutsche*, I had to slither out of the covers. I did not make one squeak, my bare feet cold, tiptoeing on the wooden ladder. Mother's noises covered me, too—her high-pitched sucking in, her shrill, "Oh, oh, oh!" I was almost down; I would help Poppa.

But his voice came like a muffled roar, "Child! No! Lovina—*schtopp graad nau!*"

I froze and half-turned, my hands and toes clenching rungs.

Mother panted like an animal—bigger than Jack when he arched his back to bark at the fox—swaying on her knees, hair in strands.

"Up with you!" Poppa hissed.

I scampered up the steps, slipping in my hurry. I could not help but bump Levi in my step under the blanket. I curled and turned from him, my chest thumping. *Poppa had yelled at me!* My heart flew to my head. *My wrong name!*

At last I wiped at my eyes and rolled to my back. My eyes blinked; it was extra quiet.

Finally, I heard a weak lamb cry. Poppa whispered loud, "Well, lookie here!" When Gideon cries, I hear him way out in the woods.

I sat up right away, but Levi was still asleep beside me.

I did not dare.

I waited for what would come next. When the other *bobblin* came, we had already been sent to Auntie Mommie's house. At last, Poppa tiptoed up to the loft again. I might have dozed, waiting. Thin light came through the cracks. Poppa shook Tobias from his sleep. "Dress at once; you must ride to fetch Auntie."

I sat up again, but Poppa said, "*Bleib schteh!*" And then a softer "Betsey." But to Tobias again, "Hurry. We have us an early one."

Ever since we have been busy. Auntie Mommie has washed bedding and rags; I helped her drape things on bushes to dry, but the air was damp. When the sun finally peeked full, she kept saying, "What would we do without sunshine?"

I did not answer; there are other things to be glad about. Poppa talks the same as before; not once has he yelled again. Tobias did not make one wrong turn with Frank on his way to Auntie's. Nor did he meet soldiers. Goldie did not kick the bucket when I milked her by myself. The little boys knew to obey; even Gideon stood still when I dressed him. But I had to be sharp with Lydia when I braided her hair. Her snarls are bad, and she had the wiggles.

After all the washing, Auntie Mommie turned bossy, "Play outside there still—mind the little boys."

We had trials. Gideon made a dash for puddles, but Tobias caught him every time. It was too muddy to traipse for trillium, though, and there was no dry place to sit and play I Spy with the girls.

Finally, we were allowed back inside. Two buckets with cloths hide in the back corner. Mother moans like she is crippled when Auntie grabs her skirts and helps her up and down from the chamber pot. Mother clenches a fist to her forehead and scrunches her eyes. I scurry to pull Mary away.

Auntie Mommie will stay until we go to the Beachys for church on Sunday. She frowned when I shook out the rugs.

"*Ei du ye, mei Kind.*" She took the same rugs and snapped them like a whip. "You must be your mother's big girl now."

My lips jerked out. She does not know all I have done since Momma died.

But later Poppa said, "*Gott liebt dich, Betsey.*" I want to hold on tight, even when his leggings are rough.

David — Shenandoah Valley, April 1862

"He is home! All of them released to worship as they please this Easter Sunday."

I had climbed a young walnut tree to saw limbs left dangling from a recent storm. Like Zacchaeus, I peered down on the good news brought by Brother Wine.

Jacob sat on his horse near the tree where I perched. "Glory, hallelujah! The men are free!" he said.

I wanted to jump to the ground and embrace the bearer of such news. "Can it be?" I steadied myself, stretched the saw down to him, and secured my jump the last few feet.

"No charges filed. Not Johnny, not the two Mennonite ministers." Jacob's voice stayed rapid; he is known to be excitable.

"Not Beery, arrested for working against the Confederacy?" I asked.

"Only ministers kept longer."

"But Johnny—free? Slow your talk. The others?"

He wiped his mouth with the sleeve of his coat. "First ones let go, marched north of town—intent on New Market. Or so they thought. Released instead."

"How can this—?"

"No one knows. One man said guards heard cannons; of a sudden retraced their steps."

"But you say ministers kept longer?"

"Perhaps to harass, keep afraid." Jacob shrugged. "No knowing what's next."

"You have it on good word, though? Johnny?"

"The tomb opened. Glory be!" He scratched fast under his long beard. "State exemption may have played a part. Our money delivered."

"Shall not be '*enforced, restrained, molested, or burdened*,'" I said. "Someone swayed."

"Brother Kline, said to have preached both Sundays. Spirits bolstered. And the singing. Our men would not desist, though wracked by coughs and sore throats. Their new song about imprisonment. Guards may have tired."

"I must hear it from Johnny. You say, home now?" I looked for any sign of exaggeration; sometimes he garbles. "Those imprisoned in Richmond also?"

"No word there. But we know there are seventy."

"Seventy men?"

"Yes, Benjamin Byerly learned that when delivering commutation money a week ago for our German Baptist brethren. A Suter did the same for Mennonites. Seventy in all."

"To carry that much money when desperate ones lurk."

"Our couriers kept safe," Jacob said.

I looked for smugness, but he left soon, eager to tell others. I retrieved my saw—the cleanup can wait. I wanted to pass news, too, cackle with my hens.

Delilah whooped and her eyes lifted from their gloom—until I said my intention.

"I must ride to see for certain. Johnny—no ill effects."

Abigail ceased her jubilation also and gripped the back of a table chair. "You care about that man more than you do your own sons!"

I stopped short and whirled to her. "You still think I sent them away, casting blame every day. There is nothing I can do about Joel and Amos."

"We hear nothing."

"That is my fault, too? You think me crazed. We all agreed it was for the best."

"You were the one—pushed."

I turned away and took a deep breath. How often have we argued thus?

"We knew we might not hear," I said. "If Johnny is released, he may still travel. Doubtless bring a letter."

Abigail went to her rocker and creaked noisily, but Delilah came to my rescue. "We knew when we gave my brothers up to their journey westward, we were subjecting them to all manner of difficulty. Only we did not know how the waiting would wear."

"We knew, but we did not know," I said.

"That is so. Not the extent," Delilah said.

Our daughter has been the arbiter before. One night, perhaps a week ago, I tired of Abigail's wild imaginings. She spoke of tribulations—starving bellies for the boys, the torrent of rushing mountain streams.

"Why not a cougar pouncing during sleep?" I asked. "Do you not see? Early word would only tell of troubles. Even bring the worst."

I regretted my words but heard Abigail say as she stumbled to bed, "You expect them to float above every trial!"

In truth I do not. I know all too well the snares of traveling in mountains, though I have spared much from Abigail. Nor have I accused her of caring too much about the boys' safety. But that night when she fled to bed, I did not follow to give comfort or ask forgiveness. Delilah went in my stead. All the week since, we have tiptoed around the rift, not sought to mend it.

She probably thinks no harm will come to me, as long as I travel *with* John Kline, her saint—the one who saved her life. Yet I am not to visit him, not to seek reassurance. There is no reasoning with her.

We have been on edge also because of unsavory-looking peddlers rattling by with their wagonloads of goods. Pots and pans clatter; muskets hang ominously from hooks on the sides. I have instructed my women: "Do not answer, if one with a loopy mustache bangs at the door."

More ominous, some say men of war make ready to execute maneuvers nearby. We hear of skirmishes far to the west in our state. And of Feds, victorious in the state of Tennessee—a terrible battle at a place called Shiloh, south and west of where our daughter lives. Thirty-five hundred men killed; more than three times that number wounded, counting both sides. I did not tell Abigail about ripped bodies strewn. But 3,500! Some say final numbers will be higher. People flock to the telegraph office at New Market, thirsting for news. A son or husband no longer heard from.

If the North gets closer—if they dare come on *our* side of the Alleghenies—the South will try to push them back. "Stop them from reaching Richmond!" is the rallying cry. One side's move incites the other to desperation. And here we sit, between. We cannot have fighting like that in our Valley. Our dogwoods and cherries, struggling to bloom, will cry out to heaven.

This dastardly weather—sleet and snow continue. Our spring planting on hold. I check the bags of flour left from last year's crop. We grab for any patch of sun, but we cannot push the plow when the soil lacks warmth. More so, not when the prospect of warfare bangs. We can only wait, praying against slaughter. *Thirty-five hundred killed.*

Abigail says a bear prowls our house. Yes, I stay restless. People do not place orders for casks or barrels. No one has time to think beyond the day's immediate needs. Delilah gave us a scare with a severe bout of dizziness two days ago. I considered riding to Mr. Hinkle's apothecary in New Market—no Johnny to consult about her treatment—but first tried a mess of mountain greens for Abigail to fry with leeks. Since cleansing her system, Delilah has regained some strength. And now our men in Harrisonburg, released! I must learn the words of that new prisoners' song. Brother Wine said, *"We'll all go home as soon as freed"* was a part.

* * *

Another blow leveled; this time J. M. brought word. I was glad to see his high-stepping stallion, until I approached and caught the gray look on his face. "The Confederate Congress has passed a conscription act. It supercedes our state's exemption for those of us who will not bloody our hands."

I had been resting with Abigail and Delilah in the summer kitchen, after another week's worth of straining milk through muslin, skimming cream off the clabber, churning to butter. All was safely stored in the springhouse below ground. When I did not return with J. M., the women came to us, halting halfway.

"Our Virginia exemption for men of conscience, voided," I said to them.

"That cannot be," Delilah said.

"No!" Abigail's face blazed at J. M.

"Do not confuse the messenger with the message," I said. At that Delilah hurried to bring J. M. a cup of water from the well.

He dismounted to speak more. "Gone in less than a month. Our exemption."

"A mistake," Abigail said. "Surely . . ."

J. M. drained the cup in long gulps. "No word has come that wiser minds prevail."

"Did you not say, Father, our pamphlet of peace principles, presented to authorities?"

I could but nod. "Along with Mennonite materials. So I heard."

"Quakers also sent a pamphlet with their views on nonresistance," J. M. said. "My neighbor . . ."

"Johnny's hard-won efforts," I said, turning my back. "No avail." *Whence cometh . . . ?*

"We cannot wilt," Delilah said. "But you say no allowance for conscientious scruples?"

"This fraud of a country," burst from Abigail. "This Confederacy!"

"Our forefathers didn't move here to be caught up in controversy." J. M. took off his hat, scratched unkempt hair, and ran his hand like a rake. "All able-bodied men, age eighteen to thirty-five, drafted for *three* years. My sons coming up."

J. M.'s grandfather, an early settler and elder at Flat Rock, able to purchase 400 acres at a nominal cost from the provisional government. Our current state of affairs—not what he must have envisioned.

"And you also?" Delilah queried J. M. "I do not mean . . . but among them?"

"Thirty-nine years," he said. "Safe, so far. Clergy and teachers, civil servants, railroad workers—the usual, exempt."

I turned back from the mountains, silent in their somber blue. "A three-year draft! Passed and done. Who could have? Why? They know our men will not fire."

"To coerce." Delilah put her arm about her mother's waist.

"Or force our men to cook. Make more shoes for soldiers," J. M. said.

"Stand with folded arms, take others' fire—" I said, "as if willing targets."

"Still lawful to provide a substitute," J. M. said. "But stricter conditions. If you hire someone to go in your place, and that man is killed or incapacitated, you're required to step in. Automatic. All money—gone. No dickering. Paid and gone."

"Disarray," Delilah mumbled. She crooned, wiping Abigail's tears with her thumb.

When all we could do was repeat our questions, J. M. left, as sorrowful as he came.

Delilah went back to sit on the porch steps this time—her face like stone. Our rock, gone silent. Abigail and I have not touched sustenance since early morning when we thought each other the worst obstacle to peace. For the rest of the day we traded time on rocking chairs with hurried steps to the necessary. The beef cows and hogs, our milk cow, and my chickens and ducks finally raised a ruckus we could not ignore. To have reached understanding with our state officials, only to have it overturned in a whiff. Our boys, spared, but where, any satisfaction?

Two days ago, I had all but looked forward to reading Scriptures, telling the wondrous story of Jesus' emergence from the tomb. I had thought to comment: we in our Valley have survived a sore time of testing, but now have garnered release for our men imprisoned. *Our help cometh!*

But now . . .

Set back in the gloom of Good Friday. And it is only Thursday. Not that this latest legislation equals the depravity of those who killed the Son of God. But how are we to bear up? Find the wherewithal?

I am to be a man of faith, but I flounder. I take the lead in despondency. Our men, soon to be dragged off. Families in the lurch. Who will grow the needed crops? We old ones. Our women and children. I cry out like David, but can barely claim the psalmist's name as my own: "*How long wilt thou forget me, O Lord? For ever? How long wilt thou hide thy face from me?*" From us?

JACOB — Iowa, April 1862

Every springtime brings life to my spirit. Buttercups lift their bright yellow faces to the sun and my step quickens. Once more the Lord brings renewal from long-lasting piles of snow and disputation. Mary promises to grow extra cabbages so our sauerkraut will last longer next winter. I take heart to encourage folks, not dwell only on grievances.

When the rains come fully, I can again use the power of my water wheel all morning, closing the gate by afternoon to keep water from spilling over the dam unused. Slow work, but satisfying, sawing one board from a log at a time. Jakob will help, closing and opening the water gate. My grandson has always been in his brother Samuel's shadow, but now Jakob has shot past in size, and since his baptism sometimes lines our hymns on Sunday morning.

For now, I stay content with the work of planting. My body aches from the bending, but seeds do not talk back. The routine of work with family settles qualms. Frederick brought his four oldest while Sarah stayed at home with the babes. Their two big ones, Barbara and Jacob, used hoes to cover the corn seeds Catherina and Delilah helped Mary and me plant. Once we finished at my place, we began the same work at Frederick's. He takes great care, marking the rows exactly; his young ones take pride also, not wasting a drop of seed from the aprons Sarah fashioned.

How different from the contentions faced all winter. The usual: John P. Guengerich finding fault; this time over my not preaching with enough specific injunctions against taking up the sword. Yes, I know fighting has picked up again in the East, but that should not be our only subject.

"Sunday mornings are times to remind us not to fall from the face of God," I say.

"But you make no specific mention of the hatred that spews from the mouths of Copperheads."

Copperheads—a magic word to utter? When others are present with John, I stay calm. "I have given public thanks for no draft in Iowa."

But in the heat of a private argument, I let loose what should never have been uttered. "You are a thorn! Why must you contest? Go to the Mennonites!"

"No," he shouts back, "you are the one, a stickler over petty matters. You dicker over ribbons when our country is at war. I could sharpen an axe atop your head."

Who can claim innocence in these times? As ordained men, we are commanded to work together charitably. I should be able to overlook. But when I think of him, I see his mouth set; his eyes question me. I am still taller, even with my stoop, but he manages to look down on me.

Winter stretched long for Mary and me also. The worst, a day I came in from choring, only to find her awash in tears. I thought it could not be: another woman, another tear-stained face.

"You never talk with me," she said.

"You have your sewing; I need time to study and be quiet in prayer."

"You do not speak at mealtime. When did you last make conversation at night?"

"I did not know."

"Your long sighs consume me."

"Church matters press."

"Only the church matters to you."

What could I say? "There is nothing more pleasing to the Lord than a virtuous woman, birthing her babies, hands to the spindle. The verse from Proverbs says it well: '*her price is far above rubies*.'"

"You could show tenderness."

"I am sorry." I reached for her hand—soft and smooth, not one blemish. "Is there anything *not* amiss? I thought we had understanding. Weighty matters, I cannot divulge."

She extracted her hand to wipe at her cheek. "You have time for your sons."

I tried to stifle my sigh. "With better weather in the offing, we will invite those from a distance to come on visiting Sundays, not rely so much on Frederick and his family. The Hershbergers, if you wish. So long as I do not show favoritism."

She rose to stir the stew, as if running out of complaints. That is what she does when she has had enough; she sniffs and gets up. Since then, I have prayed the Lord will bring peace to our hearth. I try to be attentive; I ask again about her daughter in Indiana, her years with her Daniel in Pennsylvania. I agree, the patches of dark red cloth in her new quilt are not as bright as her pin cushion.

But there is also my step, Daniel, the one who kept account of our ocean journey—a sore grief: he is also prone to dispute. The most unpleasant exchange came recently when he brought Jakob to help clean out manure from my shed.

It started innocently enough. I said to Daniel, "If we lessen our trips to town, we are not as likely to run into those with unsavory intent."

Instead of his usual grunt, he spoke. "We have no choice but to take our threshed rye to the still house."

"But we do not need to tarry."

"Relations with the English, always ticklish," Daniel said. "Better by far to mingle on occasion, than stay separate and have the mob come."

Jakob stopped shoveling. "What mob?" His big ears, not as noticeable now that he is nineteen and has longer hair to cover.

"You were abed," Daniel answered, puffing from the exertion of removing refuse to the wagon. His extra girth has saddled him with the nickname *der dick Daniel.*

"What happened?" Jakob's eyes followed his father's steps.

"A spat. Men came to harass, mostly for show. Professing worry their squatters' claims might not be respected."

"I slept through the ruckus?" Jakob asked. "Does Samuel know?"

"You were only three," his father said.

Steam rose from newly disturbed piles. "Those land speculators stirred folks up," I said. "Wanted to buy, then sell higher."

Daniel removed his glove and wiped dirt from the corner of his eye. "A few neighbors confused us with Mormons through here a few years before."

"You said a mob. I only knew about wheels stolen," young Jakob said.

"*Ja*, the wheels," Daniel said. "A vigilante group. Your mother, overcome. No means to go back to Ohio without wheels."

"Vigilantes?" I asked. "I thought you knew *not* the thieves. You only said tricksters."

"*Ja*," Daniel said. "Two wheels gone, each wagon. Acted like we came with sacks of money. Took us years to earn trust. No different now; this war makes us look suspicious again."

Jakob persisted. "You always said the wheels were returned. Put back on wagons—under cover of night."

"They were," his father replied, panting from another heave. "That first fall. Some may have felt pity. Nearly all of us laid up with fever. Bilious." He scraped his fork on the edge of the wagon, watched dung fall. "Far easier to lose, than earn trust."

"How true," I said. "Why have you kept from Jakob—all of us—the full extent?" I took a turn leaning against the wagon a spell. "People coming now only want more land, fewer encumbrances. You need to tell of early tribulations. Your sons, for certain. Back then, that first cabin—little more than a stable."

"Fourteen feet by sixteen," he said.

"No cash, but still you broke more ground, fenced in ten acres. Am I not right?" He gave no reply. "And when at last you got a start with corn—your team! Two more years, was it not? Scratching by without horses. Money still hard to come by."

"*Ja*, not easy," Daniel said. "A year, before I could replace the clapboard roof. Finally, a pair of yearling calves—trained them for field work."

"Is that when—?" Jakob hesitated. "Christena?"

"No need to dwell on the past," Daniel said. "We survived, most all. Fifteen years now, a start of money. Some income."

"Your baby sister, Jakob—less than a year old. You were only a tyke," I said. "That first August when I visited, only two other families were here at the time. It fell to me, the only minister, to take charge of Christena's funeral; the first burial, our people here. You surely know, her remains moved now from the back field to a resting place near your Grandma Barbara."

Jakob nodded solemnly. But to his father he said, "I know you bartered away your knife."

Daniel sighed. "*Ja*. When the horses died, no other way to pay someone to cultivate my corn. All is better now; that is what to talk about."

"Dire straits," I said. "That first roof, weighed down with poles before the lap shingles. But vigilantes? Bearing rifles?"

"Blessed with fertile land," Daniel said. "You say so yourself. Hard work, no curse."

I shook my head—his obstinance. Those years he lost weight before his current excess. His wife, another Barbara, unable to silence her fears, even though she comes from Bishop Benedict's seed. I can set aside her wail: "Poles of wigwams, anchored in the ground," but Daniel's nonchalance—I cannot let it take root. "Sufficient land a blessing, *ja*. But the perils of ownership and inheritance. Wartime can change everything."

"Not here," Daniel said. "Only suspicions."

"*Ja, hier!*" I could not help but pounce. "The war makes inroads. Easy money." I rubbed the tips of my fingers. "Do you not see? People chase after wealth, lose sight. More land than needful piles up. Lose sight of our godly heritage."

Daniel jabbed his shovel into the dwindling pile. "So you say, often enough."

"I do not begrudge folks their private property. Understand, Jakob? But when acreage is easy to acquire, too easy, people still buy themselves land poor. *Verschtehscht?* Owning more land but still lacking cash."

Jakob kept his nose to the task but took in every word.

"Am I not right, Daniel? Everyone was more to help each other, those early days, even as you do here today—survival." He would not permit so much as a flicker of his heavy eyebrows.

I fell in step with Jakob, making trips back and forth to the wagon. "Once a man had his children set up to do farm work, he could busy himself with other endeavors. Vill'm Wertz fashioned shoes for our horses; Crick Jake made caskets. You see? People saw a need—a bee hive—and contributed. Beautiful wedding suits, Jakob, fashioned by your Uncle Benedict. But now . . ." I grabbed his arm. "These new settlers—less willingness. A deaf ear to sharing for the good of the community."

"Uncle Chris promised to help me make a cherry cabinet," Jakob said. "He stays busy fixing others' wagons."

"That is right and good; he will get to you. But too many of these new ones—an independent spirit. And deviation. Is that not so, Daniel? Even when passing property. Priority has always been given—the rightful transition, first to immediate and extended family."

"Man to man," Daniel said.

"*Ja*, a father to his son, followed by the needs of other men in the church. You see?" I am certain Daniel knew my drift. "Now the world seeps in. Outsiders, even at the still house, offer more money. *Ja*, it creeps in."

Of a sudden Daniel pulled out his pocket watch. "Another day we will move the wagonload to your fields."

I stopped short. I could but thank them for their efforts, not chastise for interrupting. But such lack of concern; Daniel's abdication in providing warning as *Hausvater*.

The same lax discipline showed up when I had questioned Daniel about his big boy wanting to go back East. Yes, Samuel, the one who rode with me on the train to Indiana. He wants to return to his birth home, not to visit, but *to live*. Why go near the teeth of war? He insists he has no desire to join these battles that tear at our nation. But Daniel defends him—not sufficient females here to choose among.

Mary showed no alarm either, saying only, "Samuel is solidly grounded."

I had to take it up with Samuel privately. "You were granted a teaching certificate for Iowa two years ago. Where is your patience?" At first he looked mulish, the one who always has words. "Why is working in Sharon Township not good enough? Sixteen weeks out of the year, you get twenty dollars a month for your efforts."

"I need more training," he said quietly.

"You have always been quick with the numbers, steady at reading."

"But geography. I am sorely lacking."

"The East is full of trouble."

"Father says I need to find out for myself."

Such stubbornness passed on! "*Ach, mein Sohn.* You may be reaching after fire."

I have often thought of Samuel as my seed. He does the very best construction work and easily keeps himself busy when not teaching. At Abe Kauffman's place he worked much of February, even lodged there a week when that early March storm left us with twenty inches in the timber, blowing huge drifts of snow on roadways. Right now—I know for certain—Samuel has two barns and another house lined up for this summer. Yet, he wants to leave for the rat's nest.

A second time I tried a different approach. "There is a large nest of Copperheads among the Amish in Ohio. Likely entrenched in Pennsylvania also. Stay clear of vile talk!"

At that, Samuel nodded gravely and seemed more himself. "I have heard how Copperheads—a few in the county to our south—smile quietly at Union defeats."

"You run the risk of falling into the wrong crowd."

"I will be careful, Grandfather."

I might as well have spoken to the wind. This deafness—my own family! Ignoring the danger of secret influence from those posing in sheep's clothing.

The young girls at church are no better. What am I to say when I must take one to the upper room? That recent one, distraught and wailing to be restored. I did not tie those ribbons in her hair. And yet, the mother claimed I treated her daughter unfairly. These womenfolk!—tears and obstinance. Every morning I must shake myself out of the bowels, gird myself once more.

But now another dream returns—older than battle or a tilting wagon. Even before coming to Iowa, it pestered. Each time it unfolds the same way: I am back in Waldeck, our tiny village of Mengeringhausen, going on business to a Mister Folmer. I carry a tin bowl. When the man speaks, I hear his mocking tone. I pull back a curtain and see his shadow. He says my friend Christian Guengerich at Gallows Mill wants to give me gold.

Of course, my mind goes to the one with that name here in Iowa, once a young boy near Gallows Mill. Yes, a son of John P., the very minister with whom I pass the most shameful anger. Why would this son, knowing full well of disputes today, want to give me gold? I am not attracted to glitter; Mary will vouch for that.

But the dream is always the same: I proceed back along a narrow street where all is bright and clear, all the way down to my old mill. I never find this younger Guengerich. I should know that will be the conclusion; I should not need to repeat and come up empty.

The clock strikes an early morning hour and I am here again in Iowa, nowhere near to Gallows Mill. I cannot return to sleep. Nor can I make any sense, save that I am to pass along warnings, not least of which is the impulse too much land may exact on a man. Mary mumbles and turns away on her side.

ESTHER — Shenandoah Valley, April 1862

They're back! Two of mine. When we'd heard talk on Easter Sunday that the men in Richmond would be freed, I told myself and the children: *not for certain.* I spoke with a fierceness and gripped William's arm. "We can't count on the plans of men."

But four days ago, Simon and Andrew came walking in the lane. Joseph spied them first, for he was still finishing the chores. I heard a whoop and feared he might have been surprised by a rattlesnake. My Simon and Andrew are back! Andrew is all grown up, though I can't say how; it's more than thicker hairs covering his thin cheeks. He's subdued—a hard layer—more to disagree with Simon. I dare say he's seen the face of evil.

But Simon has turned around and is given to tenderness. Faith such as I've never heard from him before, and pride in our hard work. Even though it was near to dusk, Joseph and William couldn't wait till morning to show Simon the sprouts of wheat and corn; Mary Grace insisted Simon see the new lambs born on Good Friday. She's taken them as her own and won't let anyone else lift a hand, not so much as give fresh water.

When I lay beside Simon that night, I couldn't stop my tears. To have him by my side again! His arms about me, his smell. Almost as when we were first married. Only better. To let go the brave front. I tried to pull myself together, for fear he'd chide my outpouring. But he was nearly as undone as I.

"Such softness," he whispered. "No more commands from cold men."

He touched my every part; he lingered. "Don't stop," I begged. I didn't care what the children heard. My man is back!

The next morning, we scarce did any work once the animals were tended. Sunshine and a dry day prevailed, but we ate our fill of cakes and maple syrup. I wanted my men to eat and eat and never know want. Oh, never to be separated again! We sat long at the table—so many stories. How Simon had made three trips—as did others—across the swirling South Branch of the Potomac, carrying by horseback those who, like Andrew, traveled on foot. Going North.

But our heaven couldn't last forever. William took on the pout when Simon told Mary Grace a second time that she must have grown two inches in less than two months. She's sure to be a tall one. And a sulk stole across Joseph's face when Andrew boasted of all the miles he'd walked. No one said aught of Midnight—I would have pinched Mary Grace—and I only gave a short shake when Andrew asked a second time regarding Peter.

"No word," I said.

Yes, we still have a boy far from home. Not even one letter.

I was the one, though, who ventured to say, "Our state exemption has been voided."

Simon scoffed and said, "Look at me." He spread his arms wide. "I'm here because the fine has been paid. And yet, you doubt? We wouldn't be here"—Andrew nodded—"if the men hadn't come to Richmond with commutation money for all of us. Yes, there was delay. The days, long; the food, poor. But suddenly we were loaded on a train to Waynesboro. From there, we walked. And here we are."

I was afraid for his boastful tone. I said quietly, "Perhaps a rumor."

"We're *not* going back, Esther." He couldn't say it often enough. "Nor the Quakers, nor Nazarenes. Freed with us Mennonites and Dunkers."

Simon showed the same fire when he told of their interrogation. "Each man, given a choice: enlist in the army or pay $500. I admit, twenty-some of our captured group enlisted, but not one Mennonite or Dunker among them." He smacked his lips. "Not one."

"Those not church members *had* to sign up," Andrew said.

"True. Each man had to speak for himself." Simon smiled broadly at Andrew. Then he sobered and turned to Joseph and William. "Some day you may have to give account. Know your stand. What you'll say if ever told to right a wrong with violence."

Then he went silent. Sometimes a cloud comes over him, the same as reaches us all. We all mourn for Peter.

"There are men out there," Simon continued more slowly, "who don't believe as we do. They think God wants us to fight for the South. Andrew knows their ridicule. Hard labor and no water to drink. They think punishment will change a man's mind."

Andrew studied his fingers, his nails bitten to the quick. "One official at Staunton said I was a disgrace. Me and my family."

I reached a hand.

"All of us fleeing ones made him sick," Andrew said. "'You stink,' the man said. Not vile but matter-of-fact. 'You have an odor that makes this jail smell to high heaven.'" Andrew rapped his knuckles on the table like a gong. "Said we were gutless, only cared about ourselves. Said our brothers—"

Andrew folded his arms on the table and put his head atop. I could barely hear his muffled ". . . brothers die in our place."

Mary Grace went to Andrew and pressed her head into his shoulder, wrapped her thin arms about his back. He took her on his lap and pulled her tight. My tears loosed. All those weeks I didn't let myself cry in front of the children. Now my dam comes unstoppered. William scooted his chair closer and placed his cheek next to mine. I dried my eyes and patted him on the back. "Sorely touched," Mama would have said.

But Joseph stays a puzzle: willing at work but keeps his head down. When asked his thoughts, he shakes his head. Oh, that this bloodshed will be over before he turns eighteen. Where goes our Peter today? Our big boy. *A rock for a pillow?* We still hear: men from the North plan to march in these parts.

But I don't have to plan the fieldwork anymore. Simon is here! My men sowed clover seed and finished spading my garden so I could plant onions. Still, no one brings up Midnight.

Simon's faith stays stronger than mine. He sleeps soundly, while I toss. He sings a tune the Dunkers taught. It comes out half-spoken, half-sung.

> Our troubles and our trials here
> Will only make us richer there
> When we arrive at home.

He's fixed on the beyond, not singing about being here with the youngsters and me. Some days I hardly know him.

One night—all but Andrew abed—Simon said, "The worst was when we first got to Richmond. Stayed a night in a machine house before they put us up in Castle Thunder. A large room, cool; that small stove couldn't warm. No beds. I walked around most all night."

"No good to pace," Andrew said. "That place was *cold*. I dozed on the hard floor, knew there'd be no food, come morning." His voice isn't deep, but sometimes he takes a bitter tone.

"I paced to stay warm," Simon said. "Food was adequate, but late. Enough for everyone."

"Barely. Not till they moved us to the castle and gave us bedding."

"Yes, there we had more food, other provisions. That's when we answered questions before Judge Baxter, a man from the Rebels' War Department."

Andrew fiddled with his tin cup. He drinks too much for a young one, says it settles him. His hands, always on the go.

"Full of questions, that man: 'Where were you going? What for? Why do you sing at night?'" Simon poured again from the jug of last year's fermented elderberries. "I don't know that anyone's answer strayed from the truth. Going *away* from the fighting. That's what I said; that much alone. Fighting, contrary to the Gospel. I'll say this, though—" He took another swig.

"They asked the same questions, over and over. Wanted to trap," Andrew said.

"But that Baxter fellow didn't laugh at me or show disgust. A decent man, that one. Big, loopy mustache. Asked if I'd ever been in the service." Simon paused; his eyes met mine. "'Not voluntarily,' I said, but then I blurted: 'Voted for secession, under provocation.' That's not what he asked, but that's what bothers."

"You didn't mean to," I said.

Simon paid me no mind. "Admitted I'd been a teamster, two weeks last fall, but made clear: against my will."

I turned at a rustling in the loft.

Simon had a faraway look. "Another question I remember distinctly: 'Could you feed the enemy if he came to your house?' I nodded for the man, but before I could settle on words, Baxter said it for me, 'We are commanded to do so.' He'd heard it from countless others. But he never showed malice. A decent man, that Baxter. Some only tormented. But he told me right then— they would send us home to farm, sooner or later. I was slow to put stock."

"You were always slow to believe," Andrew said.

Simon didn't dispute. "I've lived too long to believe every promise. But now I'm turning to trust. We don't have to go back! God protects." He held out both arms, rubbed one, then the other. "Still alive. We are." The way he studied his hands, picked at skin, I knew he was recalling something important. Even Andrew stopped tapping on tin, drumming the table. Simon cleared his throat. "I've learned the truth: '. . . *be thou faithful unto death, and I will give thee a crown of life.*' Somewhere, it says that."

An owl called from a nearby tree.

Andrew cracked all the knuckles on one hand. "The day they marched us to Staunton, you didn't think you'd make it."

"Two days on foot." Simon shook his head. "A barrel of crackers and a few pieces of bacon for seventy-some men? Crossing the Shenandoah Mountain? How could any of us make it?" His dark eyes sharpened on Andrew. "You weren't so perfect. Distraught that time. You know what I mean." Just as abruptly Simon turned to me. "The guards trusted us at night; so much so they went off to find better lodging. Trusted our honor and said as much." He drained his mug and seemed to dare Andrew. "You young ones wanted to run off."

Color crept through the sparse hairs on Andrew's cheeks. "Could have gotten away."

"Would've made matters worse. We were under arrest."

The owl had found a mate.

I looked from one to the other. William had come down the steps to the table and said he couldn't sleep. I took him on my lap, though he's much too old.

Simon barely paused. "Go on; tell her."

Andrew scowled and half-turned away. "Some—the old ones—went after the guards. Tattled. Before we could get our wits together—bickering in the dark over how best to scatter—the guards came back. Made us line up so they could count us. That was the end of that."

"Satan might have made you dishonest," Simon said.

"And saved us thirty miserable days at Castle Thunder!" Andrew's eyes blazed at his father. "Plus Staunton."

William squirmed. "A big castle?"

"The Lord wanted us to go to Richmond," Simon said.

"I doubt that," I said before I could stop myself. I nudged William to sit on the bench.

"Given all we needed to eat at Staunton," Simon said.

"Sure, once we got there." Andrew's face turned to a sneer. "Have you forgotten? The last we saw Midnight."

Simon lowered his head, our clock's ticks extra loud. Finally he said, "On that train a full day, part of a night. Hundred twenty miles to Richmond from Staunton."

"Does the train go fast?" William asked.

"Right. A 120 miles with only a few crackers in our pockets," Andrew said. "God wanted that? Nothing goes fast when you're starving."

I've never known Simon to put up with a boy's disputing, but that evening he ignored Andrew's red face. "During those days of interrogation some members of their Confederate Congress—in session there—came to Castle Thunder to see us. Help from several important Virginia men. John Hopkins from our own Rockingham County is one, spoke on our behalf. To that very Congress. Said we were conscientious people with scruples. And John B. Baldwin from Staunton—stately man with a trimmed beard—sent up the Exemption Act to Congress. Voted on and passed."

"Not *everyone* at Richmond was kindly." Andrew was back to cracking his knuckles, one hand and then the other. "Some made life miserable. Their goading."

"Yes, pressure to drive their teams. But I've learned how to stand against their tactics. I made clear, Esther; I wouldn't change my mind.

'Course, I had to declare I wouldn't fight for the Feds either. No problem there. I've learned to be quiet, William, when guards taunt. Not fear what men can do." Simon's forehead furrowed and he studied hard again. "Some of them seemed curious about us. Looked us over, like specimens. I didn't always find words, but 'be thou faithful unto death—I will give thee a crown of life,' I remembered that."

"You say it all the time," Andrew said.

I've never known Simon to say a verse, but he sighed and studied the beams in the ceiling, as if a son's sourness was harder to stomach than taunts from a prison guard.

"They let us go because we're good farmers," Andrew said. "You know that." He scooted his chair farther back and faced the dying embers in the fireplace. "They want us to raise big crops. Feed the army. Contribute to the war machine that way—every bit as much as driving a team. Tell me that's not so!"

"Farming comes from God," Simon said. "Our surpluses from last year's crop—God gave that increase. Now we're to feed the hungry, share our wheat." A twinge crept into his voice. "Where is your compassion? You know what it's like."

Andrew turned back sharply. "Feed hungry soldiers, so they can kill more people."

I sat rooted, afraid to go to bed and leave my men alone.

Simon leaned toward Andrew. "If we'd given them the slip that night on the Shenandoah, we'd still be on the run. Or worse. Understand? Congress might not have granted us exemption." He turned to me. "Some of our kind escaped, slipping through lines. Authorities weren't going to allow any more of that. No release, I say, save for good behavior and the fine laid on us."

"But $500 for each of us! Money to buy more muskets."

"Frightful, yes. But tell me, Andrew: Do you want to be like the Quakers? Not have anything to do with paying fines? Their leaders advise them to state their beliefs and take the consequences. No separate treatment." Simon waited, as if expecting retort. "If we hadn't been in Richmond, speaking as one body, answering every question put to us—"

"Ma says there's new word of conscription."

Simon straightened, his eyes dark with night. "We've paid the fine, paid the price. It's done." He slapped both hands on the table. "Congress passed the exemption. Done."

Andrew stayed sour. William tiptoed to the chair beside his pa and asked again about the castle. This time Simon gave attention. "An old tobacco warehouse. Heavy brick walls with only a few windows. Don't know how it got its name."

"Small windows with bars," Andrew said. "Bitty. A dirty place. Rats. Guards on duty brought food in buckets, like slop."

"The building was four stories high, William," Simon said. "We stayed in the room at the east end, next to the canal. Could see the James River."

"Prisoners from the Union army kept in a separate room," Andrew added.

"Some of them friendly enough, when we had chance to speak. Seemed sorry to see us go. The singing." Simon turned to me. "Almost forgot. Those who gave aid, one brought a copy of our *Confession of Faith*, the one Peter Burkholder wrote long ago and Joseph Funk translated into English."

I nodded to Andrew. "You know the Funk he means; you wanted to see his print set-up."

"That *Confession* was read to Congress—very important, the part about nonresistance," Simon said. "Benjamin Byerly, another who helped; he's a Dunker, but we can't draw lines. Came from Dayton several times, used his influence."

I'd already told Simon how David Hartman had come here to ask for help. They needed funds for the fines, but I didn't know what Simon would want me to do. I knew where he'd hid the remaining gold—a leather pouch at the back of the top chest drawer. But two men to account for? I'd never handled money like that. We'd lost Midnight, but that wouldn't count. I ended up giving $750 from Simon's stash. He's never said aught against my decision: one full man and half the other. Out of their group of seventy, they'd lost thirty-two horses and $12,000 in gold and silver.

For a while I had felt guilty, not paying the full amount. But there are wealthier ones at church who haven't suffered the loss of manpower. Or a horse! Yet, I know, too, still others struggle with *nothing* extra. Brother Coffman said repeatedly: "Do not look to the right or left, but give as you are able. We are all one body; when one suffers, all suffer."

Some of our neighbors have sent their boys to join up. We don't ask whether they volunteered or were dragged. Genevieve and George are said to have let go their two oldest. We hardly see them anymore—so different from days past. Everyone is more to stay home and keep to their own affairs, scrambling with the late spring planting. I've held firm, though; Andrew is *not* to take a wagon into town. He's faced enough scorn.

I've sealed my lips against saying more to Simon about conscription. He'll have to hear it elsewhere. Nothing for certain anyway. Other rumors continue: Union soldiers gather near Winchester, ready to come south. And yet another one I keep to myself: Stonewall Jackson on the South's side is said to be fearless—to the point of being foolhardy with his men.

J. Fretz — Chicago, May 1862

How did we get here? This jumble war has made of life! Supposed to be over and done months ago; instead, bloodshed drags on. People live with perpetual anger and discord. Over a year already, our spirits dragged down. The pressure is endless, cropping up at work, coming from back East.

"We're on top," Ross says. "The South has had to enact a conscription law. Their men don't want to fight anymore; they're losing."

"When have the Rebels ever rolled over?"

"Fort Donelson. Did you forget?" Ross is getting a belly on him and looks shorter than ever. He keeps his sandy hair slicked down with some kind of oil. "Remember those prisoners, marching up Michigan Avenue to Camp Douglas? No shoes or coats."

How could I forget the sight of men walking along in the middle of winter, wrapped in old horse blankets and rugs? That was back in February when there was great excitement over the fall of Fort Donelson. We thought it a death blow; the rebellion had lost 10,000 men, dead or wounded. Bells rang at noon; cannons boomed. The Board of Trade passed resolutions and adjourned. Ross told of dancing with cheering people in the streets; others lighted bonfires.

I was enthused, too. This killing would be over. Almost overnight, we citizens raised $2,000 to help our sick and wounded. But I needled Ross—a reflex, since I can't avoid him. "Is it success because we *only* lost 400 men; *only* another 800 were wounded?"

"You never find any news positive," he said. "War is an evil necessity. Accept it."

"We're kept in the dark," I countered. "Did 5,000 Rebels escape at night in Tennessee? We don't know. How could thousands of gray uniforms come out of nowhere and surprise Grant's forces?"

"You ask too many questions. What's certain: we didn't lose the Tennessee River."

"True. But if our men fished Rebel minnie rifles out of that river, how is it the Rebels kept on fighting? Explain that."

"You're impossible." But Ross smiled, secure in the superiority of our Union men. "What matters: General Sherman saved the day in Tennessee."

"How are we to believe things are going well, when the government has taken possession of the telegraph service? Is it success when our papers aren't allowed to print news of troop movements anymore?"

I plunked myself at my desk; I knew better than to start another argument. I rustled through sheets of numbers, that infernal dollar error I'd made balancing the books. I would have to tell Jim. And Ross . . . I shouldn't badger one of our workers. If Beidler heard me, he'd say: "You need to encourage Ross's optimism. Disgruntled men make mistakes."

I suppose that applies to me, too. Fort Donelson happened around the time I blew up about the Anderson house proprietor telling his servants to throw swill slop and other filth on the back end of our lumber piles. I'm embarrassed when I lose control, but I don't like not knowing what's going on with the war. How am I to make a decision? Blindly sign up? How can it *not* matter if we know whether John C. Fremont has his troops in the Allegheny Mountains or somewhere else? I'm not content merely reading Henry Ward Beecher's sermon about the propriety of deathbed repentance.

When friends ask why I don't go to war, I refer to our new lumber business. But in truth, I have more questions about the conduct of the war now than when it started. Who's getting ahead, other than casket makers and embalmers rounding up hundreds of bodies? And why don't they include horses in the number of casualties?

Ross shrugs. "Stolen from unlucky farmers, I suppose. Not a concern."

He's never loved a horse. But for me, the stench would be enough. Horse carcasses with buzzards covering the fields. I've read they burn them sometimes, get them out of sight. But how can men bury piles of horses? Or humans? I can't imagine physically doing that. Wouldn't they be more than corpses, more than beasts?

I'll wager, no one imagined a full-scale war when this started. It's like a ball rolling downhill. Neither president backs down. Each side only sees the error in the other. Each side thinks it's defending something: slavery for the South, a united country for many Northerners. I'm still of the opinion that our cause is just *only* if we remove the injustices heaped on the Negro. Yet, I hear Democrats in this city deride slaves for trying to escape imprisonment. Terrible hatred spews from parts of Ohio and Indiana—filthy names for dark-skinned men. Some Northern soldiers don't want to fight beside them. And the so-called *Peace* Democrats sing their same tune: "Let the South go. This country is too large to be under one rule." All they care about is keeping whites in control.

I can't count on President Lincoln either. His son's death from typhoid fever must have affected his decision-making; he's said to have ordered the coffin of Willie exhumed twice, so he could look at his son's face. But now he grasps at any solution, tries to please every side. He'll bring up colonization for free blacks again, gradually compensating slave owners. Next time, he sounds like he'll settle for a gradual abolition of slavery in the territories. Another looney idea: some Republicans want to send freed slaves to land set aside for American Indians in Louisiana and Arkansas, have black folks apprenticed to white Northerners who've settled there.

If only the president showed genuine sympathy for those enslaved. He's like Beidler—he won't say exactly. Lincoln went before Congress in March and wanted to compensate the states ending slavery for enduring such an inconvenience. That's the way it was reported—"inconvenience." As if *states* have more burden setting aside slavery than *slaves* have living under this unjust system!

And then, after talking about alternatives, Lincoln turned around and told the Northern army in Virginia to take back Richmond. That's all-out war! How does he think they can avoid killing civilians on the way to Richmond? I can understand his being upset with McClellan's wishy-washy leadership of the Army of the Potomac. That general had asked for more troops but then stalled on the way to Richmond. The man lacks boldness. But for Lincoln to compensate by ordering a military conquest of the South? And then to think his attempt at humor can overcome people's unease: "If I were two-faced, would I be wearing this one?"

His critics are the bold ones. "The President interferes too much back East." That's better than disliking him because he's tall and gangly. And there's truth: we've fared better in the West, where generals can fight as they want. Things have never gone well in Virginia. But how will our new secretary of war, Edwin M. Stanton, change that?

Furthermore, there aren't answers to my questions about the aftermath of Shiloh on the western front. The numbers killed, wounded, and missing are astounding: over 13,000 for our Northern cause, over 10,000 for the South. The bloodiest battle ever on our soil with no decisive outcome for either side. The fog of smoke and constant noise of battle made death by friendly fire all too possible. And when I ask again—Why *did* the South abandon wagonloads of knives?—Ross changes the subject.

He'd rather talk about a new repeating rifle the troops use, invented by a man in northern Virginia. It doesn't lift my spirits to know that *right now* someone is working somewhere to come up with yet another way to kill more men, more quickly. Some evenings I can't even enjoy a bowl of last year's sour cherries with milk. Not after I've read accounts of men crawling around begging someone to end their misery. All I picture is the crazed look of delirious hogs!

For a while I took respite in a new friend, Martha Babbetts, at the Congregational church. She questions, too, how some can minimize the goal of eliminating slavery. In fact, she pushed me to think about the rights women lack, like owning property. She quoted someone named Elizabeth Cady Stanton who said a woman's dependence is parallel to that of a slave. She has a point, but I'd rather be distracted by Martha's light blue gown that matches her eyes. When she wears that, I'll agree with her about almost anything. I ask for more than I should, and she puts me in my place.

"No, Mr. Funk."

Our friendship nearly ended, though, when we fell into conversation about Julia Ward Howe's new poem, "Battle Hymn of the Republic"; it was featured on the cover of *The Atlantic* magazine this month. Howe is an abolitionist—I give her that—and Martha, of course, likes her stand for women's rights. But when Martha said the last verse showed a *perfect* blend of bravery and nobility, I huffed.

"That verse . . . my Sunday school boys sing it with such gusto; all I hear is a vengeful God and a damnable war made to sound holy."

She withdrew her hands, her blue eyes frosty. "How so?"

"Dying to make men free? Not parallel to the way God sent Jesus to make men holy."

"But death *is* a sacrifice. Why not on an altar?"

"That goes too far, to give a religious purpose."

"You think the fighting's empty?"

"I didn't say that. But as things stand now—"

"No, Fretz! It's noble, even if incomplete in intent. Don't disparage what brave men do."

"I'm not. Don't misunderstand. I like the poem's sentiments, overall. But when fighting becomes savage . . . you can't redeem it with religious sentiment."

"You want men to kill politely?"

We had to change the subject. A promising friendship nearly ruined because I refuse to accept this marriage of war and religion. I've stayed cautious—Martha hasn't needed to slap my hand again. But her attitude toward war is what I often hear in sermons at Third Presbyterian. Some Sundays I think I can't go back. Then I remind myself, the minister draws on beliefs from the eighteenth century. Early America was expected to be a redeemer nation like Israel; some people *still* think our country—white people, specifically—supposed to save the world. So when the death count goes up, they assign a higher purpose. These deaths, an instrument in God's hand. And thus, grand nobility! They'll rationalize: if innocent citizens happen to be in the way of clashing armies, that's another necessary sacrifice. The nature of war.

What makes this blend of war and religion stranger: the South does the same thing. They're convinced God is on *their* side. Southerners think God commissioned British slave traders to impose slavery in the first place. There's something in their Confederate motto about "God as our defender." And they rely on *Deo Vindice*: God will vindicate.

When Northerners hear that, the clamor gets louder again to include some mention of God in our Constitution. Each side thinks God can't favor the other side! Two equally deluded sides. Sincere, yes, but sincerely wrong. It's insane to think God ordained war to bring about peace. That's Old Testament thinking.

When I still see Martha occasionally, she mocks my dark thoughts. I play along and call it my *Weltschmerz*. How can I not feel despair at the state of the world? If she knew my naivete growing up in Pennsylvania . . . the world looked simple and inviting, waiting to be purchased with hard work. Everything was possible. Fortunes were for the taking in Chicago.

Now look at me, twenty-seven—older than Margaret ever knew. And yet my future feels less certain than five years ago. I take some hope from reading a paper from back home, *Das Christliche Volksblatt*. I've even written to the editor, John H. Oberholtzer, because of his interest in mission outreach and education—unheard of among most Mennonites. This new group—goes by the name General Conference Mennonites—is doing something positive. They don't simply separate themselves from the world. Maybe some good will come from Oberholtzer having taken the train to southeastern Iowa last year, meeting with like-minded folks there.

But for right now McMullen, Funk and Co. gives me a bigger boost. For a first year we've seen remarkable progress, a result of expert management and a willingness to do the hard task. Our lake schooner made a major difference during the winter; we had material on hand when the lake was frozen. And now we're getting a hefty bounce from lumber prices going up again. When Jim completed the books for the past year, all three of us came away with a profit of $1,576.01. We laughed about that last penny, but our business year included January, when lumber had declined to nine dollars.

I've been able to make some purchases I had postponed. My thoughts went to Father when I treated myself to a book auction and bought *Plutarch's Lives* for a dollar and *Life of Christ* for fifty cents. The latter shows beautiful pictures of Christian art. I couldn't resist stopping at Clingmans, too; I picked out dark blue pants and a vest and splurged on a cravat for fourteen dollars. The satisfaction of enough pocket money to make acquaintance with other fine ladies in the city, not rely solely on Martha.

Most of the time, I'm an orderly person, but sometimes what Phil calls "a little riot of freedom" spills out. I need a break from the stress of work and war. Gwendolyn always gives me a good time, even if afterward I feel guilty. I have to overlook her fussing with her hair, or retying a bow and pulling out a tiny mirror to inspect herself one more time. At least I'm not vain. But when I put my arm around her tiny waist, I can't help but wonder that she doesn't detest those inner garments. I would refuse to be confined like that.

But something happened in March that's left a more serious blotch on my conscience. I sued a man. This Mr. Norton insisted he couldn't pay. Suing seemed the only recourse, but it's as hard to forget as it is to remove spring's mud from the creases of my shoes. In truth, we *could* have written it off; I argued as long as I could for setting up repayment through the bank. One time Norton had come to see me alone and told me about his seven children and medical bills. I heard my mother's voice and said I'd do what I could. But Jim was doubtful the man could be trusted unless we took him to court.

When we conferred with Beidler, he was adamant. "Going to court is prudent. You'll find out if the fellow can sell off some property."

All I could muster: "I don't want the man to go to prison."

But in the end, I couldn't contradict my partners. Jim understands money matters better than I; recently he's stepped in with even more of the bookkeeping oversight and still goes around in the horse and buggy to collect bills. I've ended up doing more with sales than I'd anticipated.

I could put this episode with Norton out of my mind more easily if not for Harry, my boyhood chum. Last year it was Randolph Smith enlisting; this year it's Harry's words that rankle. He could always sled to the bottom of the hill faster than I but never showed motivation to keep up with his schoolwork. In spite of our differences, we'd kept in touch over the years. I made the mistake of admitting I'd delayed in writing back because I was caught up in business matters. His reply shocked me. He predicted I would marry a rich man's daughter, *if only for the sake of money.* I was seething. Then I began to worry: he might have stayed in touch with Salome, made inroads. I couldn't ask directly, for she's not mine to be possessive about anymore, but I thought his tone had tinges of gloating.

I waited to write back till I could take a lighter approach. I said in jest, he would get fat from accumulating a second and third farm. I was eager for his reply, but I could not have predicted. He said I used to be the first to speak of honor and affection as preeminent. His insinuation was clear: something had changed.

I should have let the correspondence go. Why do I only know these things in retrospect? Nothing good comes from someone who misconstrues; in truth, he means nothing to me. But I didn't want to slink off. So I wrote back but entirely avoided anything controversial. When he responded, he warned again, I had given in to the desire for riches. I couldn't surmise what he referred to, but the timing couldn't have been worse. I was in court over Mr. Norton. The poor man had come to me personally a second time and begged me to drop the suit. That time, I felt peeved.

"I'm part of a company; others are involved."

I couldn't be a pushover.

Nor could I forget Harry's words.

Of course, I came to Chicago to get ahead. I may have bragged of it beforehand. Father's encouragement and my brother-in-law's boldness pushed me. I wanted to be part of Jacob's circle of risk-takers. When he and Mary Ann were newly married and about to leave home for Illinois, I was the one who closed the gate in front of them. It's an old custom. Jacob grinned and tossed a coin my way—only a shilling—so I would allow their departure. We all knew the prank. But I never forgot that piece of money—worth only twelve and a half cents and no longer in circulation. Its cool feel in my palm; the ease with which Jacob threw it. He still says, "Making money is a *sacred* trust. Do it to the best of your ability."

He's right, and I have nothing to be ashamed of. The most ridiculous argument I've heard yet: "Dispose of your wealth and throw in your lot with the Union army." A recruiter said that. The fool asked us to raise a hand if we considered ourselves Christian. Almost everyone did. Then he talked about those idyllic lilies of the field—"*they toil not, neither do they spin.*" The man saw warfare as a way to follow the Bible's command: "*Take therefore no thought for the morrow . . .*" His words had the opposite effect on me: I won't contribute to what's become a destructive affair.

And yet, Harry's accusation haunts—"filthy allurement." What if I'm blind to what I've become? If Lincoln can let "saving America" become his religion and lose sight of universal emancipation, maybe my self-knowledge is equally limited.

Back in January, I used poor judgment when I took Phil along to Camp Douglas in my buggy. My new horse, Horace—I know the name's silly—stepped smartly. I thought Phil would be impressed. I know horses, so I'm not worried about Horace being more aggressive than I like. I'll train him soon enough. When he frightens Mary Ann's girls with one of his long, drawn-out neighs, I say he's starting an ode and is stuck for words. I repeat some nonsense rhyme and the girls end up giggling.

That January day, while cold, wasn't too bad with the sun shining and calm winds. Phil and I were curious about the atmosphere in a war camp, and I wanted to see how they trained their horses. Soon after we entered the campgrounds, past the post office and the commissary, we met a handsome bay horse pulling someone's carriage.

"Must be a higher-up," Phil said.

A few sentinels were warming themselves at a campfire, and other soldiers were making a show of their drills. Someone barked what sounded like, "Wheel right, wheel left" repeatedly, but I made a mental note—no complicated maneuvers like what Ross had described.

A man explained the camp's set-up: barracks all around a square with bunks three stories high and two deep. Each room has a coal stove and table, plus some seating. But 500 men make a life for themselves there.

"I couldn't put up with the commotion," I said. "No space to be alone."

Phil didn't reply, but the farther we went, the quieter we both became. He's usually carefree, his curly hair on the unruly side, but this outing never felt like a lark.

A sentinel waved a strip of wood like a sword. "This far and no farther," he yelled.

I wanted to turn around, but Phil said, "Some mighty fine women over there."

So we spent a little money and looked the ladies over. Phil drank gin and I had a pop for fifteen cents. I was getting fidgety, and the big toe on my right foot felt frozen. I was afraid he'd introduce himself to the brunette who kept glancing our way. No Rebel prisoners anywhere, but I had a sick feeling about the place. Rough-looking men—nothing like what I'd expected. I lost interest in seeing horses and said I needed to get home. I wanted to forget the entire visit. Back home, Mary Ann had me stick my foot in a tub of hot water; I was right about my toe.

Two months later, when Jacob was in the East on a business trip—he brought back a fine pair of gray socks for me—I had an unplanned conversation with Mary Ann. Most of our interactions come after she's put the children in bed; I dry the dishes while she washes. But because of Jacob's absence, I accompanied Mary Ann to a funeral for Robert Keller, the husband of a good friend of hers. He'd been missing for some time, and while Priscilla maintained hope along with most of her family, Mary Ann sewed an extra black dress for her friend, anticipating she'd be wearing black for at least a year. I didn't know this Robert, but I'm always curious what a minister will say about a fallen soldier.

As expected, the ceremony was solemn—the women and girls in Robert's family all dressed in black and carrying black handkerchiefs. The adult women also wore black veils and the men had armbands. I appreciated the dignity that prevailed—only a little weeping and no vivid recounting of the means of death. The family had chosen not to have the body embalmed—given the length of time since death—but two uncles had verified the remains when the box was opened briefly upon arrival. Even now Mary Ann says her friend hasn't come to fully realize Robert's death, but the funeral provided consolation.

By all accounts the deceased was a good man who showed his love for our country by responding to duty as a volunteer infantryman. Without fanfare he'd conducted himself with utmost bravery, following the commands as given. I have no doubt all these characterizations were true.

"A man liked by all—a patient and sweet soul," the minister said. "He fought the good fight and now a crown of righteousness is laid up for him."

Robert's life was presented as a model for us all. Just as he had followed the example of Jesus, we were reminded to give our lives for the greater good. I wasn't surprised to hear these remarks from the pulpit, infused with equal parts patriotism and Christian hope. We mourners were reminded also: the great good fortune for this servant's body to have been recovered and brought back for a proper burial. I've heard often of soldiers receiving a quick prayer by a chaplain, or an even swifter burial on the field by frantic comrades.

Later that evening Mary Ann spilled her fears for Jacob's safety, traveling by train. "One side could try to harm the others' soldiers; Jacob rides the same trains."

I nodded and felt an immediate bond with my sister. Unlike Priscilla, Mary Ann doesn't have extended family near at hand, other than me, if something untoward were to happen. Ever since, I've been quicker to lend a hand. I enjoy spending extra time with J. Michael, but I'm not as handy with Maggie or Estelle.

Yet another time when Jacob was delayed in returning home, my kinship with Mary Ann and her heart's distress stayed with me. I felt prompted to share a vision that had come to me and left me puzzled. I had waited for it to fade, but instead, the images pressed more heavily. Phil wouldn't understand, and I didn't trust Gwendolyn, so I spilled it to Mary Ann. She was large with child and had taken to reclining on the settee for the first part of the night. Since then, she's been safely delivered of a son, not long after the April night when the folks back home wrote about the surprise of a deep snowstorm.

I mentioned sleep difficulties. "Have you ever awakened at night," I asked, "having seen something so startling you couldn't sleep anymore?"

Mary Ann smiled as she does when I'm about to embark on an entertaining story from work. "No, I only dream of waking to a new babe's cry
for milk."

Of course, I have no idea what that's like—another life dependent
upon mine for sustenance. Nor am I comfortable talking about maternal
concerns. Since the birth of baby Augustus, it's all I can manage to hold my
new nephew and properly support his neck.

While speaking, Mary Ann had stirred to a half-sitting position, two
pillows propped beneath her head and neck. "Tell me your dream."

"You know the brown lily of the species that's called leopard lily?"

"Isn't the leopard lily an orange color?"

"Perhaps so. I saw it as brownish with spots and long stamens. In my
dream or whatever, it appeared larger than usual and extremely beautiful—
full-grown on a thick stalk. But here's what's odd." I regretted having started.
"We laid the lily on a board, and two or three of us carried it—much like
a coffin—into the yard. It was Father's house; I'm sure of that. We laid the
board down by the portico."

Mary Ann placed her hand on her stomach. I couldn't help staring;
it looked like movement against her hand. She mentioned no discomfort,
however, so I continued.

"That full-blown, beautiful brown spotted flower—a lily of some
kind—looked right at me, like an uplifted face. An open cup." Mary Ann
gave no response. "This is foolish to say, but it seemed to ask my appraisal:
Am I not a majestic flower?"

Mary Ann's face wrinkled in a frown. "Were you frightened? You
seem—" She gestured as aimlessly as I; her face and fingers carrying extra
fat.

"I don't recall fright. Nor revulsion. I admired its beauty. Since then,
though—"

"What is it?"

I studied the pattern within the fabric of the window draperies—large
loops and swirls. "Very strange. I hope you don't think less of me." She ab-
sently moved her hand over her belly as I continued. "On the other side of
Father's portico was a plant with green leaves—rather bushy, not tall—covered with fine white flowers. Something like a fuchsia, wreathlike or viny."
I studied my fingers. "Here's the thing. I turned around in the dream and
there stood Margaret."

"Our sister Margaret?"

"Yes. She held a small book that was open to a drawing—this same
green plant and its flowers. She pointed with much admiration: the drawing
was exact, especially the white flower. She held the book toward me, but I

couldn't read the writing. The type was large enough, but the letters were fuzzy."

Mary Ann reclined further and closed her eyes.

"I hope I'm not disturbing you. You must be tired."

"Oh, no, it's beautiful. But strange as you say. What then?"

"I mean, I hope I haven't disturbed by mentioning Margaret." I remembered tales of childbearing women, affected by thoughts of death. "I won't take long. I'm sure it was Margaret. The others?" I shrugged. "Definitely Father's house." She made no reply. "Then, I woke up."

"Oh, Fretz, it warms me to think of Margaret. Gone so young. And to picture the home place again. What do you make of the flowers?"

"I need more time." I hesitated. "It seemed, though—Margaret was my guardian angel, showing me the better thing. Yes, strange. I've always been attracted to the brown lily—or orange, as you say. An unusual species." Mary Ann covered a yawn. "The brown lily was buried." I hurried; she might not have understood. "Margaret was holding up the exact representation of the other. I felt instructed in some way. Like it carried meaning, although the words were kept from me." More quietly I added, "I still think the leopard lily is the more beautiful."

"A wonderful story. Thank you, Fretz."

That's all she said. I'd shared something disturbing, but it seemed lost, as when we're talking and one of the children runs in and the subject changes. I hadn't expected Mary Ann to shout out some meaning, or call it a vision. But she could have offered a puzzled look or shown more interest. She probably has too much on her mind.

Some days I think I may know the meaning. But I couldn't tell her of my longing. My *Sehnsucht*—whether of a religious nature or vocational. Whether grand or simple. Some vague dissatisfaction. Perhaps, in truth, only a character flaw; I *allow* these questions to put me in knots. If only I had someone to talk with, someone I trusted.

Nor did I tell Mary Ann I'd contacted Abraham Detweiler, a minister at Sterling, even though she and Jacob were the ones who'd known of him from their early days in Illinois. This Abraham had written back, saying they were having church trouble—he was very apologetic—and didn't know when they would next hold Communion. But he referred me to a Mennonite in Elkhart County, Indiana, and suggested I might travel there instead. I'm interested, but another roadblock came along with the welcome from there by the deacon, David Good; they plan to draw lots and choose both a minister and deacon the same weekend they have Communion. I'm not sure I want to attend a long, drawn-out affair.

Everywhere I turn, some obstruction crops up. I want the way to be straight. But this Mennonite church may turn out to be no more a sanctuary than any church here in the city. I tell myself to keep my nose in business affairs like Beidler does. I can't be carefree, not with a war going on. I should be satisfied with the Sunday school boys. The ones at our new Milwaukee Depot School are more difficult to settle down, but they still repeat whatever I say. Maybe some rote learning will stick with a few.

For now, I find moments of contentment, tending the four new grape roots I planted for Mary Ann: one each of the Rebecca, the Diana, the Delaware, and the Concord. Already they sprout new leaves, coexist peacefully, and wag no fingers.

David — Shenandoah Valley, May 1862

My trusty horse, Elijah—gone in a matter of minutes. All the miles he provided of safe travels! When the Rebels raid, they hand over Confederate scrip as payment, a flimsy piece of paper. But this was a Fed at my place. I did not think they would come looking this far off the main road, but I have been wrong about most things. I am down to Joel's Ruby and the colt she had a month ago. Neither army will want a skittish colt for their purposes. But Ruby . . . I dare not pile undue work on her. Nor can I replace Elijah; the Feds may come again soon.

The thick-set soldier gave me a slip of paper—called it a receipt, acknowledging he took my chestnut riding horse of seven years, a saddle, and bridle.

"Go to New Market and ask for the quartermaster, a Mr. David by name," the man said. "When the war is over, there will be proper recompense."

My fat hens could not stop their squawking.

When I followed directions, I came upon the wretched smell. From a distance I could not place the odor—sick cattle in their squalor? Now when I close my eyes, I see body parts; the stench comes back. Arms, legs, limbs of all sizes, stacked outside a tent—said to be a makeshift surgeon's operating room. Word is, so much disease in the ranks, a miracle for any wounded man to walk out alive or be carried out breathing. The main hospital in our Valley is at Staunton; this improvised camp at New Market must be for those deemed unable to survive a trip that far.

I could not proceed to find Mr. David to get his stamp. I could not. If I try again, I will go around Busby's woods, not attempt passage through New Market. I came home, spurring Ruby but trying not to call attention to her speed. I said little to Abigail and Delilah. How do you speak of destruction of the human body without retching? I had no stomach for supper. Only a cup of milk before bed and a prayer that sleep would come. I had thought losing Elijah was bad. But men have lost their minds to be part of such butchery.

I stay on the lookout, but I do not know what I can do differently. The soldier appeared out of the mist.

"You are getting a good one," I said—worth at least $200 in normal times—"sure-footed through stream and mountain path."

He nodded like he knew. What a blessing I sold the work horses a month ago!

The man was polite enough—shook hands like conducting a business transaction—but he took the measure of my place. He could return or send comrades to snatch Ruby. "Extra good-looking cattle," he said. Bile rose in my throat. My three-year-olds will make fine beef.

I need to plan. Ruby hears things before I—lifts her head sharply—but I do not know if she would hold still, cowering in shadows. I must practice. Ask Delilah to create a scuffle, train Ruby for quiet commands. Perhaps near the cove in back, so long as I do not rouse Winfield's attention.

Others of General Banks's men have said vile things to women folks when ransacking for gold. We are commanded to give what we have. But Delilah said it best: "Stripped." Sometimes my self-pity bursts afresh and I take count: two sons, three horses, a goodly measure of gold. What have I done to harm anyone? Winfield and others would blame my sons' absence for causing disadvantage. But what did I do against the North? How can anyone defend this dreadful way of settling a dispute?

And now the ongoing torment of Elijah being ridden into battle! Men on both sides said to be fond of rushing the enemy with bayonets drawn, charging directly in broad daylight. Even letting out a whoop when they drive a sword and see blood spurt.

I have only seen Brother Kline twice since his release from prison—both errands of medical mercy. We limit our travels, what with troops from both sides in our Valley, trampling stands of azaleas, as if of no value. But our scourge of diphtheria—no one can stop. We prayed for a letup with warmer weather, but the rains have stayed frequent and dampness does not lend itself to recovery. Medicines, even scarcer than before; only a rich man could afford quinine. I spend time in the woods, digging for licorice roots.

The first time I went to Johnny's house, I apologized for not having visited him in prison; I know Jacob Wine went. John dismissed my concerns with a flick of the wrist, expressing gratitude for the tea of wild cherry bark I had sent for the men. I had taken care to skin the outer bark away, and my women had boiled the middle bark down to a syrup. Some of the men had also found relief from goose grease, rubbing it on the chest. Johnny still sounds raspy in the throat—a wonder he did not get a severe case of pneumonia—but says his energy returns. I did not have the heart to ask how his wife fared while he was gone from home.

I asked though, "How did you keep the men from wavering?"

"Together—you understand? No different than when the apostle Paul appeared before the magistrate Felix and exhorted his fellow captives to obey God's law, not man's. Each of us weak at times, needing encouragement."

He showed me the new words to the song the men sang; we have used it at Flat Rock. The tune comes recently from a Bradbury man, used with the song we learned as "Sweet Hour of Prayer." But now I picture men jailed— broken in mind and body with execution threats hanging over them—singing *"Go home, go home."* Nine verses written already when the men were kept in the guard house at Mount Jackson, their heart's desire to escape conscription:

> this we did for conscience sake,
> We did not wish God's law to break.

Later Brother Kline added the chorus, as Jacob Wine had told me:

> We'll sure go home as soon as freed,
> A holy life with God to lead.

Finally, I dared ask Johnny the other question on my mind. "The mountains are crawling. Surely you will not attempt further passage."

"I have signed my loyalty oath to the Union and obtained my pass to cross through Federal troops. Yes, Lord willing, I will attend our Annual Meeting in a couple of weeks."

"But, John, we only now have you back. How can you brave the bounds of travel again?" I searched his face for any sign of faltering. "We cannot be sure where Rebel troops may be. They press north, pretending to go east over the Blue Ridge Mountains, only to end up back at Staunton by train. There is no predicting their maneuvers."

He nodded. "Stonewall is said to have a man, Hotchkiss—Jed, I believe—who has made maps, knows these mountains like the back of his hand."

"All while Union troops get befuddled. Attack and then retreat. They could mistake your innocence, take out their aggression."

"They make no progress getting to Richmond."

I could not let his dodges be the last word. "The Rebels stay determined: drive the Feds back to Winchester. They want no Northern troops in eastern Virginia. How can you . . . ?" I had to go on. "How can you expect to get past? Aberration, the order of the day."

"Do not fear for me. I must do what I can to keep our church together." He broke into song: *"Go home, go home, and that indeed / As soon as God the way will speed."*

In part I am relieved: John shows no flicker of doubt. If only he is allowed a safe return; I do not want more questions piled at my door. In spite of his foolhardiness—or because of—we may still receive word from the boys. I must maintain hope with my women, for Abigail is back to saying the Lord has blessed our early timing with the boys, now that conscription is the law of the land again.

* * *

More unwanted visitors! Late last week three Union men came with a wagon—claimed to be with General Banks—and loaded from our surplus of last year's crops: wheat, oats, corn. The latter worth nearly a dollar a bushel. I had 200 bushels before they ransacked our granary, making sport all the while.

One man waved his lighted cigar—looking long at Ruby—and threatened to set ablaze our stacks of hay. Then he thrust the pitchfork toward Abigail. "Fill 'er," he said, pointing to the back end of their wagon.

She crouched as one deaf and dumb, staring at the fork, the man, the wagon.

"Look at this old goat," the man yelled to his partners. "A stone idiot—lacking sense!" He gave Abigail a shove and stood cackling. Her fall, soft like a sack of puffball weed, the fork clattering on a stone, tines upward. I rushed to her side.

"The old codger protects his loony one," said a tall thin one, grabbing the pitchfork and proceeding to load the wagon himself.

I bent to Abigail and we huddled thus, watching until I had to shift to avoid trickles coming from her. I feared she might collapse entirely.

"There's another one," the first man said. I did not turn, but I knew Delilah must have come out on the porch steps and watched silently. I prayed she would not bar the door if the men attempted entrance. "Crying like a baboon," he said, staggering against the wagon and laughing crazily.

They continued filling the wagon, carrying bundles we had tied last fall, making hideous comments. When one talked of going inside, I rose from my crouch.

"Where's your whiskey, Old Man?" the drunk one yelled. "I need another jug."

"Come on, Durgan," the tall one said. "Keep your pants on. Gotta' get this load back to camp before dark. Come back another time—another chance."

"Look!" The crazed man pointed to the darkened ground by Abigail. "She leaks."

The two others paid scant attention, but each grabbed a fat hen, holding tight to one jerking leg. Each made a show in front of me, twisting a head while the wild one guffawed.

Then they were gone; the hens left behind continued their loud squawks. Delilah came running, and we helped Abigail to her feet. She would not respond to our questions but stepped over her puddle. Her body began to shake and she fell to me. Her cries muffled in my shirt—"Our livelihood"—until another frenzy took hold. She grabbed the pitchfork and raked scattered hay, zig-zagging as crazily as the drunk one.

I put my arms about her, wresting the fork from her grasp. I feared a bad spirit had seized her. When she first crouched, I thought she played the possum.

Delilah closed the broken bar on the granary as best she could. "Come, Mother. Tomorrow we will look to gleaning. For now, we must regain our wits."

"They said another chance," Abigail wailed.

That is how we live. The specter of unwanted men hangs over us. We thought ourselves attentive before, but now we know true vigilance. Three days have passed and the men have not returned. Their unit may have moved on, but I do not venture forth to get word at the post office. Considerable flour left behind. Our new crops unscathed in the fields. Abigail has not fully regained—she's more to sit and stare—but neither does she manifest signs of evil. I must guard against bewilderment, such as Johnny's Anna manifests.

We have started a new practice: each night we gather in a tight circle before Delilah goes to her bed in the loft. We have never been much to show affection, but now we take nothing for granted. I beseech the Lord for protection through the night—the vicissitudes of the mind—sufficient rest to be of good courage the next day.

Since then, a far different visitor appeared mid-afternoon: an elderly woman of the black race, itty bitty in size. I saw something move on the road, disappear in the row of pines. I kept watch until a hunched form slithered forward. We have harbored a runaway, near to exhaustion. Far more blessed to provide shelter than to watch soldiers grab at grain. Johnny had told me years ago of the Fugitive Slave Law; I could be fined some outlandish amount—perhaps $1,000—or be stuck in prison. The woman flees for her life.

She would not come inside, so Delilah made a bed for her in the stable where Elijah used to sleep, staying to soothe Ruby and the colt from undue agitation. Later Delilah woke the woman to offer a mess of greens with bacon, but she shook her head and went right back to sleep. We called her Lila afterwards, because our Delilah took a special liking to her. The woman stayed an extra day and left again when darkness descended. She might have been from these parts, for she knew the North Fork would take her to Fulk's Run and the Dry River. I could not make any sense of a plan, though. Sometimes she babbled, "Go to meet my man."

Yet days after, Delilah kept saying, "That woman has no rights. Where will she end?"

"Some think the troop activity makes it easier for slaves to escape," I said. "Authorities cannot look everywhere at once." I shrugged. "Only speculation." We cannot comprehend how owners or soldiers think. How slaves must fend.

Thoughts of our boys rush afresh. Three months already. Some mountain man doubtless scratched his head when they knocked on his door, said they were heading for the big rocks. Where today? *Oh Lord!* Beyond Ohio?

Given the uncertainties of travel—our beautiful Valley, reduced to a foreign place where hostile men rule—I went alone to church this past Sunday. We ministers all said our usual. I again read Matthew 11:28 for our opening. "*Come unto me, all ye that labour and are heavy laden.*" My voice broke before I could add, "*and I will give you rest.*"

Afterwards, though, I spent considerable time conversing with J. M.; he had come by himself also. For a stocky man, his voice always surprises— light in tone and soothing.

"It is not only soldiers to be wary of." He spoke like a son. "Strangers take advantage of our current state of lawlessness; they prey on innocent people."

I felt old beyond my years but nodded. "These bushwhackers stop anyone on the road, inquire as to your business." I could not avoid my shudder. "No authority whatsoever. But a man with a pistol commands attention."

"And new postings in New Market—even at Cootes store—calling for men to join a legion. Have you seen?" he asked. "Forming for guerilla service west of the Blue Ridge. A broadside advertises payment: the standard rate for military service. Extra for captured guns or munitions. Not officially part of the army but acting in support."

My thoughts ran to Winfield. I have not seen much of him lately, but I find skinned carcasses—coons and muskrats—on my land by the creek. No way to know for certain.

The way J. M. told it, these guerillas intend to stop the North's convoys and forage trains. He hesitated, looked around before adding, "Bottom of the notice—'Looking for men to shoot a Yankee as easily as kill a mad dog.'"

I rode like one possessed to reach home safely, but once there, said nothing to Abigail or Delilah. "The usual admonitions," I mumbled.

ESTHER — Shenandoah Valley, June 1862

He walked up in his scruffy outfit—a slouch hat and well-worn shoes. I don't know where he got any of it, his dirty shirt and pants. He called it a uniform, but I wouldn't want to see a whole group of men come toward me dressed like that. He gets a small amount of pay each month, thirty dollars, so he might have bought those items. A jacket to cover himself at night. He kept his haversack close by. My son and not my son. Andrew had changed mightily when he came back from prison, but nothing like this. Peter seemed taller, slimmed out. Eighteen, but barely a man.

I put down the pan of June apples when I heard a step on the porch. Any unexpected sound requires attention, what with cannons booming in the distance. A stranger peered in the window and I drew back. Then I looked again: it was him. Our prodigal, even though I hadn't seen him from afar. Straggly hair and whiskers. But a tenderness in his eyes.

"Ma," he said, his hands cupped to the pane. "It's me."

I still didn't open the door. My heart leaped to him, but my hand held back. Then I opened and could not but take him in my arms. I welcomed him. My son. Peter.

He looked me over, as if hungry for my face. "Where's Pa?"

I shrank from his hold. "He can't be here. He's away."

"It's all right, Ma. I'm no scout."

"Here for good? To stay?"

"Only the night. I slipped away from camp. We've been idle. So close, I couldn't help myself. Others have done the same without reprimand." Then he lowered his head. "I miss you, Ma, miss everybody. Everything looks beautiful—these green mountains stretch wide. Sweet summer smells, the breeze! Where are they? The others."

"Andrew can't be here either," I said slowly. "The other three, out pulling weeds. All the rains brought sudden growth." I grabbed the back of a table chair. These days I'm given to dizziness and have to use the bucket. My children do the choring, and Mary Grace has taken over cooking with grease. I manage the fire for bread, but I don't make as many loaves. We must stretch the flour.

"What is it, Ma? You don't look steady."

I forced a half-smile. He doesn't remember how I was with Joseph and Mary Grace. With William, not so troubled. "Your father and Andrew spent days in prison. Richmond." Peter showed no expression. "Back in March, gone from home, most of six weeks. Now . . . Each away, on his own." I searched his face. "I know not."

"Oh," he said, as if given sufficient information. He walked to the fireplace, stuck his head in the back room, looked up to the loft. "You say in the fields, the others?"

"Behind the smokehouse," I said with a wave of my hand.

He grabbed his haversack, then put it down again. "Would you, Ma? Can you spare some thread?" He opened his bag—much nicer than the one he'd taken from here—showed me the heavy straps on the outside, ran his hand over leather. He pointed to initials inside: R. V. M. "Would you stitch over?" And then slyly, "Other bag wore out."

I nodded as he turned to go outside, steadied myself against the door frame. I sank onto my bed, empty again, save for Mary Grace sleeping with me. I curled up and closed my eyes. From outside I heard yelps and squeals; the horses greeted him, too.

Andrew had been the first to go, almost a week ago. With all the troops hereabouts, it wasn't safe; not uncommon for soldiers to happen by. Scouts, too, asking questions, wanting food. Some days Andrew stayed in the back bedroom—no windows. He couldn't help with outdoor work. "No use; might as well be elsewhere."

Finally, one morning I knew what I had to do. I left the peas unpodded and walked to Samuel Coffman's house; I made a beggar of myself. Had Samuel been away, I would have made known my plea to Frances. Their young boys worked outdoors, but both parents kept themselves scarce. Countless threats have been leveled against Brother Coffman—his unceasing efforts to build up those of us who must resist pressure. Neighbors have unleashed their fury: rocks thrown at the house, threatening notes dropped in bags of feed.

"If you should flee to western Maryland, could you take Andrew with you?" I asked. "Another pair of eyes. Some advantage. He must find passage North. I have a brother, Matthias Lesher, in Chambersburg. If Andrew could find his way, he might hire himself out to his uncle." Simon used to say this corridor, the Great Valley, stretched beyond our valley and went north and west to the Cumberland Valley.

I must have gone to Samuel in the nick of time, for he hesitated but a minute. "Is the lad persuaded by himself?"

"Yes, but he wants nothing of a large group. I won't let him go alone."

"Tell him to make ready a bag. If I decide to attempt a trip and stop for him, he must be ready at once. I will need to get passes. How old is he?"

Sure enough, Samuel rapped at our door four nights later, one night after he led our church in our spring Communion and foot washing. At the rap Andrew rose without finishing his supper. I hurriedly stuck all the bread and cheese I could in his bag. Only the day before, Samuel had reminded us how our Savior rose from supper, laid aside his garments, and took a towel. My Andrew, resigned to the trials ahead.

There can be no better travel companion for him. Samuel will know of safe places to stop, and Andrew can be an extra pair of ears, likely taking turns sleeping in the woods some nights. Simon had said the usual pass is to go from New Market to Winchester, then another pass to Martinsburg, then to the Potomac and on to Maryland and Pennsylvania. I shuddered at the distances, but I had to release my boy.

On the day of Communion, Samuel had read the command from the book of John: "*If I then, your Lord and Master, have washed your feet, ye also ought to wash one another's feet.*" We women took our turns, weeping as we circled about the rows. The Lord's preparation to obey mingled with our uncertainties. On the other side of the building, our men—the ones left—also washed each other's feet, just as Andrew did with another young man way to the back. I didn't know the rasp at the door lay so near.

After Andrew left, Simon became more agitated. He spilled his mug and shouted at William not to dawdle. In forty-eight hours, he too was out the door. He'd moved from saying with assurance "The Lord will protect," to shielding his downcast eyes. He whispered about nearby homes known to have secret places, trap doors in the floor and such. We have nothing of the kind. I don't know Simon's whereabouts. He said it was better that way. If close by, he may come back from time to time; his food will run out. He's to rap at the kitchen window—three times, a pause, and then a tap.

"*If ye know these things, happy are ye if ye do them.*"

It wouldn't be far to Margaret Rhodes' place, her husband an invalid. She's been known to harbor men. But this spring, once Simon became convinced there might be no other recourse, he helped a Zigler man—they'd made acquaintance in prison—dig out a cave in the woods. An enclosure of some kind and hard to detect, he said. I insisted he take the rifle; he can't live in the mountains without it. I have my butcher knife.

He'd railed for days when conscription talk grew from rumor to law. His newly acquired faith weakened; he turned again to despondency.

Countless times he recited what had been told when released: "You are free to go; your fine in lieu of service has been paid."

But the notice to enlist came with no exceptions for those released. The local quartermaster insisted on a second payment and wouldn't wait for the state to refund the $500 already paid in prison on Simon's behalf. Or Andrew's. As if one day's promise had expired when the sun went down. We couldn't spare more; Simon refused to buy a substitute.

"Where is there fairness?" he asked over and over, spitting tobacco and caring not where it landed. I feared he'd slip into worse melancholy, all but give up. His departure relieved my need to make things up that might provide consolation.

Now I'm left to manage again. We give thanks on one count: our three youngsters have escaped this dreaded diphtheria. So far. But we were late sowing oats, and when we planted corn, only one seed to a hill. And now, Peter here a night. No fatted calf for him, but I simmered a small chunk of ham without stomach upset. I prayed to say, "*He that receiveth whomsoever I send, receiveth me.*"

Yes, a relief: he's alive. But he marches to another commander. I had prayed he might weary of the adventure, but he left again, even as he said he would.

"Ma," Peter said at supper, "it's not as you think. Mighty fine men in our company. We come from good families; many left a wife and children at home. Often homesick." He quickly added, "Some get packages. Letters."

His brown eyes beseeched me. A sadness, like that of an older, wiser man. How would I wrap a parcel? Who would take it to the post office? He does not realize the obstacles.

"We sat on top of Allegheny Mountain two months. Most of the men been there all winter, waiting for Feds to attack. Mumps and smallpox laid some of the men low." A smirk crossed Peter's face. "Feds thought they could get to Richmond."

Mary Grace's eyes turned to me; I lowered my head. Peter helped himself to more cooked apples.

"Long days, even though nightfall came early. No cattle to feed, no cows to milk." Joseph and William drank in his every word. "But paths to shovel in the snow, come morning. And cold winds. When March turned to April, more than ready to move down."

What might he have said to my young ones out of my hearing?

"We don't always have tents for sleeping. One time it rained three nights in a row." Peter's eyes settled on Joseph. "I got to choose the 52nd Virginia Infantry because I volunteered. If you wait for a draft, you go wherever sent."

I watched him spread more butter on his potatoes; the new ones William grubbed are little more than marbles. I don't know what Peter eats in camp, but it must not include butter. Part of me wanted to fatten him up; another part—ashamed to say.

"You must get very tired," I said. "Many miles of walking?"

"A stretch there, we marched fifty minutes out of every hour. At least fifteen miles every day, taking back towns we'd lost earlier." He paused and a grin covered his face. "On my second pair of shoes. Got them when someone else didn't need them anymore." He looked around the table. Then he added more softly, "The first battle, the hardest. Covered in smoke. Hard to see. The noise. Minnie balls sizzling past."

I sat mute. My son, exalting. I scanned his face again for scars. Sometimes when he stands, I think he favors a leg. I couldn't picture him making removal or gloating at a good fit. The haversack, the initials I'd stitched over. I couldn't ask if there'd been close calls, surprise attacks. I didn't want to know if he'd been at Shiloh. Simon had said terrible fighting there.

"You should hear us when the man at the head of the line shouts out, and the rest of us follow suit with a yell. Starts low and deep, ends high—a wild shrieking. Goes all the way to the back end of our unit. Curdles the blood." Peter put down his fork, and I was afraid he was going to demonstrate. Instead, he smacked his hands. "We know we'll prevail. No one can outfox our Stonewall. God's Sword, that man. Not a one of us thinks twice to do his bidding. Long fast marches and lightning strikes." He slapped his hands again like a whip cracking. "Like that."

My potatoes swam like soup. I regretted taking my usual helping, pushed my plate toward Joseph. He cleans up whatever is left from anyone.

"We captured so much of Banks's supplies at Winchester—medicines, ammunition, even sugar and salt. Took a week for everything to get dragged back to Staunton."

That might be the same booty some of our men had been forced to move as teamsters. I sat stunned, idly glancing outside to see the day's light fading.

"The explosion, Joseph, when we burn a bridge. Fire and wood bursting. Whoosh! Then the splash and sizzle—hot boards hitting the river." I looked, in spite of myself. Peter's eyes danced. "Feds tried to chase us south; we knew what we were doing. They might have more men—fancy outfits— we've got guts." He laughed. "We know these mountains. They thought we'd give up and turn tail. Not with Jackson—we're smarter, stronger."

I caught Peter's eye and put a finger to my lips. Mary Grace had come to me and leaned into my shoulder.

"One more thing, Ma—I promise. We burned nearly every bridge we crossed." He scooted his chair back and jumped up. No one made pretense of eating; we watched in a trance. "The Feds, stuck on the wrong side." He turned his body slowly and clapped his hands over his head like beating a drum. "Couldn't get to us. They're the ones had to retreat. Nowhere to go but back where they came from." He threw back his head and laughed again. "All the time, they thought they'd sweep us out."

Just as suddenly, he turned sober. He went out the door and walked back and forth on the porch, his footsteps heavy. Early evening's insects began their buzzing. Joseph started to get up, but I said, "No."

We waited at the table.

When Peter came back, his face had changed, as if he'd seen a ghost. "Have to get back. My buddies need me." He sagged against the door frame. "One of 'em, Jude McCarver, took a ball to the eye. Told him I'd be back. Once you've seen the elephant—" His eyes looked straight ahead, stark. "Did you hear about our men at Shiloh? Thunder and lightning, most of two days. Some at the front, turned and ran. Shells exploding. Have to get back. Might march again soon."

"Peter, I wish you'd cast it aside. Putting yourself in harm's way. Not God's intent."

"It's a righteous cause, Ma," he said. He sat at the table again, subdued but looking at each of us, his hands gripping the table's edge. "We can't fail. We won't. God won't let us down." He spoke with the same certitude as Simon, after he'd renewed his faith. "Some reverses—a testing of sorts. But we won't let Yankees take our Valley. Ma, believe me. I'm a better man than when I left. We hear sermons, have revivals." I could barely listen. "Fear. Fear's the worst."

I didn't know this man. *Believe him?*

He spared me from answering. "I meant to tell you, Ma; I met that Hildebrand bishop's cousin. The Jacob who's not the bishop. Old man brought a new pair of shoes for his boy, Benjamin. Couldn't put my finger on it first off, but thought this Benjamin looked familiar. He didn't remember me either. But the old one brought us together. Friends now—Benjamin and I. This Jacob comes every so often. A fine man—quiet way about him, like a Mennonite. One night he stayed over. He said—listen to this, Ma—he said he'd be with us every day but for his bad heart. And before he left he offered a prayer. He made Benjamin and me kneel down, right there, and put a hand on the shoulder, each one of us. Said something like, 'May the Lord protect you and deliver you from Lincoln's hireling tools.' That's what he said."

My heart heaved. It was my turn to go outside; I walked down the lane and back up. Till I came back, Mary Grace had cleared the table.

As it turned out, Peter stayed the night. His frenzy tamed. As if healed by telling of Hildebrand. He bedded down by the fireplace and rose again at the break of day. That's when they always get up—his company—even in the cold of winter.

"Don't worry, Ma." His eyes begged, but I couldn't say one word. Before he left, though, he opened his shirt and showed me a scrap of paper he'd sewed to the inside. Big, jagged stitches. *Peter Shank* is all it said. Then he closed again and reached for his hat and haversack. "Nobody wants to die unknown," he whispered. "If it's mine to do, and far from home, I want you to know—I'm ready."

My mother's heart riven. His words meant to reassure—not tempted by unbelief or despair, not caught unaware. But how can life be so simple, good and evil straightforward, when he wears a paper with only his name?

I thanked him for coming—I did that much—but I couldn't say a prayer like Hildebrand. I'm glad Peter has this friend, a Benjamin from our own kind. But I could only stand outside and watch him walk out the lane, sadder by far than the first time.

My son.

I don't understand, but I pray silently. I pray for R. V. M and his family, too. My black crisscrosses of thread. Somewhere, someone mourns the man I removed.

I've tried to undo damage with Joseph and William; I've asked about their talks.

"He took my turn with the hoe," Joseph said, "gave us each a rest."

"That's good," I said. "And what of the war? Did he tell of the command to rise in an instant and charge?" William's eyes widened and I wanted to swallow my words.

"He told of a musket that uses bullets in the shape of a cone," Joseph said.

"It shoots farther than Pa's rifle and never misses," William added.

My queasy stomach rumbled.

"Don't worry," Peter had said, as if a small matter to think of your child prepared to face an enemy's bayonet at close range. Only a minor inconvenience to be here without Simon. "Don't worry." As if the child that takes form within will be born into a home of safety and contentment.

* * *

Simon's been here and gone again! Like a thief in the night. Such stealth, I nearly swooned. Three raps, nothing, then a short tap. I sat paralyzed.

Someone had guessed our code! As was my custom, I'd barred the door and closed the extra lock when darkness descended. But that night I sat mending a shirt Joseph had ripped in the armpit. We have no extras—not with three men gone—nothing bigger for Joseph. We must take extra care with our flax this year.

Later, Simon said he whispered my name loudly. I couldn't hear right. He rapped a second time; he followed the code. That might be when Mary Grace mumbled in her sleep. And suddenly Joseph was by my side; I hadn't heard him creep down the ladder. I clung to his arm, but he pulled away and tiptoed to the window. He said in his deepest voice, "Who's there?"

"Your pa," came the reply. I stumbled to the door, unlocking and embracing Simon. In all the fuss William awakened and hustled down the ladder. Only Mary Grace slept through the hubbub of whispers and low tones. She took on the pout when she learned she'd been the only one not to see her father. I promised to wake her, if he ever came again in the night.

He stayed but a few hours; we whispered back and forth. His beard scraggly, his eyes bloodshot, he insisted he's well. He had to see for himself that we were safe. He needed food. It's the cave, but no hint as to where. Nighttime most of the day. He only ventures out to gather firewood or check their trap. Surprised by a patch of wild asparagus. Sometimes a stray joins the two men for a night. Sore surprised to learn of Peter's visit, disappointed at no word from Andrew. I remind him: our oldest travels with Brother Samuel.

All too soon Simon retraced his steps. Half a moon. We sent cheese and bread, refilled his flask. I slept no more that night. What four-footed beast might cross his path? What two-footed, armed with bad intent?

The next day my thoughts turned anew to Andrew. I sent Joseph the long way around to the Coffmans' farm. Had they heard anything? Exposing one son to danger in order to have reassurance about another. As it turned out, Joseph met no soldiers, but Frances had no word. Simon's right; it's not knowing—what might have beset—that most sears the mind. Before he left, he asked again about Peter's well-being. No one mentioned the end of our meal, the Hildebrand man's prayer.

The work at hand gives my mind surcease from sorrow. We had to replant corn in low spots; now the bag of seed is empty. Ghosts come at nighttime. Not Mama on the rocking chair, but a wild cat's cry. Worries over Joseph. Those looks on Peter's face, his loud laugh. His name written on a scrap.

I said nothing to Simon about my trips to the bucket—enough on his mind. Besides, a sudden fright could change my innards, bring everything to a halt. No one knows how long for the men. This Zigler sounds steady enough, but Simon's not the patient sort.

David — Shenandoah Valley, June 1862

Things have quieted, but I am awash. I still miss Elijah and try to still the tremor of my hand. While the danger from armies is no longer immediate here, we do not know about elsewhere. They called it Stonewall Jackson's Valley campaign. Day after day, soldiers by the thousands moved up and down our Shenandoah Valley. All of May into June. A Southern general by the name of Robert E. Lee is said to put great stock in this Stonewall.

The unruly ones never came back to raid my whiskey, but others came for grain and chickens. My seven best-laying hens! Now we take turns: one day I fix Delilah the few eggs that show up; the next day's take goes for Abigail. I am entitled on the third day. Whatever accumulates by Saturday goes for baking.

Some say as many as 20,000 of Banks' men marched in these parts—Yankees all the way south into Harrisonburg. Polite at first, they gave receipts. But when Stonewall's men attacked them—their whoops!—and sent them farther north, the Feds became unruly. They make no distinctions, but consider us enemies, for we fed both sides. They played cat and mouse, one side then the other, taking horses and food. I could not keep up with movements, which general took troops where. Reports of fighting at McDowell and Front Royal. One time Stonewall got as far north as Harpers Ferry with his men, causing panic in Washington.

In the midst, Jefferson Davis called for a day of humiliation and prayer. As if one day's supplication could bring men to their senses. But after the reprieve, right back to their drumbeat. Victory, uppermost. Calling on the name of the Lord to kill? I am not meant for such questions, but my mind works extra. Can this killing be ordained, as easily as a hawk destroys a rodent? One man meant to seek power over another, even as a fox chases a rabbit? Brother Kline reminds me of the blister beetle in Hardy County. When a skunk snatches this beetle, the bug releases a fluid that causes blisters in the skunk's mouth. In a matter of hours the skunk writhes and dies. Even if the skunk quickly spits out the beetle, it will suffer a raw mouth and may die anyway.

Not until June 9th did men say, enough. A terrible battle at Port Republic that Confederates claim they won. Heavy fighting at Cross Keys, too, where many German Baptists live. Some said Fremont's soldiers were not nearly as *considerate* of the locals as Banks's men had been. I would not have used that word for Banks's men: pillaging smokehouses and ransacking trunks in search of valuables.

In the end, the North got sent back. Or as Winfield said, "Kept from Richmond! Sent the cussed devils home." Those captured, taken through Harrisonburg to Staunton.

But not all was victory for the South. The Confederates lost an important general, Turner Ashby, a colonel and commander of their cavalry. Rebels poured out their anger on people living near Harrisonburg; Ashby's death came close by. A makeshift hospital in a school building said to be frightful. Larger but no worse, I wager, than New Market. Brother Neff and I went to offer consolation, but I could scarce complete the rounds. Pus dripping from wounded men, torn to pieces, lying in rows on a barn floor. Sawing off limbs—still the first line of treatment by doctors.

How dare I put that scene aside and go about daily living? Guilt creeps, even with Abigail's warm body nestled next to mine. Revulsion.

The worst may be over, but there is no end in clear sight. I am not the same. I pay heed to everything. On a recent Saturday, my women washed each other's hair at the well. First, Delilah soaked and massaged her mother's long hair, bent over my bucket. Then Abigail washed Delilah's hair, gently rubbing her scalp. I sat on the porch steps, immersed in their warm weather rapture, remembering the first time Abigail's long tresses fell over my naked body. All morning I felt derelict; the women went about with locks swirling. Delilah's take on a curl in their wetness. By noon, though, order was restored—their hair pinned tightly, save for unruly strands.

But by evening, questions returned afresh. I reread the passage from Job of God speaking from the whirlwind. During the winter Delilah had read the entire book aloud for Abigail and me. One calamity after another: boils, reproof, betrayal. Why? I cannot say I expect to hear a voice out of the thick fog that can blanket our mountains. I still lack the heartfelt faith of a child.

Not that I rail in public. Only Delilah and Abigail know I have raised a fist to the heavens: "For what end?" But even they do not know how I sometimes turn from Brother Kline's admonition: "We are called to endure suffering—to be misunderstood and reviled as was Jesus." His words are too hard. I have trouble assessing.

Being thought odd for our plain dress is customary. For over ten years we banned short curls close to the head, or beaver fur caps. Nothing fancy allowed; not like Methodist ministers who have forsaken the simplicity of their founder, John Wesley. Some of them wear ruffles or powder their hair. Our women also—no fashionable bonnets or hoop skirts.

But to be misunderstood, looked on by neighbors as traitors—condemned as Union!—when we do not fall in line with popular thought on slavery and warfare. A severe test. As more die for the Rebel cause, those left behind—even while claiming victory—seem more anxious about the ultimate outcome, even desperate, looking for any excuse to pin their troubles on others.

I have not complained about nuisance carcasses, but I grow tired, trying to explain. I am not equipped. Winfield calls me simple-minded to take Jesus's command seriously.

"Love!" he shouts. "You will let anyone run over you, if you see no one as an enemy."

I would not be surprised if he is some kind of spy, turning his trapping skills to people. These guerillas are known to name names, eager to catch anyone hiding or having useful information for authorities. And bushwhackers continue to make me think twice about going anywhere, even to church. John Imboden—from Augusta County and viewed as a hero ever since Manassas—is said to have raised up four companies of irregulars in two months' time. They doubled the havoc against Northern troops.

For a while, when the Union army had taken over, the local newspaper stopped printing. But now they are back to gloating. A writer made sport of any exemption, even for those with a disability such as nearsightedness. They consider deserters the lowest of beings, fit only for "petticoats and curls," one scribe said. "Croakers," they call those who have fled.

Many of our German Baptist men had no other recourse but to forsake families and property for safety in Pennsylvania. Those who stayed still hide in the mountains. We do not know when it will be safe for departed ones to return. On a Sunday morning at Flat Rock I still look out on a handful of old men, women of all ages, singles like Delilah, and the children. Those few who paid a substitute and now dare go out in public—my friend J. M. is one—face scorn, derided as rich men, able to buy their way out.

Recently, Johnny divulged his back-and-forth with the newspaper. Already while confined in prison, he had written a letter to *The Rockingham Register*, answering the charges they printed against the men. Their heading had been "Union Men Taken," but Johnny explained why we do not take sides. Quite simply: we must obey God rather than man. He showed me a copy wherein he also made the point that putting men in prison on false charges makes *more* expense for the Confederate government and prevents imprisoned men from being useful in their homes and fields.

But the newspaper did not print the letter! When he asked after released, regarding the omission, no one gave a worthy answer. Instead, the paper printed false insinuations, saying the jailed men had used their influence against the Confederacy. They refrained from formal charges, but the writer gave no evidence—no where, when, or what for the claims of contrary acts. We know Mr. Beery is not entirely innocent, but the charges were leveled against all, and the accuser made no affidavit as to their truthfulness. As Johnny has repeated often, "That is contrary to the Constitution. The law may be at an end, when misrepresentations can be printed."

But now he is gone, heading for the Annual Meeting as planned. We are left to fend for ourselves again. Why? I do not know if any calamity could have kept him home. Those of us who remain pray the Lord's will be done. We sing as best we can at Flat Rock: "*Am I a soldier of the cross?*" But voices drop out with the words: "*Increase my courage, Lord.*"

* * *

Johnny is back from his trip North! He rode Nell to our place this morning. Abigail had become more and more anxious as time went on.

"We will not hear; I know for certain. Lost in the wilds."

Her lament might as well have been a daily dirge: *Look on us with your pity.*

But Johnny came early, while we still dawdled in the kitchen. I went out at once to greet him with our usual Christian salutation. He told how one of Nell's shoes had come off on the trip, and she had to proceed lame until shod again.

Once inside, a cup of spearmint tea to warm him, he looked directly at Abigail and said, "You must be eager for word. I am pleased to set your minds at rest, all of you."

At this Abigail clasped her hands and said, "Thank you, thank you. I knew you would bring good news."

Brother Kline reached inside to his inner pocket and pulled out an envelope. "I do not know the contents, of course; I was not privileged to see your boys, but our plan worked."

He smoothed a bent corner of the paper, folded to make an envelope, and pushed it toward me.

I recognized Amos's handwriting at once: the angular slant of letters. "To Mister David Bowman, Flat Rock, Virginia." I passed the letter to Delilah. "Would you, please?"

"Hurry," Abigail said, her fingers interlocked.

Delilah fumbled with unfolding the single sheet of parchment. I do not know what I expected. A day-by-day account? Answers to all our questions? We received twelve sentences.

> Dearest Mother, Father, and Lilah,
>
> We are both well. Joel bears watching, but that is not news. We barter work for food. Far better than frog legs or clover. We never know if blue or gray next.
>
> Ohio does not have the beauty of our mountains. But here, we face rugged oaks and narrow ravines. Huge sheep barns offer shelter for hiding, but the stink clings. Even the woods scare up hissing possums at night.
>
> Our plan is to set out for Indiana in another week, when we have finished the brother's planting. That is, if we have not turned around under cover of night. We sorely miss all of you on the home place.
>
> Fondly, Your Sons,
> Amos and Joel

We sat stunned. The smile on Abigail's face turned to squinting eyes.

"They are safe," I said, my voice wavering.

"Do you know the brother's name?" Delilah asked. Her eyes scanned the sheet as if she had missed a clue. "The one for planting."

"I cannot say." Brother Kline only glanced briefly. "Brother Yost handed me the letter—we stayed with him and the Sister in Dayton—and asked me to provide safekeeping to the person intended. He knew I was expected to be the courier. You must wish for more. Is there a date?"

"Yes, of course." The paper slipped in Delilah's hurry. "The first day of June, 1862." She turned the missive over, as if she might have neglected more words scrawled on the back.

"We arrived in Dayton on June 3rd," Johnny said. "No one else stayed with the Yosts that night. Only Brother John Wine and myself. You say, no location given?"

Delilah mouthed the sentences silently, then with deliberateness repeated only, "'. . . set out for Indiana in another week.'"

Abigail fumbled in her pocket for a handkerchief. "But 'turned around,' you said."

"So little," I said. "That was only *if*. Not so?"

"I cannot explain—the boys, no more information. Perhaps . . ." John paused and drank more of his tea. "I do not want to speculate. The good part: we know they made it to Ohio and were following the plan to go on West."

"But would they think to return?" Abigail asked, her eyes wide.

Before I could reply—the boys would have to fake a pass—John offered to say a prayer and we bowed our heads at once.

"Bless this father, and mother, and sister, and bring them peace." Abigail's nose wiping turned to a sob. I reached for her hand and clutched Johnny's also. He in turn extended an open palm to Delilah; we sat there, linked by inner petitions, eyes tightly closed. "And grant the boys safety in travel, if it is your will."

"We may never hear again," burst from Abigail.

Brother Kline did not scold but said, "We are to remain hopeful."

"At a loss," I said, halting.

Johnny scratched fast at his beard. "Perilous times remain, although the boys should be beyond the reach of fighting. Indiana." He drained his tin cup.

We must have looked as glum as diphtheria patients.

"You faced perils also?" I asked. "Many soldiers along the way?"

"When we left on the 29th of May, we faced uncertainty. But the next day we were allowed to pass through part of General Fremont's army. That first Sunday we spent with Brother Clark and his son in the Alleghenies, greatly enjoying the fellowship there."

If I had gone along, I would have persisted with others at the Annual Meeting until I learned more. *Who saw the boys? How did they look? Was it for certain?* But I had had no desire to travel with Johnny that far; tales of Ohio have spread like fire. Far worse than possums.

"I know my brothers," Delilah said. "Amos will prevail—his solid thinking."

I nodded for Abigail's sake. Yes, I could have taken Ruby. But the problem was buried inside: no desire to mingle with soldiers or ride train cars. How could I have seen fit to leave Abigail and Delilah in the hands of Banks' men? When Johnny had said Brother John Wine would ride with him—not our Jacob Wine at Flat Rock—I felt relief. Would not any man?

John's voice droned on around the table. "Brother Clark accompanied us to Oakland, made certain we boarded the cars as planned. He kept our horses during the time we traveled by train."

"What is that like? A train?" Delilah asked, polite in spite of her drawn face.

"All was commodious, although my coat suffered new holes—sparks flying in the window."

"The boys may have ridden such," Abigail said dully, her eyes red with fear.

I reached for her hand again. "We do not know."

John showed no impatience. "We wish we knew what manner of transportation your boys used. Whether only on foot. Many ride the cars and do so safely. Officials often sit in the back, but no soldiers rode the trains we were on."

He shook his head at Delilah's offer of more tea. "On the way back we traveled toward Pittsburgh, the same car as a number of brethren from eastern Ohio and Pennsylvania. We all partook of a fine Love Feast the Sunday near to Milford. Oh, this is of interest: a Brother Thomas was there from Preston County, only a short distance south of the Pennsylvania border; that would be the western part of Virginia. He told of meeting two lads from the Shenandoah Valley—of our faith."

"Yes? And what else?" Abigail asked, sitting forward, her hand squeezed in my vice.

"Did the brother say, one with brown hair and the other, black?" I asked. "Medium build?"

"The brother said naught of their looks. But the location suggests Amos and Joel might have made their way over the Seneca Rocks, as planned."

"Oh." Abigail's fingertips pressed hard to her chest.

"We know so little. But following the plan. Surely some work will be had in Indiana." I tugged on my long beard. "Yes, farm work aplenty." Yesterday we would have rejoiced at any word. Now nothing fully satisfies.

"We know they are safe." Delilah squeezed her mother's arm.

"They *were* safe in Ohio," I amended. My left hand fluttered. "Yes, they are *safe*."

"And heading for Indiana, as planned," Delilah continued. "Some farmer will be glad."

"Might they head instead . . . ?" Abigail stopped. "Reckless," she whispered.

"They will seek advice before doing anything rash," Johnny said. "As you say, Amos—"

He pushed back, as if to rise, but I felt obligated. "How did business matters proceed? A smoothness?" I knew thorny questions were expected for discussion in committees. As moderator, Brother Kline would hold preeminent his charge to keep all together. He likely reminded those gathered: Methodists and Presbyterians have divided into Northern and Southern factions. The Baptists, no better, and rumors suggest strains among Moravians, too.

"All went as expected," John said, his voice even. "Four days, hosted by the Wolf Creek congregation in Montgomery County, but meeting in a large tent on a farm. Huge, o'erspreading trees formed a natural canopy also. Thousands of general attenders came."

"Thousands?" I could not picture so many Brethren in one place.

"Large congregations of German Baptists in that area. Northerners eager to attend again; you recall, so few came our way last year." He rubbed his hands—stubby fingers, always clean. "We had to table our mission plans another year—distractions. But more sorrowful, the farewells, knowing we may never meet again." I could not lift my head. "Cheering, though, to know we will meet again if faithful, in that happy land where parting shall be no more."

I know when he withholds. His face stays calm, but his words fly to future promises.

"These are perilous times," he repeated and slowly rubbed the back of his neck.

"You know of fighting while you were gone?" I did not say we had gone to the cellar two times.

"Yes, my hired hand told."

"And Ashby? You heard?"

"The colonel, killed near Harrisonburg? Yes."

"The noise has quieted, but people stay enflamed."

"Yes, I am aware. Scouts at Cootes Store now."

I grabbed Abigail's hand again and held tight.

Brother Kline continued. "You will rejoice to know, we participated in the Love Feast at Elklick in Somerset County also. Three persons baptized—much answered prayer."

I could not so much as nod, regarding the three souls. I wondered about churches in Indiana and beyond.

"We were able to make adjustments—the difficulties in the church at Elklick. Amicable."

Delilah murmured warmly; I cared little.

"From Frostburg—that is Maryland—we took the cars to Cumberland and then to Oakland, staying at Rogan White's tavern as usual and hiring a spring wagon the next morning to pick up our horses. From there, blessed to see brothers and sisters along the way home; our blind Sister Parks is doing well." John's voice stayed subdued, his recital measured. I feigned no interest. "Three days later, Brother Wine and I parted ways. Twenty-six days altogether. The Lord saw fit to bring me back to our beloved Valley, my dear wife again."

I cleared my throat, but no words came.

"She is well?" Delilah asked.

"Yes, her usual state of health." He abruptly looked to the door. "I must be getting on. You know, I suppose, we need to raise more money. Those able, have paid for substitutes. But others, once imprisoned and having paid

$500 to the *state* of Virginia, are now being asked by the Confederacy—another $500."

I straightened. "We must stand against double payment."

"Yes, with God's grace," Johnny said quietly.

"A heavy burden." My voice trailed off. I did not want to hear exact numbers; I have determined not to touch my silver.

"It may wean us from worldly treasure," Brother Kline said.

I could not say Amen. I have given so much. Even if our crops develop. Even if my back stays strong.

"We cannot make as much money this summer, lacking the boys' labor, lacking work horses." I may have sounded peevish.

He nodded. "We but commend our lives and hearts—our money matters—into the hands of God."

Delilah's long face nodded soberly, but I could not hold Brother Kline's gaze. I wanted to cast off this burden of being a minister. I cannot set the proper example; I am not the man. It is all I can do to refrain from complaint. "*Come unto me, all ye that are weary and heavy laden.*"

The best I can say to Abigail: *the boys are safe!* They were. There is that much. They made it to Ohio; they were keeping to the plan. How foolish to have expected assurance from a letter. We know little of the boys' spirits. *Amos will prevail!* Further word *could* come—some unknown source, some later date. For now, though, what is there for the hand to do but push the plow? Another crop, another laying hen. What other glimmer remains? Surely they will *not* turn around . . .

Since Johnny's visit, I have learned more. He faces additional charges since his return! Those lined up against him say he was gone to help the North side. Why can they not understand? He carried out the business of our denomination. Unity—his only desire. Nothing devious. He brought an innocent missive from our sons. A letter that left us straining for certainty.

Author's Note — Fall 2019

Charting my path in writing this novel is a complex task that goes back over ten years. When I began reading American Civil War material and plotting, I was still teaching, so my time for research was limited primarily to summertime. After reading Steve Nolt and James Lehman's book, *Mennonites, Amish, and the American Civil War*, I recall talking with Nolt in his Goshen College office and returning home with borrowed tomes about the Southern Claims Commission's findings after the war. Their task was to decide whether to recompense claims of damage or property loss from Unionists living in the Shenandoah Valley. Equally vividly, I remember being swept up reading the novel *Cold Mountain* by Charles Frazier and thinking: *if only I could create something half as enthralling.* Based on my early research of what had happened to Anabaptists during the war (in this case, to Amish, Mennonites, and German Baptists/Brethren), I made lists of potential characters living out conflicts in the North and South.

A turning point—from serious interest to resolve—came after I read books like David Goldfield's *America Aflame* and Drew Gilpin Faust's *This Republic of Suffering*. If nonfiction writers could succeed in marrying the stories of warfare, politics, and religion, why couldn't I do something similar with big-picture fictional knots that the literary world often deems too dangerous to touch? With ample parts of courage and fear I proceeded to blend history and fiction, while recognizing the dilemmas of a broad scope.

Three of my narrators are based on actual people who lived during the Civil War: Jacob Schwartzendruber, John (Fretz) Funk, and Betsey Petersheim, although I changed the latter's first name. I found sufficient historical information available to build tensions true to these people's lives. Accounts of them and their families helped me translate their inner thoughts and feelings into fictional desires that led to actions capable of capturing readers' attention. However, after perusing some of Funk's formal-sounding Civil War diaries and later autobiographical writings, I took some liberties with his voice. Other minor details have shifted slightly throughout the trilogy, like which year he received a pair of gray socks from his brother-in-law.

The two other narrators, Esther Shank and David Bowman, come from my imagination, but their experiences are composites of multiple accounts of what happened to Anabaptists living in the Shenandoah Valley from 1859 to 1865. Many other characters, including family, friends, and neighbors of narrators, also enlarge the story by illustrating both supportive and resistant perspectives toward the war and government demands. Some of these characters come from a blend of fictional and researched clay; others are well-known figures, such as John and Anna Kline, whose words and recorded histories also required interpretation for fictional purposes.

The novel unfolds amidst this diversity of viewpoint, taking place where military and government action affects civilians' lives physically, or where psychological stress builds, as delayed information becomes known. In addition, conflicts within churches and across denominational lines complicate the concerns of individuals, adding inconsistent practice to the tension. This overlapping complexity illuminates the interplay of war's impact with distinctive religious beliefs.

My own views of the conflicts that divide us in 2020 have been stretched and enriched from my reading, thinking, and inventing. Whatever your ideas about race, class, gender, religion, militarism, or patriotism when you first picked up Book I, I hope this series invites you to connect some dots across centuries. History offers a wide lens to see how these systems interact and how we all benefit from a generous *and* thoughtful understanding of our shared humanity.

I am indebted to Denise Giardina's *Saints and Villains,* as a model of historical fiction about Dietrich Bonhoeffer's resistance during World War II. In her afterword she conveys the novelist's desire to write a work of the imagination while determined also to write a story that is true. May it be so again.

Acknowledgments

A series of books like *Scruples on the Line* takes on life over many years and with essential help from many individuals. My gratitude begins with assistance from Denise Ehlen, Research and Sponsored Programs at the University of Wisconsin-Whitewater, and with support from the Languages and Literatures Department, UW-W, for an Academic Staff Development Grant, used toward research and travel expenses in 2008–2009.

During my travels I benefited from the resources of museums, librarians, and book collections at Mennonite Historical Library, Goshen, Indiana; Menno Simons Historical Library and Virginia Mennonite Conference Archives, Harrisonburg, Virginia; Mennonite Church Archives, Goshen, Indiana; and Iowa Mennonite Historical Museum, Kalona, Iowa. On multiple trips I welcomed research tips and memorable conversations with Steve Nolt, James Lehman, Lois B. Bowman, Paul Roth, Christopher and Marti Eads, Marie and Paul E. Yoder, Joe Springer, and Lois Gugel. I also had the pleasure of driving adventures and discoveries with Sarah Piper and family in the Shenandoah Valley, Virginia; Mary and Merlin Grieser in eastern Pennsylvania; and Andrea Wallpe along today's Route 50 in West Virginia.

I owe particular thanks to readers of early drafts of my manuscript who often became consultants throughout the process: Marilyn Durham, Alex Hancock, Carol Lehman, Andrea Wallpe, Brenda Smith White, and Wesley White. Other friends and colleagues provided advice at critical times: Kathy Walter, Lisa Weaver, Joanne Yoder, and Suzanne Wolfe, teacher along with fellow fiction writers at the 2016 Glen Workshop, Santa Fe, New Mexico.

Many professionals at Wipf and Stock Publishers contributed their skills, including Matthew Wimer as Editorial Project Manager. I'm indebted to the time and energy of many others as well. Alice Schermerhorn, John Nyce, Jodi Brown, and Hannah Sandvold participated in various stages of formatting the text, creating family charts, and offering advice about layout. Mark Louden applied his advanced knowledge of Pennsylvania Dutch and German to my efforts of including a sampling of the language the narrators of my novels would have been steeped in. Jeanie and Steve Tomasko brought enthusiasm, patience, and technical skills to their mapmaking. And finally, over these many years my sisters, Lois Brubacher and Dorothy Yoder Nyce, have provided enduring support. Inevitably, errors work their way into the finished products; for that I take full responsibility.

CREDITS

(first words of quoted material and sources, if not identified in the text)

"Am I a soldier" begins the song by the same name, written by Isaac Watts, in the Mennonite *Church Hymnal*

"Full many a flower" comes from Thomas Gray's "Elegy Written in a Country Churchyard"

"[G]ive an inch" from *Narrative of the Life of an American Slave* by Frederick Douglass

"I would prefer not to" from "The Scrivener: A Story of Wall Street" by Herman Melville

"Lord, make me an instrument," attributed to St. Francis of Assisi from "Peace Prayer"

"My dearest friends in bonds" begins the farewell hymn, "Parting Hand," found in *Papers from the Elder John Kline Bicentennial Celebration*

"Nor shall any man" from the U.S. Constitution and printed in Daniel H. Zigler's *History of the Brethren in Virginia*

"Our troubles and our trials," identified in *The Olive Branch of Peace and Good Will to Men* by S. F. Sanger and D. Hays, as a song from a Brethren Hymn Book

Phrases ("this we did") and lines ("We'll sure go home") from the verses and chorus of "The Prisoners Song" found in *Papers from the Elder . . .*

"When we asunder part" comes from John Fawcett's words in the song, "Blest Be the Tie That Binds," *Church Hymnal*

(first words of Scripture references, KJV, if not identified in the text)

Ps 13:1 - "How long wilt thou forget"

Prov 31:10 - "her price is far above rubies"

Matt 5:44 - "Love your enemies"

Matt 6:28 - "they toil not"

Matt 12:25 - "every city or house divided"

Matt 25:43 - "I was . . . in prison"

Luke 6:31 - "And as ye would"

Luke 15:8 - "what woman having ten pieces"

John 13:14, 17, 20 - "If I then," "If ye know," "He that receiveth"

John 18:36 - "if my Kingdom were"

Rev 2:10 - "be thou faithful"

Glossary of Pennsylvania Dutch and German

Ach, mein Sohn — Oh, my son

alliwwerrum — every-which-way

ausgfeegt — feeling exhausted

Bischt du deitsch? — Are you Dutch?

Bleib schteh! — Stay standing!

Bobbli — baby

dappich — clumsy

Das Christliche Volksblatt — title of newspaper: *The Christian People's Paper*

Des is addlich wichdich! — This is exceedingly important!

Deutscher Bund — German Confederation

Dieners-Versammlungen — ministers' meetings

Du musscht! — You must!

Ei du ye, mei Kind. — Oh, my goodness, child.

Fernweh — longing for far-off places

Gott liebt dich. — God loves you.

Guck nunner! — Look under!

Harrich mol! — Listen!

Hausvater — head of the household

Ja, hier. — Yes, here.

O, Gott! Halt uns in Deiner Hut. — Oh, God! Keep us in your care.

O, Herr, in Deiner himmlischen Barmherzigkeit! — Oh, Lord, in your heavenly mercy!

Ordnung — discipline

Ordnungsbriefe — written document of discipline

rumrutsche — restless movement

Schtopp graad nau! — Stop at once!

Sehnsucht — longing

Spiegel der Taufe — title of book: *Mirror of Baptism*

unbekimmert — careless

Unser Vater — Our Father

Verschtehnt dihr? — Understand?

Was sin Schlipp? — What are bows?

Weltschmerz — grief for the world

Zimlich gut. — Pretty good.

CPSIA information can be obtained
at www.ICGtesting.com
Printed in the USA
FSHW021854240320
68430FS